Lock Down Publications and Ca$h
Presents

TIPPIN THE SCALES 4

Fear Of The Unknown

Written By
Christopher "Diesel" Hornezes

Lock Down Publications
P.O. Box 944
Stockbridge, GA 30281
www.lockdownpublications.com

Like our page on Facebook: Lock Down Publications
www.facebook.com/lockdownpublications.ldp

Stay Connected with Us!

Text **LOCKDOWN** to 22828 to stay up-to-date with new releases, sneak peaks, contests and more…

Like our page on Facebook:
Lock Down Publications

Join Lock Down Publications/The New Era Reading Group

Visit our website:
www.lockdownpublications.com

Follow us on Instagram:
Lock Down Publications

Email Us: We want to hear from you!

CHAPTER 1

JAVI

Frozen. Unable to move. He didn't even feel like he could breathe. Time stopped. Everything ceased. There was no pain. No white-hot sting. He couldn't believe that out of everybody that had been gunning for him, in the end, it was a cop that got him.

So stuck on the drama with his pregnant fiancée and the pregnant jump off he had been smashing that had put a steak knife in his chest and left him for dead, Javi's head had been stuck in dark gray clouds in his late-night ride to attempt to beg his future wife to forgive him, to let him come home, to hold her, to kiss her. He was trying to get to their big luxurious mansion to kiss that butt until she forgave him.

Javi was caught off guard. Like a deer caught in bright headlights, he had frozen up when the detective upped his cannon and pointed it at him.

He closed his eyes, then he heard the gunshots. He thought he would feel it for a second, before life as he knew it was over, but he felt no pain at all.

"Aye, nigga!" He heard shouted a second later.

Javi frowned, eyes still closed.

"Javi! Open ya' fuckin' eyes, yo! Fuck is you doin'?!"

Ain't no way... There just ain't no way my cousin's up here too, Javi thought to himself.

"On God, nigga, if you don't open yo' fuckin' eyes, on my dead homies, I'ma fire on yo' ass, man!"

4

Javi opened his eyes then. He blinked them and saw he was still in his Monte Carlo SS, sitting on the shoulder of Green Bay Road, a hundred or so feet away from the beginning of 33rd Street with Wadsworth Road dead ahead.

"Jaaaviii-fucking-eeerr!"

He turned his head to the right and saw his heavyweight boxer built cousin there, at the passenger window. And he looked royally pissed.

"Hello! Hello! Hello! Can you hear me now, nigga?!"

Javi nodded.

"Great! Now…. now get the fuck out and help me get this bitch ass cop in my trunk!"

Javi was still dumbfounded to see his slightly older cousin there. He had expected to see angels, not a demon.

"I-Is he dead?" Javi asked.

"No! Come on before anybody rides this way!" Macho shouted.

Javi found the mental strength to get out of his G-Body. He made his feet move him around the front of the SS to the passenger's side. He saw Detective Barrera, laid out, but no blood was anywhere.

"What did you do to him, cuz?" Javi asked, as the big, tatted-up, Steel City Mafia goon put the detective's own cuffs on his wrists.

"I shot in the air then ran up and knocked his bitch ass out – the same thing I'ma do to you, cabrón, if you ask one more dumb ass question instead of grabbing this chunky muthafucker's ankles!"

Javi did as Macho demanded. He grabbed Barrera's ankles and helped carry the hefty Mexican. They hurried the unconscious man past his unmarked Dodge Charger, the strobes still flashing, to where Macho's white Bentley Flying Spur was parked, just behind the cop car.

"How the fuck you pull up and ain't neither one of us hear nor see you, nigga?" Javi asked as Macho hurried to get his trunk opened up.

"When a nigga finna get his shit blown back, he ain't focused on nothin' but death." They tossed the cop into the trunk, and Macho slammed it closed then looked at his shorter and slimmer green-eyed cousin. "And when the one wit' the gun is 'bout to put a muhfucka in the dirt, all he sees is victory. Now get in ya' whip and get ready to go!"

~   ~   ~

Almost three minutes later, sitting back behind the wheel of his Chevy, Javi heard Macho's big twin-turbo V12 engine rev then the sound of his tires screeching. He saw the Bentley speed off from behind the Charger. Macho hit the horn as he blew past. Javi hit the gas and made all seven hundred horses of the race-built engine that the G-Body had catapult him forward like Superman picked it up and threw it.

Javi's engine roared angrily. Macho's taillights were ahead of him.

Boom!

A loud explosion sounded. A bright flash of orangish red in his rearview caught Javi's eyes.

"What the fuck?! This nigga blew the cop's car up?!"

Then, he burst out laughing at how crazy his cousin was.

Javier Valdez, a now twenty-five-year-old Dominican, was the product of rich cocaine importing and trafficking parents as was his younger brother, Xavier, and even younger sister, Evelyn. A businessowner, a thoroughbred, and a lover boy, all at the same time, Javi lived a wild life, as did his family, but none of them would trade their action-packed lives for the world. They were all caked up and very connected. People like them only existed in hood movies or hood novels.

Javi's big cousin, Macho, a half Dominican, half Puerto Rican monster, was the wildcard of their family. He was even richer than Javi, Xavier, and Evelyn and still in the trenches like one couldn't believe a man of a certain wealth status would still be. Macho was as wild as an untamed tiger, and he lived by one rule and one rule only: There were no rules.

Javi was a slightly compact version of his blue-gray eyed cousin. They both had golden-brown skin with long hair in braids, were tatted all the way up, athletic, muscular, and had colored eyes that turned women into putty.

Born and raised in Waukegan, a predominately Hispanic and African American suburb about forty minutes north of Chiraq, Javi was all about the Ill-state, while his cousin, born and raised in Pittsburgh, P.A., repped the Steel City like the 4-1-2 was the key to life.

Though born and raised in different cities and states, the two cousins couldn't be closer. They were like brothers. They moved tons of cocaine together, hundreds of millions in cash and other illegal goods, and they killed anyone that opposed them, or they beat them to bloody pulps and made it so that they never made that mistake again.

The latest and greatest beef Javi had been constantly having to deal with was brought forth by Victor Gomez, prince of the Rojas-Gomez Cartel, a Mexican drug organization out of Tijuana. The man just would not leave Javi be nor would he honor the peace and understanding put into place by the three Valdez ol' heads that built the family's multi-billion-dollar empire, all off of the pure cocaine that they grew and cultivated into white-gold then shipped to the United States from the Dominican Republic. Then, they had it shipped around in their eighteen wheelers to their mighty list of clients. So, after a man's most common downfall, pussy, had gotten Victor right where the queen of the family wanted him to be, he was snatched up and joined his grandmother and his father in death.

Javi knew it was only a matter of time before his family's next opponent stepped up. He just wished he could have gotten at least five minutes before someone else tried to kill him. But that was life for him. Kill or be killed.

~ ~ ~

Reaching the light at Green Bay and Wadsworth, Javi followed his cousin as Macho banged a hard left onto Wadsworth and floored it.

A call came in from Macho as Javi hit sixty miles an hour in mere seconds.

"Yeah?" Javi hit the 'answer' icon on the touchscreen.

"Yo, cutty, you do realize ChaCha is going to be livid about this, right?" came Macho's voice out of the Kicker speakers.

"Uh... maybe we should hide?" Javi replied as they passed the private Waukegan airport on their right.

"Damn," he heard Macho say then.

"What?" Javi asked.

"These palsas do not give up, yo. Homies, cuz, they got the fucking road blocked off like they 5-0 or somethin'!"

Javi swerved over into the oncoming lane. Sure enough, about ten to fifteen seconds ahead, a line of SUVs stretched across the road, blocking him and his cousin.

Immediately, even more than he already was, Javi grew so pissed that he felt like he could breathe fire.

"On my mother's grave, cuz! Que se joda! We goin' through they asses, yo!" declared Macho, as Javi got right next to him.

Javi looked to his right and locked eyes with his cousin for a second. He nodded his head then looked back straight, out of his windshield, and braced himself for impact.

~ ~ ~

"Fire!" shouted Nino to his crew of twenty as he saw the target speeding toward where he and his crew were blocking the street off.

Twenty automatic AR-15s opened up and started dumping in a fire line at both of the cars.

They blew round after round at the white Bentley and the blue SS Monte Carlo relentlessly. NATO slugs flew like hundreds of metal bees chasing after an intruder that had destroyed their hive and killed their queen.

But after nearly ten seconds of non-stop dumping, Nino saw that neither of the cars slowed down... at all.

"Hold your fire! Deten el fuego!" he commanded his men.

They stopped shooting, and as the Bentley and the SS got even closer, all at once, Nino and his crew realized that the two vehicles were bulletproof.

"¡Hijole chingao!" Nino gasped as they kept coming. Realizing what was about to happen, he yelled, "Muevanse! Muevanse! Look out!"

MACHO

"Wooooo! Listo o no, mamahuevos, ya' voy!" he shouted as he hit one hundred six miles per hour. "Y'all better run like la migra's comin' for you!"

He could hear Javi's laughter come out of his Bentley's speakers, as they got within a hundred feet of the roadblock.

They positioned themselves with a foot or so of space between them, locking in on the Lincoln Navigator in the middle. The Steel City Mafia goon saw the shooters all making a run for it. Gritting his teeth, Macho gripped the leather woodgrain steering wheel, and right as he rammed the front end of the SUV, Javi rammed the rear. They hit it so hard that it went flying, while they went under it in their invisibly armored cars.

"Yeeeaaahh, bitch! Fuck y'all thought this was?! Easy?!" shouted Macho as he and Javi blew past the block and came up on the intersection of Wadsworth and Lewis Avenue. "Aye! Mr. Officer in my trunk! You aight back there, bitch?!"

They reached Lew and shot across it, ignoring the red light. Javi sped up, passed his cousin, then darted over in front of him.

"Well, make my Bentley look like a Honda, why dontcha', cabrón?" Macho said as Javi started creating a gap between them.

"I gotta get to my girl, cuz! She's not safe by herself, nigga!" He heard Javi say.

Macho chuckled. "On the contrary, lil cutty. Yo' lady is very safe, and she ain't by herself, but I'm wit' you, yo. Just remember we ridin' real dirty right now."

Minutes down the dark, curvy, two-way road, the tree-lined property of his and his woman's home came up on the left. Javi hit the brakes then slid sideways into the stone driveway and floored it into forest-like property with Macho right behind him.

They came to the large circular parking area that was in front of the massive log cabin designed mansion with the matching ten car garage across the way from it. Parked in the center of the circle were two black H2 Hummers that had the mob of AK-47-wielding Jamaicans posted in front of them, looking in Javi and Macho's direction, while the teams of more armed Rastas were positioned all around, hidden from plain sight.

Javi slid his damaged Monte Carlo to a stop at the stone steps to the front of his house, while Macho stopped his banged up Flying Spur at the Hummers. Hopping out, Javi saw the boss Rasta come out of the cut with his two big Rottweilers on thick chain leashes with eight more of his Shower Posse goons behind him with choppers fitted with drums.

Javi ran up the stairs to the tall wood and glass front door. He entered the security code and pushed his way inside.

"Michelle!" he yelled out, running through the grand abode's high ceiling opened up great room to where the stairway to the second floor was.

Sitting at the top of the stairs was Demon and Diamond. The two big, Sicilian mastiffs, both with clipped ears, big pit bull heads, and tall bodies with black and brown brindle fur, looked down the stairs at him. Demon, at over one hundred pounds and a bite force that rivaled a hyenas, was the beast, while his just under one-hundred-pound mate was his ride or die. They were both trained to immobilize and kill with no fear, nor hesitation, when Javi or his fiancée' gave the command.

Javi ran up the stairs and passed by them. He ran to where his and Michelle's big master bedroom was. He found his unexplainably gorgeous, brown sugar complexioned Dominicana sitting up on their bed, looking his way, with a frown.

"Why are you here, Javier?" the New York born and raised belle asked with a major attitude.

Even with a scowl on her face, Javi could not believe how amazingly beautiful Michelle was. On top of her beauty, her 5'5" tall, thick and curvy frame, and her long, dark brown, and silky hair added to her exotic looks. She was stunning to say the least.

A year older than Javi, Michelle was originally from Washington Heights, the famous Dominican section of Manhattan. She was a street chick through and through that had taken the wet-work profession at a very young age. She became a hit woman, not by choice but by destiny. Her best friend, that she came up with in the Heights, had been raped and brutally murdered. Michelle avenged her best friend and was ultimately given the job by her best friend's very plugged father, who had been like an uncle to her. To say the least about Javi's future wife, Michelle was not the average hood chick.

Javi walked up to his woman. Her eyes narrowed even more. She looked like she was ready to smack him.

The dogs entered the room, running and jumping up onto the bed with Michelle.

"We have to go, Michelle. Right now, baby," Javi urged her as Demon sank down and snuggled next to her.

"Why?" Michelle asked, patting Demon's side and Diamond's head.

Javi explained everything that had just happened in the last thirty minutes. As he did, Michelle's jaw dropped.

"What the fuck?! And he is in Macho's trunk?! Like right now?!"

"Yes, bae. We don't know how deep this shit goes, so we need to go!"

"But… Victor Gomez is dead, yo! And his fucking father and his grandmother! You think the cop is cartel?"

"I'd bet on it. We'll figure it out but for now, get up and come on!"

Michelle got up off of the bed. The dogs hopped off with her.

"I'm still not talking to you, charlatan!" she told him, then she ran into their big California walk-in closet and came back out with an AK-47 equipped with a drum. "Let's go see what this piece of pork has to say," she then said.

"Thought you wasn't talkin' to me?" Javi asked with a sly grin on his face.

"Shut up and let's go! Asshole!"

CHAPTER 2

MACHO

"You are all fucked! I hope you know that!" said the detective while on his knees in the center of the circle made around him.

SMACK!

"Bitch, ain't nobody ask you that!" Macho snapped. "And I think that it's you that is fucked, mamabicho! With no Vaseline!"

An older Lincoln Town Car backed over toward them and stopped. Four more of Jamaica's goons hopped out, ready to take the crooked detective away to his final resting place.

Jamaica looked at them and nodded.

"Last chance, bitch. Who sent you at my cousin? Tell me and you can get a bullet in the back of your head. Keep actin' like you tough, I'ma soften you up by puttin' you in a meat grinder, feet first, while you're still alive," Macho told Barrera.

The detective started smirking. "Chingate, puto, y chinga tu madre."

Wham!

Macho rocked Barrera's jaw as hard as he could. He broke his jaw with ease and made the left side of his face sag.

The Rastas grabbed Barrera up and tossed him into the Lincoln's trunk and slammed it shut.

"Make 'de bomba-clot pussy-hole mudda fucka feel de worse pain eva'," said the ol' Jamaican to his goons just as Javi emerged from the house with his fiancée and their dogs.

The dreads jumped back into the Town Car and dipped off. Macho looked at his cousin and future cousin-in-law.

"What happened? Did you get anything out of him, cuz?" Javi asked.

"Yeah. A laugh," Macho told him. "ChaCha's expectin' us though. Time to go see another angry New York chick."

Michelle let out a sarcastic laugh. "Is it really ChaCha you should be worried about, Antonio?" she asked, calling Macho by his government name.

"Oooooo... You are evil!" Macho exclaimed.

Michelle burst out laughing at the look on his face, knowing he knew his ass was grass when his woman caught up with him.

Xavier

"Kenzie, come on, Ma. It's okay. Stop cryin' please," Xavier pleaded as he gave his woman a back rub. "You don't got nothin' to be embarrassed about. Fuck them jealous ass hoes. Real talk."

The cocoa-toned twenty-three-year-old was doing his best to bring back the peace and comfort that the thick and gorgeous red head had finally began to have since he had taken her and her four-year-old daughter in and had her abusive baby daddy dealt with.

Sitting on the humongous bed in his luxurious home in the Zion area of northern Illinois' Lake County, the 6'3" Dominican and the stacked 5'10" tall Cuban Armenian were joined by Xavier's one-year-old female Dogo Argentino, Precious, while Kenzie's multi-heritage daughter, Neveah, was asleep in the bedroom that Xavier turned into a young princess' wonderland.

Earlier that night, after arriving at the new Valdez Transport yard, three of Xavier's honey-dips had popped out from seemingly nowhere, led by his pregnant jump-off, Nena. Xavier was even more shocked when he laid eyes on his childhood girlfriend, Vanessa, working for his brother's company as the supervisor. Xavier had been crazy in love with the now tall and oh so voluptuous Persian-Puerto Rican beauty when they were growing up. She also happened to be the queen of his family's younger cousin. He was dumbfounded to say the least. And then, Pamela, Keisha, and Nena appeared, and all hell broke loose.

"Bae, please stop cryin'. Your tears are really hurtin' my heart," Xavier told her, meaning it sincerely.

He sighed to himself as she continued sobbing. He knew Kenzie was beyond embarrassed, but he did not see it as her fault at all. The way he saw it, while Kenzie, like a straight gangster, duked it out with Pamela and Keisha at the same time when they attempted to jump him while Nena stood on the side lines and Vanessa freaked out, Keisha had happened to hit Kenzie in just the right spot and made the red head shit on herself in front of all of them... again.

"Keisha got a lucky hit in, bae. It happens," he continued trying. "You are human."

"No!" Kenzie suddenly yelled. "It's different for me! I have Crohn's, Xavier!"

He groaned then. Shaking his head, he remembered what she told him about her bowel disease, which was incurable.

"You know what... I'll leave," Kenzie said, standing up.

"Wait... What?! Leave?!" he questioned, getting up as well. "Why?!"

"Because, Xavier! There's no way that you really want a girl that has a disease like mine when the caliber of women you get are what every guy fiends for! So, I'ma leave you before you leave me and break my heart!"

"Kenzie! Chill, Ma!" He went to her, taking her hands and halting her as she tried to go pack her things. "Why the hell

15

would I get down on you like that over somethin' you can't control?!" You can't compare me to those in ya' past that did you wrong! I'm not none of them dick-head-ass niggas, Ma!"

Kenzie looked up into Xavier's eyes. She saw hurt in them, frustration, but even more than that, she saw fear. It was exactly what she felt. Kenzie was terrified to lose who she felt was the best man she could have ever met.

Her feelings for him were so incredibly deep. To lose him would be her undoing. To add salt to the wound, her daughter was already calling Xavier Daddy after just a week of being around him.

"I'm... sorry. I just... I'm so sorry, Xavier," Kenzie said as her tears started to fall again.

He gently pulled her to him and wrapped her up in his big, bulky arms. She leaned her face into his chest and let it all out. He comforted her like a man should when his woman needed him.

"It's okay, Ma. I'm not gon' leave you. I swear," he told her, holding her so tightly that the safety she had felt because of him instantly came back to her. "I love you, Kenzie."

Those three words. At first, she thought she was tripping. But he said her name behind them.

She pulled back a little and looked up at him, her eyes meeting his. Pools of deep sincerity glistened at her, full of passion and full of love.

"I... I love you too, Xavier. I love you! I love you, baby!" Kenzie cried, as her emotions poured out of her.

"Then show me you love me. Stay with me, Ma."

His deep voice did something to her. Butterflies fluttered around in her stomach, tickling her. In an instant, she grew hot for him. He was making her melt like she was a stick of butter, and he was a hot skillet.

Xavier tipped her chin up with a finger, making her look at him in his eyes. Their eyes met. He then leaned down, and he pressed his lips to hers.

Kenzie moaned as their lips met. The soft feel of his sent her off to the moon. Xavier was like a drug to her, delivering such a euphoric high that she never wanted to come down from.

The scent of her Sweet Pea body wash smelled so good to Xavier. It invigorated him. He placed his hands on her bare sides. Only a sports bra concealed her succulent melons.

Xavier deepened the kiss, as a cool breeze blew in through the open windows of his lavish master bedroom. He felt his lady's body tremble, as his hands slid down her slim waist to her wide hips. He cupped her phat, juicy ass through her skin-tight Fabletics leggings. It was so plump and soft. His dick grew so hard in his jeans that it throbbed.

Kenzie's temperature shot sky high as they tongued each other down, like horny teenagers skipping one of their classes.

Xavier backed his woman toward his massive luxury Maree bed. As they moved toward it, the heat between them increasing, Xavier reached behind Kenzie and lifted her bra up and over her flaming red locks. Her perfectly round breasts and hard pink nipples were freed.

His hands dropped to her hips. Stopping at the bottom of his bed, Xavier slid her leggings down to her ankles. She wore no panties nor a thong on under them. Her shaved box was so fresh, leaking in anticipation. Pussy lips swollen, her core on fire. Their sex was hot, dirty, and quadruple X-rated. Kenzie was ready for some good love, and Xavier was ready to give it to her.

Kenzie stepped out of her leggings all the way. Xavier stripped out of his tank top, his jeans, boxer briefs, and socks. He clapped three times. The lights in the crystal chandelier that hung down from the center of his ceiling dimmed, and music came on. *Trip Downtown* began crooning through the studio-quality surround sound speakers of the exclusive Sennheiser home audio system.

Her body was beautiful. It had him hypnotized. From her sexy red hair, gorgeous face, her voluptuous frame, a few tattoos giving her a 'bad girl' appeal, to her pretty feet, the twenty-five-year-old was the total package in Xavier's eyes.

He closed the gap between them, his thick, long hardness now pressed between himself and Kenzie's flat stomach. She felt him, and it excited her. She couldn't wait for him to be inside of her.

"Fuck me, Xavier," she whispered, horny as hell for him. "I need some of this love, baby. Please."

Kenzie gripped his shaft. Xavier groaned as she gave it a jerk.

"Diablos, mami. That feels good," he told her, making his voice go even lower. "Let me make you feel good, Ma."

"How you gon' do that, baby?" Kenzie purred, still jerking his dick, squeezing as she did.

"I'm finna turn you around and fuck you hard from the back," he told her, then he took his dick from her and spun her around.

Kenzie giggled when he smacked her ass.

"Ohh, shit, Papi! I like that!" She leaned her head down, bending over, and tooting her bubble booty up for him. "Do it again."

Smack!

"Beg for it."

"Please, baby! I need it! Please gimme some of that good ass dick!"

"Just some of it?"

"No! All of it! I want it all, baby!"

Xavier grabbed his shaft, and as Kenzie reached back, pulling her booty cheeks apart for him, he slid his thick, ten-inch tool into her tight, wet pussy.

"Oohh, yeeesss! God!" she moaned, as she felt him fill her up.

"You like that, baby?" asked Xavier, as Rick Ross's *Hit You From The Back* came on. "You like how that feel?"

18

Kenzie cried out his name, shouting that she loved it. Xavier drilled her, going deep, power fucking her as hard as he could. He grabbed her hair with one hand and gave it to her the way Kenzie wanted it: Rough as hell.

He went hard on her. Xavier's eyes rolled to the back of his head. The pussy was just too damn good. He wanted to never have to come up out of it.

"Fuck! This pussy is so goooood! Wooo, shit!" Xavier shouted, as he was overwhelmed.

"Shit! Bae! I'm gonna cum! Oohh, God, I'm gonna cum!" Kenzie cried out.

Xavier jackhammered her until she exploded all over his dick. She drenched him with her sweet nectar.

He pulled out, surprising her. Kenzie was about to beg for more until she felt him drop down to his knees behind her. A second later, his face was in her pussy.

"Oooo! Oooo! Xavier! Oh, my God! Fuuck!"

"Tell me how good it is!" he demanded and started eating her from the back.

"Oh, baby, it is soooo muthafuckin' good! I love you! I fucking love you, Xavier!"

He reciprocated his love back then sucked her pussy until she climaxed again.

"Fuck my ass! Fuck me in my phat Cubarmenian ass!" Kenzie begged.

Xavier burst out laughing at her. "Yooo, you're funny as hell! Cubarmenian though?"

"Yes! Now put that dick in my ass goddammit and fuck me until I start talking gibberish!"

Xavier stood up, ready to oblige her. He spread her ass cheeks apart and spit a wad of saliva onto her pink asshole. He stuck his finger in it, getting it lubed up. Kenzie clenched around his finger, eyes closed, biting her lip. Anal was one of Kenzie's favorite things to do. The dirtier, the nastier, the freakier sex was, the harder she came. And Xavier was exactly the type of horn ball that she needed in her life.

He pulled his finger out, then holding his hardness in his hand, Xavier aimed the bulbous tip at her puckered up back door.

Kenzie felt him gently ease in, slowly inching more and more inside of her tight anus. She squinted at first because of the pain from how his size stretched her out. But it was a pain that she welcomed. Pain was love, and she loved pain.

"Mmmm, shit…. God, that feels so good, Xavier!"

He started slow stroking her, looking downwards at her juicy butt. The sight of his dark brown dick going in and out of her phat ass made him almost bust his nut off sight alone. Kenzie clenched around him, squeezing, to add to his pleasure. His groaning and cursing got even louder.

"Goddamn, bae! This shit is so good!" he said to her.

"And i-it's all y-yours, Papi! A-All this ass i-is yours!"

Xavier brought her to another orgasm in just minutes. Soon after, Xavier felt his nut coming.

"Fuck, I'm finna bust! Shit!" he moaned, as his whole body tensed up.

Kenzie had been waiting for this. She reached back and yanked him out of her, then she spun and dropped to her knees. She opened her mouth wide for him, looking up into his eyes. Xavier took his wet cock and put it in her mouth.

With no hands, Kenzie started sucking his dick, going balls deep. Xavier cursed as she worked him. He put his hands on the sides of her head and began face fucking her. His balls smacked her chin as he touched the back of her throat. Kenzie gagged but didn't stop.

Seconds later, Xavier busted his nut. He came so hard that his knees nearly gave out.

"Oohhh, fuuuuck!" he shouted as Kenzie took his dick in her hand and jerked him off while sucking the last of his semen out.

Her mouth was full of hot globs of cum. She spit the sticky load out on his dick, then she slurped it all back up like a straight up freak!

TIPPIN' THE SCALES 4 | DIESEL

"Damn, Ma. Yo ass is a muhfuckin' beast, yo!" Xavier exclaimed, looking down at her, as Kenzie licked his dick clean of cum and pussy juice. "A nigga gon' have to put a rock on ya' finger."

Kenzie stopped and looked up at him. She smiled broadly, elated at the thought of being Mrs. Xavier Valdez.

Xavier took her by the hand and helped her up. He put his hands on her hips. Kenzie wrapped her arms around his neck.

"Whenever you're ready to make me wifey, I'm ready to be her," Kenzie told him.

"Oh, yeah?"

She nodded. "Yes, baby. I know you are for me, and I'm for you. My daughter loves you more than her punk bitch ass dad."

At the mention of Stacks, Xavier's eyes went dark. He wished he'd been the one to take the so-called Chiraq goon out.

"Hey. Come back." Kenzie released his neck and cupped his face. "Dontae is dead with his bitch ass friend, Rambo."

Xavier nodded his head. "Sorry. I just hate that there are men out there that beat on women because they some insecure ass bitches. Real talk."

"I know, I know. Some girls do deserve to get the taste slapped out they mouth, but it don't mean you have to. But fuck all that. Can we go out when you come back from your trip tonight?"

"Anywhere you and Neveah want to go, we'll go," he said.

Kenzie lit up. "Cool. I just wish I didn't have to go back to work yet. I need to make sure my baby's gonna be okay."

"My g-ma and g-pa gon' make sure that lil' mama never stops laughin' and smilin'. Now, can I have some more of my pussy before I go?"

"You know you don't gotta ask, Papi," Kenzie purred. She grabbed his wrist and put his hand between her thighs, so he could feel how wet she still was. "This pussy is always ready for you to beat it up, baby."

Xavier picked her up and tossed her onto the bed. The sudden move caught Kenzie off guard. She burst out laughing then, as Xavier did a running jump onto the bed, landing right on top of her.

CHAPTER 3

EVELYN

Evelyn cried her eyes out as she drove her special edition Alpina B7 BMW 750i out to Gurnee where she and her Dominicana lover's big four bedroom house was, close to Six Flags: Great America.

The threat from Stacks to knock members of her family off, which included employees of her oldest brother's company, if she didn't bring him coke, had her so conflicted. Normally, she would've laughed and even pulled her gun, knocking his shit back.

But everyone already thought he was dead. He wasn't. And worse, he turned out to be the cousin of Prince, the chocolate treat of a man Evelyn had recently tasted and gotten so addicted to. The man had gotten shot by some unknown shooter, as they came out of a hotel. She had given the pussy up to him there. Prince had rocked her world. He'd been the first man Evelyn had sex with in years. She'd been in a relationship with her girlfriend since the seventh grade.

Five foot seven, the same golden-brown skin tone as her big brother, with long, luscious, golden blonde hair, she was so damn curvy and thick that when she told someone that she was a truck driver, hardly anyone believed her. She wasn't just a lady trucker though. Evelyn was the boss of her own division in her brother's company. Both she and her middle brother, Xavier, had their own crews up under Javi. As a trio, they worked like a well-oiled machine. They made serious money hauling legit freight and illegal goods. The twenty-one-year-old beauty was richer than most could believe. But having come from big money, she wasn't a bougie, materialistic chick. Naw. Evelyn was just crazy, especially when it came to her family.

Calls from her girlfriend kept coming in, as Evelyn rode west up Grand Avenue toward Gurnee. She knew Gloria was going to keep calling, so she finally answered.

"What, man?!" Evelyn snapped.

"¡Para quien piensas que te habla, puta!" Gloria shot back. "Yo' ass ducking my calls 'n shit! Dipping off with some fucking dude! Disappearing for hours! And you got the fucking nerve to talk to me like that!? Bitch, wait 'til I catch yo' ass! I'ma beat chu' the fuck up!"

Evelyn sighed. "I'm sorry, Gloria."

For a good minute, there was just silence. Gloria was shocked. "Okay… What the hell is wrong with you? You never say sorry for nothing,"

"Nothin'. I'm on my way home. I don't wanna fight with you, baby. Real talk."

"How far are you? You eat?"

"Ten minutes and I'm not hungry. I'll be there soon," Evelyn said and ended the call. "I can't believe I got myself in this shit. How the fuck am I gonna do this?" she asked herself, lost like never before.

JAVI

Leading the way to ChaCha's truck yard, Jamaica, in the first H2 Hummer, drove the big square vehicle rolling on beefing monster truck wheels, his eyes peeled, AK-47 on his lap, his dogs in the rear. His three other men were also on the lookout as were the four in the H2 Hummer bringing up the rear.

Riding in between the exclusive brand new, completely special ordered, and built over in a Brabus factory in

Germany, was the Mercedes Benz G65 AMG, gliding on twenty-four-inch Forgiatos. Both the truck and the rims were painted in the wine-colored Designo mystic red paint. The Brabus edition G-Wagen's exterior styling set it apart from all others rolling around the Midwest. The interior was one of a kind, as well as its features. The Bi-Turbo V12 engine under the SUV's hood put out more power than the highly coveted Dodge SRT-8 vehicles. Nearly half a million dollars rolled on twenty-fours. Behind the wheel was Michelle, cruising her sweet ride that Javi had gifted her with on the same day he proposed to her. Macho sat in back with Demon and Diamond.

Riding shotgun, Javi leaned his chair back a little, stoic and trying to come up with a thought for what ChaCha may say… or do. She was pissed. Not only at how a dirty cop had slipped through her fingers but for how Javi could have gotten himself killed… again.

~   ~   ~

"Maaan, hell naw, folks. Nigga on the D. Yo' ass tweakin', fam! Fuck I look like frontin' you a whole brick, and yo' ass hotter than actual fire?!" exclaimed Crazy D, a Satan Disciple from out south in Chicago that had migrated up to Wauk-Town to get money in a slower paced suburb instead of the fast paced kill or be killed Chiraq.

"You dun' turned into one of these scary-ass Waukegan-ass niggas, huh?" asked the tall, dark skinned Unknown Vicelord standing before Crazy D in the driveway of Crazy D's house.

Right across the street from an elementary school and a massive soccer field on Lewis Avenue, in between Ridgeland and Grand Avenue, traffic buzzed by Crazy D's crib, not paying attention to the two men posted next to a Chrysler 300C SRT-8 parked in front of an old school, drop-top Cutlass 442 on big chromed rims. The late hours of the night – or to some, early morning – had nobody paying any attention to anything but getting home to bed.

"On the D, nigga." Crazy threw the pitchforks up and then kissed them. "I'll never be one of these bitch ass Wauk-Town lames, fam. I'm just brought up to be careful about who I jam wit', you feel me, Lord?"

An old Buick turned into Crazy D's driveway just then. He and his visitor turned and were nearly blinded by the headlights.

"Expectin' company?"

"Hell naw. It's almost five in the mornin', and my baby mama inside sleep," Crazy D said, reaching behind him and pulling out his Glock 21. "Hold up real quick, Lord. Be right back."

Crazy D walked toward the car cautiously, gripping his thumper behind his back. The passenger window rolled down as he got closer. When he was a few feet away, the interior lights went on. Behind the wheel was a dark-skinned chick with long dreads, the tips dyed red, balled up at the nape of her neck.

"You need somethin', shorty?" he asked, relaxing when he saw how small she was.

"Yeah. Me and my baby daddy needs all that coke and cash you holdin' up in yo' crib," she said with a sly smirk.

Crazy D's eyebrows furrowed up. He went to put his Glock to her face when he felt the kiss of steel touch the back of his head.

"I'll take that," he heard his visitor say from behind him.

"That's crazy, Lord. We go way back, and you gon' get down on me like this?" Crazy D asked, as the guy took his pistol from him.

Crack!

"Aaghh!" Crazy D yelped, as the butt of the gun opened up a deep wound in his head.

He fell against the car, dazed. The dread-head chick was still smirking at him, as he slid down to the ground, bleeding profusely. On his back, he looked up and saw the man he had known from down in Chicago stand over him, looking down at him. Crazy D could see the smirk on his face, and knowing exactly what the man was capable of, his bladder let loose out of pure fear of the unknown.

STACKS

"Check it out, folks," Stacks said sarcastically to the bleeding Disciple. "Me and my BM gon' help you up and get chu' inside. Run everything you got up in here, and don't for a second think I don't know exactly what you're holdin'; yo' baby mama likes to bump her gums when she's drunk, and she loves Black dick. If you make it through this, you might wanna get you a new bitch."

Stacks' baby mama got out of the stolen car with her semi-auto, dressed in a black hoodie, red leggings, and black mid top Air Forces. She helped her son's father get the Mexican gangbanger up off the ground, then they took him into the house where he discovered his daughter's mother waiting inside with an evil smile on her face.

"You conniving ass bitch!" Crazy D said to her as the reality of her setting him up set in.

"Fuck you, nigga! Yo' bitch ass deserve this shit wit' cho' snitchin' ass!" Teresa spat. "You think I ain't know the real reason why you had to get up outta Chicago? I found out you ratted on yo' own guys when you went down for that dirty gun, bitch ass rat!"

"Aight, joe, enough of all that!" Jazmine snapped at Teresa. "We got shit to do, so shut up and play yo' position!"

Teresa scoffed at how Stacks' baby mama had just come at her neck.

"Chill, 'Resa," Stacks chimed in, then to Crazy D, he asked, "Where's the merch? Give it up or I will turn the stove on and burn it out of you. You know who I am, so do not try me, my dude."

"Aight! Just be cool, fam!" Crazy D pleaded.

Wham!

Stacks kicked him square in the face.

"Be cool these nuts, bitch nigga! Where it at?!"

He gestured for Jazmine to go turn the stove on. Crazy D saw her obey him. When the glow of the flames coming out of the burner appeared, Crazy D pissed himself even more.

"Nasty bastard," Teresa said, curling her lip up in disgust. "You's a bitch, joe! I can't believe I got pregnant by a square like you!"

"Shut the fuck up, bitch!" Jazmine snapped, pointing her Taurus at Teresa. "You talk too fuckin' much!"

"I'm waitin'," Stacks said to Crazy D, ignoring the women.

Crazy D gave up the whereabouts of his merch. Stacks told the girls to go get the shit. They did as told. Teresa led the way to the baby's bedroom. She was shocked to find thirty kilos of cocaine under her daughter's blanketed mattress with her daughter in the crib.

"Damn... Yo' baby daddy is a real bitch ass nigga," said Jazmine, shaking her head.

"Tell me about it."

Teresa went and lifted her sleeping toddler out of the crib and carried her over to the changing table. She laid her down gently then grabbed a big bag with handles.

Jazmine stood by while the Mexican chick put the bricks in the bag. From the kitchen, she could hear Teresa's baby daddy pleading for his life, then his pleas turned to screams of agony.

"Shut the fuck up!" She heard her baby daddy shout.

"I hope Stacks burn his whole body off," Teresa said as she went to the closet to grab clothes to pack and take for her baby..

Boc!

Without hesitation, Jazmine put one in the back of her head, blowing her brains out of the gaping hole in her forehead.

The toddler screamed awake from the loud bang, crying her eyes out on the changing table.

Jazmine went and picked her up and cradled her. "Shhh. It's okay, mamas. Mommy's just sleeping. Come on, you can come with me and my dude. You'll love livin' with us."

Stacks came in the room just then. He looked at Teresa's body then at Jazmine holding the baby and grabbing the bag. "You good?" he asked her.

"Yup. Let's go introduce Dontae Jr. to his new little sister," Jazmine said with a smile. "Then, we can put your plans into action."

Stacks started grinning diabolically. "Bet," was all he had to say about it.

CHAPTER 4

JAVI

Jamaica led the way from Javi and Michelle's house, through Zion, out to where ChaCha's truck yard was, sitting on the Illinois-Wisconsin border. She was the boss of RJ & D Transport, LLC, a gargantuan trucking company started by the three Valdez brothers back in the seventies solely to transport the massive amounts of pure Dominican cocaine that they were bringing into the country. ChaCha's yard was her own dispatch location that housed nearly one hundred trucks and trailers plus her own.

As they all turned in, a line of semis were rolling toward the exit. A number of trucks and trailers were in rows across the huge employee parking area. They all rolled up to ChaCha's big diesel service and repair garage that was connected to her office building/dispatch center, which also had a few non-blue printed spots down below where some people that had seriously violated came and never left.

Michelle followed Jamaica's H2 over to the building. She parked next to the colomborriqueña's matte-black Rolls-Royce Drop Head coupe. She hadn't even put her Brabus truck into park when the Amazon-warrior tall New York gangstress came bursting out of the office door with both fear and anger etched into her face.

The six-foot tall beauty was one that intimidated most men, let alone women. Her demeanor told no lies. Ximena

Sandoval, a.k.a. ChaCha, was a straight goon, protective like a lioness over her cubs and just as nurturing.

The thirty-year-old was a billionaire in the flesh. Cocaine had gotten her filthy rich, while her fearlessness had gotten her the reputation of a new-age Griselda Blanco mixed with JLo. She was the daughter of a hitman from Colombia and a dope girl from Puerto Rico, was raised in Jackson Heights, Queens, then had migrated to Pittsburgh, where she met Danny Valdez and became his righthand goonstress.

Michelle, Javi, Macho, and the dogs all hopped out of the G-Wagen. ChaCha, still in her work clothes with Timberlands on her feet, her long hair in two braids to the back, and a New York snapback on her head, turned backwards, ran right to Javi, and threw her arms around him.

"¡Dios mio, papacito! Yo, what the fuck?! Are you okay?!" she asked, hugging and squeezing him like a mother did to her son after nearly losing him in a tragic way.

"I'm good, prima. Cuzzo saved my ass for real," Javi told her, keeping it a buck.

ChaCha kissed Javi on his forehead then turned toward Macho as he grinned…

Wham!

"Aye!" Macho jumped back when ChaCha jabbed him in his chest. "Coño, what the hell was that for, yo?!"

"Because goddammit! Why the fuck you let him leave the house when I told you to keep him in?!"

"He was asleep, ChaCha! I didn't think I needed to sit in a chair next to his bed and watch him!"

ChaCha looked at Javi then. "What the hell were you thinking, Javier? Did you forget how people are looking for you?!"

"I do not give a fuck!" Javi snapped. "I had to see my woman, cuz! I had to! She is my life! I'm dead without her!"

Michelle started smiling at his words. She found herself taking his hand into hers and holding it.

"Plus, I knew if I wanted to come home, I had some butt to kiss, and Yessy's punches really hurt."

Macho burst out laughing as did Michelle. Via a text message from Macho, Michelle had heard that when Javi showed up at Macho and Yessy's house after she kicked him out for having a wayward dick, Yessy had cleaned Javi's clock with a punch to his jaw, sending him to the floor on his ass.

ChaCha shook her head at Javi. The reason he had gotten kicked out in the first place still had ChaCha wanting to pop off on him.

She looked at Macho then, seeing him still laughing at his younger cousin.

"Mamao, I wouldn't be laughing if I were you," she told him. "Javi ain't the only one the bad 'Rican gon' get at."

Macho stopped laughing then right as he heard the unforgettably exquisite sound of the insane twin-turbo V12 engine under the hood of his woman's rare, one-of-one, four door rocket screaming out of its monstrous exhaust pipes.

In seconds, they all saw the headlights of the dark-tangerine-colored Pininfarina Gran Lusso coupe concept BMW M7 as the big 7-Series whipped into the yard as if it was on rails.

"Aww, come on, Mena! You called Yessy on me though, yo?!" Macho legitimately panicked, as the Beemer slid to a stop just inches away from him.

The driver's door flew open then and out hopped the caramel-skinned 5'9" tall Nuyorican, so pissed at her man that as she immediately gave chase to a fleeing Macho, Javi, his fiancée, ChaCha, and the dogs all took steps back, staying way out of Yessy's way.

"Antonio!" They all herald Yessy shouting as she hawked him down in the middle of the parking lot.

"Wait. Hold up. Why is she mad at him?" Javi wondered right as they all saw Yessy jump up into the air and land on Macho's back, taking him to the ground by one of the H2s.

"Because he blew up a cop car on the side of the road after he rescued you," ChaCha told him.

They all watched as Yessy rained down fists of fury on her man. That was how they got down. They were nuts, but they were also deeply in love with each other. Yessy was all for riding with her man until the wheels fell off, but when he did some crazy shit, she never hesitated to give him a Bronx beatdown to keep him in line.

Seeing her whoop ass, shoot guns, and get to regulating on anyone that thought shit was sweet was like watching the famous actress, Gina Rodriguez, getting on some gangster shit. Everyone swore up and down that Yessy had the most uncanny resemblance to the *Jane the Virgin* star.

The Nuyorican had gotten the call from Michelle after she had called ChaCha. Yessy jumped right out of bed, threw on one of her Army sweatsuits that she had gotten from the Great Lakes Navy base where she was stationed as a 1st Lieutenant. Her long hair was pulled into a bun, and on her feet were her most comfortable running shoes, all for running her man down to make him see how upset she was with him.

"It's not like he did it just because though, prima," Javi said to ChaCha, coming to his cousin's defense.

"Okay. You gonna go help him out then?" ChaCha asked.

Javi looked over at them again. Yessy was on top of her man, pinning him down, spazzing on him.

"Heeeell naw! Eh eh! As I said before, Yessy's punches really frickin' hurt!"

They all heard Macho shouting just then.

"Yessy! Chill out, yo! Goddamn!"

"Then stop blowing up cop cars then, motherfucker!" she yelled back.

Javi, Michelle, and ChaCha all burst out laughing.

~   ~   ~

33

ChaCha ended the phone call and looked at Javi, Macho, and their women.

"You're all goin' east," she told them. "The Steel City awaits you. I have two loads of cash that you'll take to the Murrysville yard then from there, vacation."

"Sheeit, you ain't gotta tell me twice! Homies, I'm ready, yo!" exclaimed Macho, geeked to be going to his hometown.

"Straight up!" Javi added, equally hyped up to be going to Pittsburgh. "I haven't been to the 'Burgh since... Damn... a year ago."

"Well, the faster you two get moving, the faster y'all can get on the road."

Javi and Macho nodded, then Macho told his cousin to follow, as he headed over to Yessy's $800,000 BMW.

"You better not ram no fuckin' roadblocks in my car, Antonio!" Yessy hollered to him, as he and Javi hopped in.

"Then no roadblocks better not get in front of me," Macho said back.

He put it in drive, mashed the gas, and made the rear wheels smoke. He tore up out of the yard like he was chasing a dream that refused to come true. Jamaica hollered for two of his crews to go with them, even though Javi's truck yard was minutes away, and Macho's truck was at his own parking spot, not far from either of their yards.

MICHELLE

Michelle leaned against the front of ChaCha's building, sighing to herself. Demon and Diamond stood in front of her. Diamond nuzzled her hand, licking it to get her attention. Michelle patted her big head, smiling at Diamond and her brutish mate.

"No long faces, mamita," ChaCha said to her. "Everything is gon' be aight, yo. I promise you that."

Michelle chuckled. "I know everything's gon' be aight, Mena, until the next group of dickheads wanna get to tryna knock us off."

Yessy remained quiet. She often thought the same thing herself: When would it end?

"Yo, look. This is the life we all live, kid, 'yah mean? You heard what B.I.G. said. The more money muhfuckas get, the more problems come. That's why we gotta stay on our toes and keep our eyes open. When we come across a threat, we eliminate it. Fuck tryin' to do it. We do it,"

"I can tell you who I would love to eliminate," Yessy said then with an evil look in her eyes.

Neither Michelle nor ChaCha had to hear Yessy say the name. They already knew.

"Narco," they both said in unison with looks on their faces as if they had just seen someone eat dog shit that hadn't even came out of the dog yet.

"If Antonio involves him in any more of his family's business again, yo, I'm beating his ass, then I'ma chop that fat fucker into pieces and feed Maliante and Dreams chopped bitch."

Michelle and ChaCha burst out laughing at her.

"Yo, how come I never hear you call him Macho?" Michelle asked Yessy.

"Because I fucking hate that damn name! Macho! Macho! No! His name is Antonio! What the fuck type of name is Macho anyway?!"

The two laughed so hard that tears ran down their faces. Yessy was truly a monster when she got taken to the dark side.

Ten minutes later, Michelle heard the sound of a truck's engine brake roaring from close by. She and the other two looked toward the entrance and saw Javi's brand new Pride and Class edition Peterbilt 389 turning in. It sported a glossy, royal blue paint job with chrome front fenders and a long list of other custom exterior chrome and stainless-steel parts that made it turn heads on the streets and on the highways. And it came from the dealership decked out already, but the type of big truck enthusiast that Javi was, he needed his Pete to embarrass all the other ones on the road, especially since losing his custom-built Kenworth W900L to a hit crew ambush and acquiring his least favorite type of truck thanks to his fiancée forcing him to buy the nearly $400,000 Peterbilt.

Michelle watched her man coast the big, flashy Pride and Class toward where she and the ladies and dogs were. It seemingly sailed on water from its all-air ride suspension, giving it a near bump-free ride.

He came to a stop a few feet away from where they all were. The loud whoosh of air shot out when he applied the brakes. He got out, and ChaCha filled him in on what he and Macho would hook onto a couple of her step-deck trailers. They were similar to flat-bed trailers but were even lower to the ground, enabling tall cargo to clear under overpasses, bridges, and tunnels.

Javi nodded then glanced at his future wife, who purposely looked away. He went and climbed back up into his truck, released the brakes, and rolled off, heading toward where ChaCha's trailer yard was.

"Girl, how long you gon' give him the silent treatment?" ChaCha asked Michelle.

"Ximena... Javi got a traga pregnant. I'ma give his ass that burn until I feel like he's had enough," Michelle said.

"If you want, I could knock him on his ass again," Yessy offered just as they heard another truck's engine-brake, this one waaay louder, as the driver down-shifted gears like they had just been doing one hundred miles per hour and had to stop fast.

"Here comes Antonio," Yessy said, knowing the sound of her man's crazy driving anywhere.

"He drives like he thinks he's me or somethin', yo," ChaCha chuckled, as the candy powder blue 2007 Legacy

Class edition Peterbilt 379 extended hood whipped into the yard like it was a Lamborghini.

No expense was spared when Macho fixed his limited-edition up. Just like many others in the family, he was a big truck lover and decked his rig out like a dope boy did a box Chevy or a Benz. The custom paint and all the custom lights, its stretched frame that gave it a long and tall hot-red stance, and a completely done up interior, made Macho's Legacy Class one of the only one thousand made a showstopper. It wasn't what he did to the 379 that made it nearly priceless to him and his older brother. The value in it came from it being what gave their mother the best last few weeks of her life before cancer took her away from her boys.

Macho slammed on the brakes and made his Pete skid to a stop in the middle of the lot. Michelle, Yessy, ChaCha, and the Rastas all watched as Macho started revving up the monstrous high-performance Caterpillar C15 engine under the long square hood.

The truck shook and flames shot up out of the huge ten-inch diameter exhaust stacks, as 1,350 horsepower begged to be let loose. The rear wheels started spinning seconds later, creating thick clouds of white smoke, then the eardrum-piercing train horns blasted.

"Your man loves showin' off," Michelle chuckled, as Macho started doing donuts in his Legacy Class.

Yessy shook her head. "I can't lie… He does it very well."

"If it wasn't for the fact that his truck had given Cristina the best times of her life on the road with 'Tonio and Tool, I would pour water in his fuel tanks for tearing up my damn parking lot," ChaCha said.

Macho stopped doing donuts a minute later. When the smoke cleared, he rolled his rig over toward where the ladies and the dogs were. He came to a stop a few feet away.

Michelle watched Yessy go to the passenger door and reach for the handle, which was at the front of the door, not the back. She opened it, suicide style, and both her big, male

German rottweiler named Maliante and Macho's female chocolate-red tiger-striped female Ood family red nose pit bull jumped out, running right up to Demon and Diamond, excited to be back around them.

Macho pulled off after ChaCha to go hook up to a step-deck. Jamaica and two of his men walked up and got word from ChaCha on what was going on.

"Thank you for bein' here for us, tio," Yessy said and gave Jamaica a hug. "Means a lot to us all to have you as family."

Michelle and ChaCha then gave the fifty-six-year-old Shower Posse goon boss hugs, thanking him emphatically. In reply, he nodded his head of thick and long graying dreadlocks.

"Notta problem, ladies. Family rides for family. Me love you all like ya' share me blood," Jamaica said to them, then he headed to his H2 to get ready to roll.

JAVI

Already backed up to a forty-eight foot long step-deck trailer, Javi was outside getting hooked up. He connected the two airlines, the electrical line, and made sure the trailer's king pine was locked all the way in the tractor's fifth wheel. With a small tire thumper, he checked all eighteen of his tires and the wheels, then he checked that all of the lights on his tractor and ChaCha's trailer worked and shined brightly. As he was heading back to climb up into his cab, Macho's Legacy Class rolled in his direction, already coupled to an identical step-deck.

Javi jumped up behind the wheel of his Pete, releasing the trailer's brakes only. He let air flow into the trailer's air brake system until he saw on the dashboard that the air pressure in his truck's air tank had risen back up from being released to charge up the trailer's system.

He did a quick brake check, then he pulled out of the spot with the step-deck following behind him. He followed his cousin over to the garage. They both made wide, swinging turns then backed their rigs to two separate bays.

Javi saw in his mirror, his woman, ChaCha, and Yessy standing in the space in between his truck and his cousin's.

The bay doors behind them began raising up. Parked inside the bays were two brand new Volvo 630s, both of them with PJ&D Transport decaled on their small mid roof-style sleeper berths.

Javi got out of his rig and made his way to the garage along with Macho. The ladies stepped in behind them. More PJ&D trucks and trailers were in other bays, needing repairs. ChaCha's yard operated twenty-four hours a day, but for the evening, she had shut it down so as to keep private family business private.

"Yo, I know you two can't stop competin' with each other to save your lives," ChaCha said to the two look-a-like cousins, giving them both eye contact, while Michelle and Yessy stood with their dogs. "But keep in mind there is $35 million in each truck."

"Word?" Macho asked.

ChaCha climbed up into the driver's seat of the Volvo Javi was taking and pulled the lever to pop the hood, Volvo's being the only big trucks where opening the hood wasn't as simple as unlatching the exterior engine hood straps like all other trucks had. She got out, went to the driver's side fender, and lifted the fiberglass hood up.

Under the hood, there was a big block of plastic wrapped cash, the size of the D13 Volvo engine that had been inside the engine bay before being swapped with the gwop.

"The rest are inside the sleepers, stashed inside the rear wall," ChaCha finished, closing the hood back down.

Javi and Macho both nodded. They got to it, going to the fronts of their trailers and unhooked the strong winch lines from their hooks. Yessy and ChaCha laid out ramps at the rears of both trailers, then Yessy went and got an airline from a big air compressor close by.

While Javi hooked the front end of the 630 he was taking, and Macho hooked his up, Yessy filled both trucks air tanks up with air, so the brakes could be released.

ChaCha got up behind the wheel of the one for Javi. When enough air was in the system, she pushed in the parking brake knob, put the shifter in neutral, and held the steering wheel.

Yessy did the same. Javi and Macho got up on the trailer decks and watched carefully as ChaCha and Yessy steered the Volvos, while Javi and Macho winched them forward and up onto the decks.

Minutes later, both trucks were resting on the center of the step decks. ChaCha and Yessy put the brakes back on, shifters in gear, then they got out.

They all worked together to chain the trucks down, blocking the wheels, then re-checking each chain. Accidents were not needed when $70 million in cash was at stake.

"Okay. Go," ChaCha told them. "Cops and troopers are either sleeping or getting paid to stuff their faces at Pilot or a TA somewhere. Use the wee hairs and fly straight through."

They all knew that even if it was daytime, their only worries would be the Illinois, Indiana, Ohio, and the Pennsylvania State Police. From Indiana and eastward, it was all toll roads and turnpikes; there were no weight stations on them.

"Okay," said Macho as a cheesy-ass grin grew on his face. "We'll do the speed limit."

ChaCha twisted her lip up at him. She saw Javi with the same look on his face, as well as Yessy. Michelle was even smirking in a sly type of way herself.

"Mentiroso," ChaCha called Macho. She looked at the Nuyorican then. "And this means you too, loca," she added, knowing that Yessy, who drove big rigs in the military with her best friend, G-Baby, had a lead foot just like her boyfriend.

"Who? Me?" Yessy asked with a cheesy grin matching Macho's.

"Yeah you, fucking speed demon!"

"Maaan, I knooooow you ain't comin' wit it like that, prima," laughed Javi. "Yo ass be speedin' in that X-edition like Diabla's a Bugatti," he said, calling ChaCha's wickedly fast Peterbilt by the name she had chosen for her.

ChaCha turned and looked at Javi, hands on her hips. "¡Cabrón, yo soy la bichota y yo hago lo que me salga de los cajones! ¿Me entiendes, lil' nigga?"

Michelle and Yessy both burst into fits of laughter.

"Get on his ass, biiiiatch!" cheered Michelle.

"Treated yo ass, niiiggaaaa!" Macho teased.

Javi waved his cousin off. "Shut cho' ass up."

"Tell ya' mama to shut up, foo," Macho countered.

"My mama is your cousin, foo!"

"So?"

"Aye, aye, aye! Goddamn, yo! Shut cha'll asses up and go get the fuck on the road! Ahora!" ChaCha shouted, shutting the two up asap and making Michelle and Yessy laugh even harder.

CHAPTER 5

XAVIER

Cruising up Russell Road, Xavier gangster leaned in his black and chromed-out '94 Cadillac Fleetwood Brougham, as it glided so smoothly on the chromed twenty-two-inch, hundred-spoke, wire wheels toward the yard. He nodded his head as Verse Simmonds' *Shake Dat* featuring Gucci Mane thumped hard from the woofers in the trunk.

He had a big smile on his face, and behind the green lenses of his gold Aviators, his eyes were filled with excitement. All he could think about was getting to work, getting done, and getting back home to Kenzie and Neveah. He was happy that Kenzie was going back to work. She needed to get back to her life and teach her daughter how to be responsible, but the minute she expressed wanting to be something way more than a cashier, Xavier already had a plan for her to boss up.

Reaching Kilbourne Lane, Xavier hit a right, and just up ahead, turning out of ChaCha's yard, he saw his brother's shiny blue and chromed Peterbilt making a wide turn out, pulling a step-deck trailer, loaded with a semi on it. Right behind Javi, Xavier saw the bright light blue Legacy Class Peterbilt pulling an identical step-deck with an identical semi on it.

Right as he rolled past Javi, his brother tooted his loud air horns then came the extra loud train horns that Macho's 379 Extended Hood had.

Xavier went into the phone log on the touchscreen in his dash and called his brother.

"¿Qué lo qué, 'mano?" Javi answered, as Xavier approached the entrance to their yard then turned in.

"What up? Where you 'n cuz headin'?" Xavier asked.

Inside, he immediately saw the Alabama twins, Kiara and Jada, both of them with long, blonde-dyed dreadlocks, that were drivers in Evelyn's auto transport crew, pre-trip inspecting their brand new Peterbilt 389 ten-car hauler trucks.

Also in the yard, preparing to head out and make some cheese, was a few of Javi's own intermodal/dry-van freight squad drivers, hooking up to fifty-three foot long dry-van box trailers. Xavier's two heavy-haul homies, that drove for him, were already gone, en route to go pick up the oversized loads he had scheduled for them.

"We shootin' to the City of Steel, tiguere," Javi said.

Xavier coasted toward where his heavy-hauler was. "I know y'all niggas is geeked for that run. Where my future sis-in-law at?"

"Hiii, big little bro!" He heard Michelle holler out.

"Yo, sis, what's good? How's your head doin'?" he asked, wanting to know how she was doing after she'd been in a wild truck chase and crash with Javi.

"Still hard as fuck," Javi answered for her, chuckling then.

"Shut ya' ass up, punk!" Xavier heard her shoot back.

He laughed. "Yeah, y'all asses are meant for each other."

"Don't I know it," Michelle said, as Xavier pulled up to his three Kenworth W900Ls, two of them heavy-haulers, one a plain spec'd tractor. "How's Kenzie and Neveah, bro?"

Xavier paused, as he saw the purple drop-top Porsche 911 Turbo rolling up to the office to park just then.

"Bro?" Michelle called out.

"Huh? What did you say?" he asked, seeing her behind the wheel.

"Kenzie? Neveah? They okay?"

Xavier parked next to his new ICON edition W900L, his brand new heavy-haul tractor, but didn't get out yet. He looked at the 911 and felt his heartbeat speeding up, as he grew so anxious to see her.

"Yeah, they good, sis," he finally answered, seeing the driver's door open up. The second Xavier saw the voluptuous woman step out, clad in a sexy, sleeveless dress, with high heels on, and her ink-black hair hanging loose, he was instantly hit with a bad case of the jitters. "Uh… Kenzie goin' back to work today."

"That's a good thing," Michelle said. "Did you give her that gift? I know it'll mean a lot to her."

"By the time she leaves out of the house, it'll be there in the driveway. Payton's dropping it off now."

"Wish I could see Kenzie's face. Go ahead and get movin'. See you when we get back," Michelle told him.

"Yup. Y'all ride safe."

"You too, bro," Javi said, then the call ended.

Xavier looked at the office and saw the lights in the windows were on. He thought about the woman, their history. He had been crazy over her back when they were young, and she'd been crazy over him as well. It was only the other night that Xavier discovered his ex-girlfriend was now working at the company, supervising day-to-day operations and fleet management. He saw her the same night that his other chicks jumped Kenzie. She was the reason why Xavier hadn't noticed Keisha, Nena, nor Pamela sneak up on him. Her sexy smile had hypnotized him, making him oblivious to anything but her.

He cut his engine off and hopped out. He needed to get his truck and trailer per-tripped, so he could go. But dammit, he wanted to see her. So bad!

"No. I know what's gon' happen if I go in there. Que se joda," he said to himself, going around to the driver's side of his truck and opening the door.

He jumped up inside of the sleek leather interior. The Apple iPad he used to log his trips set up on the dashboard, connected to the charger. He picked it up, went into his app list, and selected his driver trip log app. He pressed the icon for 'On-Duty/Not Driving: Pre-Trip', the feature that displayed that Xavier did a pre-trip inspection on his truck and trailer before getting on the road. He and every trucker in the country that was mandated by the Federal Motor Carrier Safety Administration's laws had to make sure their trucks were safe to drive. Lots of people got seriously hurt or killed when accidents involving commercial vehicles, that shouldn't have been on the road in the first place, happened. And the owners had to pay millions and could maybe even face criminal charges.

Xavier did a thorough check on his heavy-spec'd ICON and his specialized hydraulic-powered Removable Goose Neck Low-boy trailer. It was somewhat like a flatbed but sat very low to the ground from the front to the rear. At the back, there were three axles and then a fourth that flipped up onto the top of the trailer's rear deck. All the extra wheels, and its heavy steel build, was what gave it the ability to haul 110,000-pound loads. Heavy weight meant big bucks.

When he finished thirty-odd minutes later, Xavier sat behind the wheel. The beefed up, 750 horsepower ISX Cummins engine idled smoothly. Air pressure was up at 125 psi. All other functions were operational. Xavier was ready to head out, go get his load, and make the $15,000 he'd get for delivering it.

But he didn't move. Instead, he looked at the office. A few cars pulled into the yard. Other drivers were arriving for work. Xavier paid no attention to them.

"Fuck," he cursed, then he opened his door to get out.

The second his Timberlands touched the ground, he heard her voice.

"Hey, Zay."

Xavier looked up and saw Vanessa there in all her sweet, sexy, butter pecan-brown Puerto Rican and Persian splendor. The gorgeous woman stood five-ten without heels on, so with her sexy pumps on her feet, she stood almost as tall as Xavier.

Her professional office girl style dress hugged her curvaceous body like it was a second skin. Her sexy legs, big breasts, luscious hair, and her beautiful face had Xavier staring in awe at her.

"Goddam… Is that really you, 'Nessa?" he asked her.

She smiled at him. "It is. It's really nice to see you again. You're still so handsome and… big… Wow, you're big. What do you bench press?"

"Uh…. four hundred twenty-five pounds," he told her and made his pectoral muscles flex.

Vanessa bit her lip, as she grew aroused. "Hmmm. That's a lot of weight. Um… I'd like to start exercising again. Maybe we could… ya' know… workout together?"

"Oh… you… You think you need to workout?"

"Well, I got a little extra I don't need," she told him, then to show him what she meant, Vanessa gave him a slow turn.

Goddamn! That ass is phat! Coño!; Xavier thought to himself, as Vanessa's big, round bubble came around, poking out so far in her tight-ass dress.

Facing him again, Vanessa smirked. "I need to drop a few pounds. You are ripped, so you could help me. I've got a lot of energy, Zay. I can keep on going." She wiggled her eyebrows suggestively at him.

Oooowee, she wants the dick! I'ma fuck the… No! No! Kenzie is my girl! I'm not cheatin' on her! But goddammit! 'Nessa so thick!

Xavier was stuck. His old playboy instincts were kicking in.

"Tell ya' what. We can talk about it over dinner. I'll drive," Vanessa said. "See you when you get back, handsome."

She turned and sauntered off, swaying her hips extra hard, knowing that if there was any guy she wanted gazing at her plump derriere, it was her ex-boyfriend, who she planned to get back as hers really soon.

EVELYN

Evelyn looked down at her naked girlfriend. Gloria laid splayed out in their bed, snoring lightly. The second Evelyn got home, Gloria was on her. She was a ball of horny Dominiciana, hot and in need of some love. Evelyn wanted to go to sleep, but a few orgasms didn't sound bad. They got it on, twice in a row, before they both passed out, their bodies wrapped up in each other's, hearts beating as one. Evelyn loved her girlfriend more than she could describe. Thinking about how she'd just so recklessly gotten herself in deep shit, with a man who was like a ghost, had the girl terrified. The guy knew how to get at her loved ones. She had no clue who he was or how to even the odds. All she could do was get Stacks some coke. Her family had a lot. Surely nobody would question her if she showed up at one of the distribution spots, bagged up some yayo, and took it with her. Right?

Evelyn went into her big, walk-in closet, stopping at a tall eye-retina scanner safe. As she put her eye to the scan pad, Oinky trotted in. His tail wagged rapidly as he saw his human opening her safe up.

She got out the two brand new automatic Clock 18 pistols that Michelle had gifted her with on her twenty-first birthday. Evelyn locked in two thirty-round clips, loaded with hollows, then took four extra clips, and for good measure, she grabbed a Rambo-style bowie knife from the safe as well. It went into a leather sheath and down into the side of her sweats.

"See ya' later, cutie pie," Evelyn said to her piglet and walked past him, heading toward the stairs.

GLORIA

Gloria's eyes were open, but Evelyn hadn't noticed. She heard her girlfriend slapping magazines into guns, which woke her up. Lying in their bed, as still as she could be, Gloria watched her lady leave out of their room, heading out to the stairway.

Shaking her head, Gloria got up out of the bed just as Oinky entered the bedroom. The piglet came to her side of the bed and stood up on his hind legs, squealing for her to pick him up.

Gloria reached over, scooped him up, and grabbed her iPhone off of the nightstand. Letting Oinky snuggle in her lap, Gloria brought up the name of who she kept informed of Evelyn's moves.

"She just left out of here like she about to go hit a bank. What do I do?'

Gloria sent the message and waited. She rubbed Oinky's face, making him snort happily, stretching out across her lap. Her phone dinged a minute later from a response.

"Gold Mouth's following. Let her be. Whatever she's doing, we'll find out. You just go ahead to work and don't worry."

Gloria sent a thumb's up emoji then looked down at the piglet.

"Wanna ride with Mama today, cutie pie?"

Oinky snorted at her, wagging his tail.

"I'll take that as a yes. Let's go eat some breakfast then off we go," Gloria said, then she scooped him up and carried Oinky out with her, heading down to the kitchen, still in her birthday suit.

KENZIE

Kenzie checked herself out in the full-length mirror in the bedroom. It'd been a while since she'd gotten dressed in work clothes. Looking at herself, she smiled, loving what she saw despite how plain her uniform was.

The dark blue top with yellow insignia significant to Wal-Mart's branding on the back fit her tightly. She wore khaki-colored leggings that made her look so much more thick. On her feet, she wore metallic gold flats, and her hair was pulled up into a high ponytail.

Her job as a cashier had been held while on a leave of absence. It wasn't a glamorous gig, nor did it break the bank, but she was proud of the fact that she was a working woman and didn't rely on a man to feed her or her daughter. She did, however, have plans to look into getting herself into classes to become a real estate agent.

"Mommy!"

Kenzie turned around right as Neveah ran into the bathroom, wearing the bright green denim jean and jacket outfit with purple flowers on it, purple Air Forces on her feet, with her curly hair in two pigtails. Behind her was Precious, tail wagging, as she playfully gave chase.

"Hi, Mommy! I love you, and Precious loves you too!"

"Aww! I love you both too, baby!" Kenzie crouched down and kissed her daughter on her cheek then kissed Precious' nose. Just as Precious ran out of the bathroom then shot right back, Kenzie heard her new iPhone ringing.

She hurried out of the bathroom to grab it off of the dresser. It was an unknown caller. She hesitated to answer it but ended up doing so right before it went to voicemail.

"Hello?" Kenzie answered cautiously.

"Hey, is this Kenzie?" asked a woman with a southern twang.

"Y-Yes… who is this?"

"My name is Payton, and I work for Xavier's lil sister. I'm outside for you."

"Uh… outside of his house?"

"Yup. Got somethin' fa' 'ya. Can you come out?"

Kenzie looked at her daughter. Neveah was playing with Precious.

"H-Here I come," Kenzie said then ended the call. "Neveah, come here, baby girl."

Her daughter did as her mother told her. Kenzie hugged her then gave her the iPhone.

"One of Auntie Eve's friends is outside for me. Look at the screen. You see what time it is?" Kenzie pointed her little girl's eyes to the time. "It's 7:30 a.m. If Mommy doesn't come back in to get you, when you see a seven where the zero is," she paused and showed Neveah how to get to Xavier's name then how to call him, "press 'call' when you see this and tell Daddy that Mommy needs him right away. Can you do that?"

"Yes." Neveah nodded.

"Okay. I love you, baby." Kenzie kissed her daughter's forehead, then going to her nightstand, she got the new FN Five-seveN out of the safety case that Xavier got for her.

She made sure a fresh twenty-round double stack clip was in, cocked it, then tucked it into her new Michael Kors handbag but kept her hand gripped around the semi-auto just in case it was a trick.

Stepping out of the house, which was in a cul-de-sac, Kenzie saw the dark and lovely five-foot-nine-inch-tall trucker girl wearing her long, black hair in two-strand twists. She stood at the curb. Behind her was a brand-new Porsche Cayenne Turbo, sitting on twenty-two-inch HREs, painted dark green to match the Porsche truck's dark metallic green paint.

In the middle of the circle was Payton's brand new, 389 Peterbilt car-carrier, empty now that she had delivered her last vehicle.

Payton smiled and tossed Kenzie the key fob. Kenzie gasped, jaw dropping to the floor.

50

She ran out to it and checked it out. The interior was so exclusive and luxurious with beige leather, rare-inspired dash, and a sunroof. Climbing into the driver's seat, Kenzie hit the push-start button. The powerful twin-turbo charged V8 engine barked exotically, as it came to life. Kenzie hit the gas pedal and revved it, making it roar. She screamed again, overjoyed.

"Oh, shit!" Kenzie panicked, seeing it was 7:38. She ran back inside just as Neveah was about to call Xavier. "It's okay! I'm here!' she told her, taking the phone from her. "Mommy's got a new car! Daddy got it for us, baby!"

Neveah shouted, "Yaaay! Daddy! Daddy! Daddy!" She clapped her hands.

Kenzie's phone rang again. Another unknown number was on the screen. She answered it, less apprehensively, more excitedly.

"Heeelloooooo!" she sang, taking her daughter's hand.

"Don't think I forgot, bitch. You dead when I catch you," a whisper said, then the call ended.

Kenzie's heart dropped. She looked at her phone and saw the caller had hung up.

"Mommy? What's wrong?"

Kenzie looked down at her daughter. She put on a smile that was in no way authentic.

"Nothing, my love. Come on. Let's get you ready for Gamma. She's coming to hang out with you and Precious."

"Yaaaaay! I love Gamma!" Neveah cheered.

Kenzie's smile turned into a real one. Her adorable little girl always made her smile. But the creepy call had her legs trembling.

Who the hell was that? she wondered to herself, as fear of the unknown began to settle in.

JAVI

Javi pushed his rig past eighty-five miles an hour down the Edens Expressway. Just outside the city limits of Chicago, he was doing all he could to stay ahead of Macho's eighteen-wheeler Lamborghini.

A few truck lengths behind, Macho cruised at seventy. He steered with one hand, nodding his head as Lil' Wayne's *Pussy, Money, Weed* pounded from the thunderous sound system in his sleeper. Six competition, twelve-inch, JL Audio brand W7 subwoofers hit so hard that Yessy's breasts bounced every time the bass hit.

Macho laughed and turned his music down. He reached for where his Cobra CB radio set mounted on the custom woodgrain and chrome accented dash's center, unhooking the mic.

"¡Oye, tiguere? ¡Que te tratando pa' hacer, cabrón?" Macho asked.

Yessy started laughing, as she flung her big red bird at the annoying green pigs on her iPad.

Seconds later, they heard Javi's voice come back.

"Kickin' yo ass, foo'! Duh! Haa!"

Macho burst out laughing. "Cabrón, vete pal' carajo. You ain't doin' shheeeaaaat!"

"That's why yo' ass all the way back there," Javi laughed.

"Aight. When we get to the Skyway, ya' ass is grass."

"Bet some donuts from Dana's Bakery on it?" Javi wagered.

"Sure. I like glazed pretzels and cinnamon bows; Yessy love them fruit filled joints."

"Good, 'cause yo ass gon' lose! Bye-bye-bye-bye, cabrón!" Javi shouted.

Macho and Yessy watched as Javi put even more space between them. They both started laughing.

The signs for the upcoming Chicago Skyway toll booth came up. Macho smirked. He couldn't wait to embarrass his little cousin.

Up in the Pride and Class, Javi could see the Skyway about a quarter mile ahead. He cursed, knowing that although he had an I-Pass fixed to his windshield and could go through the I-Pass lanes without stopping, slowing down would allow Macho to catch up.

Suddenly, from the passenger's seat, Michelle burst out laughing. Javi glanced over at her. "What?"

"You should see your face right now! You look like you're in hard thought about how you can beat him."

"I am gon' beat him! Watch!"

"I hear that crazy shit. You got money, baby. Why you ain't do the same thing he and ChaCha did to their trucks?"

"I just got this muhfucka, Michelle," Javi reminded her. "Don't 'een trip," he said, as he got all the way into the left lane for the I-Pass users. "Tool gon' get me together. I'ma take my truck out to his shop in Jersey while we out east."

Javi then came upon the I-Pass detection sensors. He slowed down just enough for them to detect him. As soon as he saw the green *thank you* light, Javi put the pedal to the floor, taking off with all six hundred horses galloping.

Chuckling came through the CB just then. Macho's voice came next.

"Let the games begin, little cousin! Ready or not... here I come!"

Javi climbed gears until he was in high eighteen. His dash read to him that he was doing one hundred. He smirked to himself. Michelle shook her head, reading a text from Yessy.

"Javi is funny," was all she said.

Michelle replied back.

"Don't be tryna talk about my baby, Bronx Biatch."

Yessy sent a LOL then a SMH.

Javi caught an orange glow in his mirror. Glancing in it, he saw the Legacy Class. It was coming. Flames were shooting out of its monster stacks, as it blazed up the hammer lane.

Macho closed the gap in seconds, as Javi passed a line of traffic in the granny lane. Seconds later, Macho blew past Javi. Yessy hung out the window, sticking her tongue out at Javi and Michelle.

Javi cursed as his cousin pulled away from him, leaving him in a trail of thick, dark, diesel smoke.

Laughter came through the CB.

"Daaayuuum, cuzzo! Where you go? I can't see you through all my smoke, yo!" Macho teased.

Javi grabbed his mic and ignored Michelle's snickering.

"I got some smoke for yo' ass. Watch!" he told Macho.

"Boooy, stooop!" Macho shot back and burst out laughing.

CHAPTER 6

STACKS

"Joe, y'all ass better get the fuck up here asap! On the Fin, jo! I got shit that needs to go down to the Raq!" Stacks barked into his iPhone.

"On Ghost, we on the way now, Lord," his young wolf, Lil' Five, replied. "We already on the E-Way, joe. We stompin' this muhfucka too."

"Aight, hurry up."

Stacks ended the call then went into his text messaging app. He went to Kenzie's number and typed.

"You love red. You gonna be covered in it when I get through with you, bitch," he texted then sent it, smirking devilishly.

Stacks was from out west, down in Chicago. He was an Unknown Vicelord from the K-Town area. Six-feet tall, his dark skin tattooed all over, and very physically fit. he rocked a bald-fade haircut with a low-trimmed beard, lined up sharply. The twenty-six-year-old was a tried and true jack boy. Growing up out west, from a young age, Stacks had been schooled by the old school hustlers, businessmen, and the gangsters. He'd had a homie that was like a brother from another mother, but a few weeks ago, Rambo had been killed by bullets dumping at him and his bro by the hands of the Valdezes.

It was after a fight in a Burger King. Stacks had seen a thick, pretty-ass chick come in. Always having been a fiend for a phat ass and a pretty face, Stacks couldn't resist driving on her. Rambo was with him that morning. They'd been on their way to one of their dope spots where they'd stashed a huge score after hitting a lick on a Rojas-Gomez Cartel stash house.

But as Stacks tried to get at the golden-haired beauty, another woman even more beautiful came up and got to going in on him, snapping because he was ogling her little sis. She had quite the mouth on her too. Stacks had also grown up around pimps and players. He wasn't for no bitches talking reckless.

Stacks was about to get on her ass after the gold head issued a threat in Spanish. But before he could, three guys walked in, looking like angry bulls in designer clothing and diamond jewelry. All three of them were looking directly at Stacks and his homeboy.

The shortest of the three, a green-eyed man with braids and golden-brown skin, walked right up to Stacks, while the second tallest, a blue-gray eyed, braided up man, and an even taller guy with dreadlocks stood on 'S'– meaning *security* – with looks of death in their eyes. Green Eyes got on Stacks' ass. Stacks found out really fast that the golden-haired chick and the green-eyed man were sister and brother. The other woman, that had kicked it off, was green eye's woman, and the two big dudes were his cousins.

It went down in the BK. They did not have it their way.

Stacks and Rambo stood their ground and fought, but they had gone up against real goons. They both got trashed, tossed over the ordering counter, and left there. Stacks, still somewhat conscious, could hear one of the goons ordering food as if there was no need to get up out of there, then he flirted with the store manager to get the security camera recording.

After he and Rambo had dipped off in Rambo's Tahoe, they both plotted revenge. It was Rambo that realized that the posse had to be the Dominican cocaine family they had both been wanting to catch up with and hit the biggest lick ever on them, even bigger than the one on the cartel house.

As Rambo was hurrying to get away, a white Bentley appeared alongside them, and a twelve-gauge was hanging out of the passenger window, held by the massive dread head.

Rambo got hit when the shotty blew through his door. He tried to spin around and shake them, but another blast took his face off and splattered it all over Stacks.

Stacks did all he could to get out of there. He got turned around and hit the gas, but coming right at him was Green Eyes and his crazy girlfriend, blowing at him through the roof of the Donk'd Escalade pickup with a machine gun.

Stacks had no choice but to go off-road but ended up jumping a hill then plunging into a pond in the center of the park. He managed to get out through the blown-out windshield and swam for dear life until he reached a little island in the middle of the pond. Stacks surfaced just as Green Eyes went back to his Escalade and jumped up inside. He climbed out of the water, unseen by the four Dominicans; before they all dipped off, Stacks had seen a cop car pull in. But not even ten seconds later, the car screeched off, as if the driver had seen the devil.

All four of the Dominicans stood where they were, guns ready to pop if the cop even looked like he would reach for his radio.

Stacks was gobsmacked by the quad. He waited until they were gone before swimming to the other side and hurried off just as other cops came speeding up to the park.

He'd called his big cousin, Prince, and told him what had happened. Prince was heavy out west with a gang of young killers and a drug connection most dope boys in the hood dreamed of having. Prince got right on the road to come get his little cousin to safety.

Sometime later, as Prince was going to meet up with a chick he'd bumped into on the way up from Chicago to save his cousin's ass, Stacks thought his eyes were deceiving him when he saw the same golden-haired beauty from the Burger King.

Immediately, Stacks realized his plan to get at the Valdezes' coke connection, which he'd heard about during a very brief visit in the Lake County jail and then gained even more info on the cocaine-rich Dominicans from one of his ride or die bitches, Magali, about their routine, was still possible.

Through Gold Head.

So, he followed his cousin when he went to link up with the bitch. Stacks waited outside of the hotel Prince had taken the thick chick to where he was sure his big cuz was fucking her brains out.

A few hours later, the two emerged. Stacks had been posted in his cousin's Audi A8, parked a few spots away, when suddenly, gunshots rang out.

Not knowing where they'd come from, he ducked on instinct. Once he heard screeching, Stacks rose up. He looked and saw his cousin on the ground. Gold Head was screaming and crying for help. Panicked, Stacks sped the Audi over to them and hopped out. When Gold Head saw him, her face nearly flushed of all color.

Ignoring her, he got his bleeding-out cousin into the car. She demanded that she was coming. No time to argue, he allowed her. He sped his dying cousin to the closest ER, saving him.

A week later, Stacks went to check on his cousin and found the young Dominican beauty there. While his cousin was still comatose, Stacks used what he knew about the girl's family, the location of her brother's company, to force her into agreeing to hit him off with bricks. The tactics he used, he knew would work. The way that her family rode out together that crazy day, Stacks knew if he put it in her head that he could strike where it'd hurt worse, that she'd do as he demanded.

He put the fear of the unknown in her heart. She was now his slave, and he would soon be up millions. Big dog in the streets was the title he wanted. And now, he was close to making it happen.

Stacks pocketed his iPhone back into his Balenciaga jeans and stood, looking at the flashy Mercedes Benz S600 sitting on chromed twenty-one-inch AMG rims, wrapped in Lo-pros. It was blood-red with dark tints. Stacks wanted it. It was a 2013 model with a $82,000 price tag.

Out at a Mercedes dealership by Stokie, he was car shopping. His SRT-8 was too hot to drive, and he'd grown tired of driving Prince's Audi. He needed his own. He was still up; a secret stash house, that not even Rambo had known about, held hundreds of thousands of dollars in cash, guns, and bricks of different kinds of drugs.

Buying the Benz would be his first major purchase. And it was painted in his colors.

"You gettin' this?" asked the mother of his one-year-old son, Dontae Jr.

Stacks turned to see his baby mama, Jazmine, walking up, looking good as a big plate of golden fried catfish, wearing a lavender colored snake skinned bodysuit with a spaghetti-thin neck strap, open back, and a big slit over her melons. White Louboutin pumps were on her feet. Her red tipped dreadlocks were tied up into a ball on her head. Her hazel eyes were red from the potent kush blunt she and Stacks had smoked on the way to the dealership. Her dark chocolate skin radiated beauty. A few tattoos on her arms, one over her breasts, and one on her neck gave the five foot one inch tall belle a sexy thug-misses appeal. She was carrying a bookbag with Gucci symbols all over it.

"Yup. This me right here, bae," Stacks said, pulling her to him and smacking her phat bubble booty. "You gon' suck this dick while I push this muhfucka home too."

Jazmine giggled. "Yo' ass bet not crash."

A salesman came out then. Stacks inquired about the Benz and got the info. He was offered a test drive afterwards.

"Naw, joe. I ain' need nothing but the keys, my man. Bae, give him the bag," Stacks told his BM.

With a smug smile, Jazmine handed the man the Gucci bag. He opened it up and saw bundles of cash inside.

He grinned like he had discovered a pot of gold. "Alrighty then, folks. Let's go get you those keys."

"Lead the way," Stacks said and took his baby mama's hand to follow.

EVELYN

Evelyn pulled up to a tire retreading warehouse a little past noon. It looked like a plain building on a small commercial street out in Evanston. But Evelyn knew that the whole three blocks of businesses lining the street belonged to her family.

Snipers were all around. Security, strategically placed, and a few other high-tech defense mechanisms, invisible to those who had no clue they were there, made sure nobody who didn't belong there made it out alive.

At the building's tall garage door, she waited as it began raising up. Pulling inside, Evelyn saw so many rows of truck tires, all brand new, wrapped in plastic. To her left was an office. Lights were on inside. A group of men stood outside, around a forklift, with one guy sitting on the machine.

Evelyn got out of her car and was instantly approached by the warehouse manager. He was a tall, lean, Dominican man with dark skin, graying hair, and a clean-shaven face. He smiled welcomingly at his good friend's granddaughter, greeting her with a hug.

"Evelyn. ¿Como haz estado? Hace mucho tiempo que no te veo," he said, voice deep and raspy.

"I know, right? Too long since we've seen each other, Leo. I've been good too. How you been?"

"I been okay. You know Anilla passed a few months ago."

Evelyn gasped. "¡Dios mio, Leo! I'm sorry! Your wife was so beautiful and nice!" She gave him a hug, sympathizing with him.

"Thanks, Evie. Well, what's going on? Wasn't expectin' you to come here."

Evelyn took a deep breath then spoke, getting right to it. "I need a hundred bricks right now."

Leo's eyes went wide. "A hundred? Hold on... why? You're not in that field, mamita. That's ours."

"My friend screwed up her shit up in Racine. Had to dump her stash. I'm replacing it with my money, Leo. I'm not gonna leave my girl hangin', so my big cousin thinks she's skimming. You know how ChaCha is."

Leo took a minute to think about it. He was very unsure about it. Evelyn didn't touch coke. Never did. She transported it along with her brothers, cousins, and ChaCha.

"I don't know, Evie. It's gonna mess my count up," Leo said.

Evelyn opened up her trunk, grabbed the U-Haul box out of it, and handed it to Leo. He opened it and saw it was full of cash.

"Um..." He was speechless and not because of the money; he'd seen fifty-three foot long trailers filled from front to back with money. He was speechless because this was Diego's granddaughter purchasing a hundred kilos of, technically, her own cocaine. "Let me just call and..."

"No!" Evelyn immediately panicked. "Leo! He's just gonna call ChaCha, and she's gonna go get at my homegirl! Come on! I need you to trust me on this! No funny business, man."

Leo, like any other man, couldn't hold his stance the second Evelyn gave him those puppy dog eyes. He was there when Evelyn was born. She must've really wanted to save her friend to do something so drastic.

"Alright, Evie. This better not come back and bite me in my ass," Leo said then ordered one of his guys to fill the order. He looked back at Evelyn. "You puttin' them in that flashy-ass car?"

"I got a trap set under my rear seat," she said and went to the driver's side door, opening it up. Leo followed and saw her pull a fake seatbelt strap in the center. The sound of a lock popping came, then Evelyn lifted the rear seat. Leo saw an AK-47 inside the secret space with three drums. "See? I'm on the E-Way all the way to Racine, and I'm ridin' with my escort. I'm all good."

Leo nodded. "Okay then," he said and stepped back as his worker brought big duffel bags with her coke in it. "Drive safe, little lady."

"I will. Love ya," she replied, stashing the bricks and putting the seat back in place. "Thanks again and please don't tell anyone. It will get back to ChaCha."

Again, Leo nodded. He watched her get into her Beamer and back out as the door opened for her. Looking at his workers, they all stood quietly, not knowing what to make of what they'd just seen.

Leo pulled out his iPhone and scrolled down to the name he would never hide anything from and pressed call.

XAVIER

Aw, come on, man! Goddammit! These bitches is crazy! thought Xavier, as he saw Pamela's red Audi A4 tailing him. He could see Pamela behind the wheel and riding shotgun was Keisha.

Xavier was en route to one of his family's businesses to pick up a very heavy load to deliver to a family friend for his grandfather.

He had the tunes on blast, as he cruised with the southbound traffic to get down to Joliet. He was keeping his eyes on the road, but every so often, checking his mirror, he could see the beautiful Venezuelan freak behind the wheel of the little red car, still trying to tail him while thinking he had no clue she was there with Keisha.

The music cut off right then, as a call came in. Xavier smiled when he saw her name on the touchscreen Pioneer.

"What up though, my peanut butter thick Justina Valentine?"

Her sweet-sounding laughter flowed through the speakers and filled his cab sleeper up with what made him smile even harder.

"Boy, we gon' throw hands if you call me her again," Kenzie joked. "And then, I'ma suck the shit out that big dick and fuck you 'til yo' eyes close for gettin' me this sexy ass Porsche truck!"

"Porsche truck?" Xavier questioned.

"Yeah, Xavier. That girl, um… Payton, the dark-skinned chick that drives for yo' sister. She delivered it here this morning, right before I was about to hop in my putt-putt and go to work."

"Uh… I don't remember buyin' no Porsche truck, Ma."

"Hold up… What?"

"Who you said delivered it?" he asked.

"Payton!"

"I don't know anybody by that name, Kenzie."

Xavier did everything he could to keep from laughing. He heard Kenzie gasp, then she fell silent. Seconds later, Xavier could no longer hold it in. He burst into laughter, wishing he could see her face.

"Ugh! You's an asshole, man! Wait 'til I get my hands on you!" she said then, sounding salty as hell.

"Oh, yeah? What chu' gon' do?" Xavier asked, seeing the merge off from the Dan Ryan to I-55 for Joliet and farther south of Illinois.

"I'ma beat cho' ass, then I'ma lick you up and down."

Xavier burst out laughing. "I think that as your man, I'm the one that's supposed to lick you up and down."

"Well, we can do it together, baby; sixty-nine is our best friend. You and me can put a whole new meanin' to licks."

"Wow. Yo' ass cray-cray, Ma,' he chuckled, getting into the exit lane to jump onto the Stevenson Expressway. "You get a chance to put ya' new ride on the road before work?"

"Hell yeah. After yo' grandparents came to get my baby, I put it on 41 and pissed everyone off, joe."

"I bet you look good in it too."

"I'll look better when I'm bouncin' up and down on that dick if you come to give me a quickie."

"I cannot disagree, but if I did that, it won't be a quickie." Kenzie purred sexily. "I know. Love you, Xavier."

"And I love you… Justina."

She burst out laughing again. "Asshole. Drive safe, baby."

Xavier chuckled. "You too."

The call ended. Xavier rolled with the early morning riders of 55, closing in on the pick-up point. As Lil' Wayne's *Leather So Soft* started playing, he glanced in his mirror again and could still see the Audi. It was maintaining its distance yet sticking out like a sore thumb. He shook his head at the two then focused his eyes ahead of him.

CHAPTER 7

STACKS

"Woooo! Shit!" His eyes rolled to the back of his head, as Jazmine deep-throated his length like a pro while on her knees in the passenger's seat of the Benz, ass up high, head down in his lap, bobbing up and down. "Suck this muhfucka, bae! Get all this dick!"

Northbound on 41, Stacks pushed his big V12 Benzo back toward his stomping grounds. He had a new, fly-ass whip, a thick ass ride or die chick, a free re-up, and a team of young, hungry ghosts that came up to help him become the Black El Chapo.

Thankfully though, after a few promises, Jazmine was no longer pissed off at him for making her drop Teresa and Crazy D's baby off at the hospital. He had to make her understand that having the stolen baby of two people that they had robbed and murdered… would not be a good thing if the cops caught them up.

Yo Gotti's *Standin In The Kitchen* bumped from the stock Bang & Oluffsen audio system. Stacks caressed Jazmine's ass, squeezing it as he felt his nut rising. She sped up, feeling his dick pulsating in her mouth, tasting his pre-cum as he got closer and closer. Less than a minute later, Stacks busted his nut, cursing loudly as he filled her mouth up with cum.

"Fuck! Goddamn, baby! Yo' ass finna make a nigga crash 'n shit, joe!" he said to Jazmine as she swallowed.

"Don't ask for what you can't handle then, nigga," Jazmine replied, sitting back up in her seat. "Just make sure I get mines before we get Dontae Jr."

A call came in, interrupting the music. Stacks hit the 'answer' icon on the L.E.D. screen in the dash.

"What?" he answered ignorantly.

"Fuck you mean 'what'?" Nigga, where the fuck is you at?!" came the voice of the angry Dominicana.

"Bitch, number one, watch yo' mouth or I swear on the Five I'll slap the fuck out cho ass!" Stacks shot back, as he neared the Great Lakes/North Chicago area. "Don't get that shit twisted, ho! You on my time! I run this! You dig what I'm sayin'?"

She didn't answer. Jazmine laughed at how her baby daddy had no problem putting bitches in their place.

"Bitch! Answer me when I talk! I said do you dig?!"

"Yeah, man! I'm fuckin' here, joe! Yo' lil' friends think I'ma just hand the shit to 'em like I'm Boo-Boo the Fool! I don't do hand-offs with the help, so hurry the fuck up and get here!"

The call ended, leaving Stacks wishing he was already there, so he could strangle her. Jazmine looked over at him.

"Yo' ass need to control that bitch, bae," she said to him.

Stacks called the young gunner that he put in charge of the clique of Unknowns.

"What 'ain, Lord?" Lil' Five answered.

"Leave the bitch alone, bruh. I'm almost there."

"On the Five, if this bitch wasn't so muhfuckin' bad and thick as hell, I'd have knocked her muhfuckin' noodles loose right now."

Stacks laughed. "I know. We need her though. That bitch is our golden goose. After we get all the yay' we need, then her brothers gon have to pay us if they want lil' sis to be alive this Christmas."

"Say less. Almighty, nigga."

"Mighty," Stacks replied back then ended the call with a diabolical smirk as the plans he had for the Valdez princess swam around in his head.

JAVI

At a travel plaza rest stop in Gary, Indiana, Javi and Macho made a stop for fuel, then with everyone needing to eat, they parked their trucks in the crowded truck parking area and headed in for breakfast at the Hardee's inside.

Jamaica and his goons stayed posted outside, keeping their eyes on the trucks. There was way too much money in them to leave them unattended at any point.

Ordering their food, Javi and Macho took bags of breakfast sandwiches, beverages, and hash browns to the Rastas then got their dogs into their harnesses and leashes to take them with them to eat as well.

Joining the ladies outside at a patio section, with the dogs chilling with them, Javi and Macho sat down to eat.

"Why you look like someone stole ya' favorite baseball card, lil' cutty?" Macho asked Javi, seeing his cousin seemed to be in deep thought, staring down at his croissant.

Macho called his name twice. He still didn't respond.

"Bae?" Michelle nudged him then, which brought him back.

He saw everyone looking at him. "Why is y'all starin' at me?"

"Because you look like you got a heavy mind," Yessy said. "And Antonio, in a way, asked you why you look so sad."

Javi shook his head. "I hate feelin' like a coward."

"A coward?" Michelle questioned with a raised eyebrow.

He looked at her. "Bae, we are runnin' from the trouble when we normally run to it and face it head on."

"It's a lil' different this time, cutty," Macho said. "Five-O is involved, somehow connected to ol' boy's side. This ain't nothin' to take lightly, yo. Homies."

Javi's eyebrows rose in shock. "Wow... did my cop-car exploding cousin just say that? The same one that stuffs cops in the trunk of a Bentley?"

Yessy shook her head at her man. "Just dumb!"

Macho ignored her. "I'm not a stranger to logic, cuz. Soy un gangsta all day 'eryday, but I'm smart too. We don't know who all that fat fucker was tied to nor do we know if it was just him on your ass or if there will be others. We have to be careful with this, yo."

"ChaCha reached out to Danny, and he's making calls," Yessy informed Javi. "She hit me while we was rollin'. From what's been discovered so far, he's been investigated for bribery, extortion, tampering with evidence in certain cartel member arrests, and prostitution. Supposedly, he has ties to the Rojas-Gomez Cartel."

Javi and Michelle's eyes went wide with shock.

"How?" asked Michelle before Javi could.

"Not know yet," Macho answered. "But we'll soon find out."

Javi nodded his head then brought up something else that was bothering him.

"Gloria told me that Eve left out this mornin', thumped up like she was finna go hit a lick."

Macho's, Yessy's, and Michelle's eyes all went wide.

"What the hell?" said Macho, not liking that at all.

"That's what I said when he told me," Michelle chimed in.

"Something is up wit' baby girl, so we put extra eyes on her... At least we tried to. She shook her protection while she was on the E-Way to Chicago."

"Put a tracker on her car," Yessy suggested.

"She'll find it," Javi said. "Especially if she feels like she's bein' followed. Eve is a worrywart for real. I'ma just keep Gloria on her ass."

Michelle laughed out loud. "Javier, she does that anyways."

"Aye! Yo!" Macho burst out laughing suddenly. "Who can answer this question?" he asked, as the three looked at him with confusion.

"Ask away, mutt," Yessy said to him.

"Shut up. But, yo, what is the one show on TV still where you can still see Queen Latifah wearin' dresses 'n skirts 'n shit?"

Javi and his fiancée burst out laughing at his random question.

"¿En serio, Antonio?" Yessy said with narrowed eyelids.

"Yeah, punk. For real."

"I'm stumped," Michelle admitted.

Macho was about to tell them when he got a text. They all watched him read it, then he looked at Javi.

"Guera has a big shipment comin' in tomorrow night. You ridin' wit' me?" he asked.

"Hell yeah!" Javi replied eagerly. "To help put a Venezuelan on is somethin' I know our ol' heads would love, cuz."

"They our people too. Juan Pablo Duarte made it like that when he got exiled to Caracas," Macho said, giving his cousin a little bit of Dominican history. "He was one of three in the group *La Trinitaria* back when shit was goin' down between Spain, Haiti, and Santo Domingo. Then came *Las Mariposas* when Rafael Trujillo got on his Fidel Castro shit."

"Didn't the C.I.A. kill him?" Michelle asked.

"That's what I was always told, in 1950 or '51."

Yessy suddenly scooted over and got onto her man's lap. She kissed his face and hugged him tightly.

"I'm guessin' I'm not in trouble for blowin' the cop's car up anymore?" he asked with a chuckle.

"I've decided since you are so smart and so cute that I can let this one slide, but," Yessy cupped his face and made him look up at her, "don't do it again!"

He started smiling at her. "What if one just happens to catch on fire?"

"Antonio... I will punch you in your eye."

"No, you won't because you love my eyes," Macho shot back.

Michelle started laughing at Yessy's delayed response.

"Maaaan, I can't wait for you two to have kids. On God, they gon' be wild as hell," Javi said.

"You know what else is on God, lil cuz?" Macho said with his arm wrapped around his woman.

"What?"

"I will fuck the dog shit outta Queen Latifah, yo! Homies!"

Yessy smacked her lips, then she muffed his face, which made Javi and Michelle laugh their asses off at him.

Ready to go, they left the Hardees and headed back to their trucks.

"The hell? Yessy's drivin'?" Javi asked, as he opened his driver's door, Macho opening his passenger-side door at the same time.

"She threatened me with no sex if I didn't let her drive," Macho told him.

Javi burst out laughing. "Salty!"

"You will be."

Javi climbed up into his truck and closed the door. He saw his woman had her iPad out and was already playing a game. Diamond sat next to her, panting with her tongue out.

Looking to his left, he saw Macho wasn't all the way in his truck yet. Javi smirked to himself and hurried to release his brakes, put it in low gear, and pull off, attempting to put more distance between himself and his cousin.

Michelle looked at him, as he swiveled his head all around, making sure he was clear to glide along the interstate's re-entrance ramp and get back on the road. He speed-shifted gears, splitting the high-side to get as much speed as he could.

She snickered to herself, admiring his never give up attitude. But she already knew that the real speed demon was now behind the wheel.

YESSINIA

Yessy gripped the woodgrain steering wheel and shifted Macho's eighteen-speed transmission like she was attempting to set a new land speed record in a semi. Macho sat back and wore a smirk, as the distance between him and his woman and Javi and Michelle very rapidly decreased.

"Blow his doors off, bae," he told Yessy.

She nodded, already having planned to do so. She reached eighty-two miles, and quickly, the 1,3 50 horses that the high-performance diesel upgrade that Pittsburgh Power, Ine gave it were hard at work. Thick black diesel smoke shot out of the pipes as Yessy drove the big rig like she stole it. Years as a truck driver in the military had given her the whip skills that most seasoned male truckers didn't have.

Swerving over into the hammer lane, as she closed in on Javi, Yessy hit the button and blasted the train horns, as she flew right past Javi, now doing just over one hundred miles an hour.

Macho hung out the window and shouted to his cousin, "Hasta la vista, cabron!"

Michelle laughed so hard that she could barely breathe. Javi shook his head.

"I'm guessin' you just lost… again?"

Tool's voice came out of the speakers via Bluetooth call.

"Maybe," Javi capped.

"Naw, the way Michelle's laughin', you just got smoked," he said, then he burst out laughing.

"Los dos de ti pueden besar mi culo," Javi replied, salty, as he watched Yessy pull far ahead of him through the trails of black smoke she left behind her.

XAVIER

Xavier parked his rig in the section designated for semis to pick-up or deliver. It was all the way inside the massive business. As he'd entered, Xavier caught a glimpse of Pamela's car parking at the car wash across the street from his grandfather's heavy machinery sales and repair business. He wondered to himself if they really actually thought he wasn't in tune with his surroundings at all times.

An hour later, Xavier's heavy-duty low-boy trailer was loaded with a big off-road articulated Caterpillar rock truck that weighed just over sixty-thousand pounds by itself without the extra three-thousand pounds of cocaine hidden inside the six huge master-truck wheels the giant rump truck rolled on.

He got it chained down properly with thick heavy chains, orange flags at the outer four corners of it, then at the back of the trailer, and the front of his tractor, Xavier hung yellow banners with *Oversize Load* in block letters.

Back up in his seat, Xavier grabbed his log and put himself back onto 'Driving' duty-status. He released the brakes as he shifted to low then gently pulled off with almost seventy-five thousand pounds of weight on his trailer.

Peeping the ladies in Pamela's car as he rode past, once he exited the business, Xavier continued to play dumb. He got back onto 55 to head north, falling in line with a few semis rolling like they were in a rush.

A few car lengths behind, Pamela followed. He couldn't continue to allow it due to the nature of his load.

"I gotta get these bitches off my ass," he said to himself.

Then, another thought popped into his head. *Nena been real quiet and ducked off... Her ass better not forget about my windshield*, he thought to himself.

Then, he realized that he really did need to reach out to her. She was carrying his seed. He had to man up. His father would not approve of a deadbeat daddy.

Checking in his mirror again, he saw Pamela switch lanes and get right behind him, now blocked from his line of vision by the big rock truck.

"Oh, yeah?" Xavier smirked, then he slammed his brakes on. The Audi darted back out from behind him before it collided with his rolling brick wall.

"Yeah, bitch, get cho' ass back. Pendeja," he chuckled, then a minute later, an idea came to him on how he could get them off of his ass.

CHAPTER 8

EVELYN

Sitting in her Alpina B7, Evelyn shook her head at how the young dudes were milling about, looking like they were up to no good. Shaking her head again, she could see why people got targeted by cops so easily. They were damn near having a block party in the driveway, while she was loaded with cocaine.

Just then, a shiny red Benz pulled into the driveway and parked next to the house's side entrance door. She saw Stacks hop out from the driver's seat, fresh in Balenciaga with a fresh fade. The long gold Cuban link chain around his neck gleamed like the gold Rolex on his wrist. Diamond studs flicked in his ears as well. Evelyn actually found Stacks to be an attractive man. He was like a thuggish Morris Chestnut in her eyes but a straight up dickhead.

She watched him go around to the passenger's side of the car. He opened the door up and assisted a dark-chocolate complexioned woman with long, red-tipped dreads out of the car. They both walked up toward the house's door. Evelyn nodded to herself in approval of the fly-ass bodysuit the short girl was rocking. She was gorgeous. Evelyn still very much liked women. Instant visuals of her and the thick sexy chick bumping coochies filled her mind.

Evelyn's attention went back to Stacks, as she saw him snap his finger at her. She shook her head, beyond tired of him thinking she was his bitch.

Right now, you got it, playboy. You gon' learn real soon though that I'm not just beauty and booty, Evelyn thought to herself, tucking her two pistols into the custom holsters in her sweats which concealed the extended clips as well. With her Rambo knife still on her side, Evelyn got out of the car.

"Ain't no time fa' bein' slow, joe," Stacks said as his baby mama went to open the door. "Let's get a move on, shorty."

"Naw, homeboy. Check it the fuck out," Evelyn said, staring at him with fire in her eyes.

Stacks looked at her, as if her words had just smacked him. His baby mama looked like she wanted to thump. Evelyn ignored her and told Stacks to step over to her.

"Shorty, yo' ass gon' quit talkin' lik..."

"Ah!" Evelyn shushed him with her hand. "I said check it the fuck out. That means stop talking and come look at how messy this shit looks."

"Hold up, hold the fuck up, joe," Jazmine snapped, walking toward Evelyn. "Bitch, who the fuck is you..."

Crack!

Evelyn waited for her to get within a foot of her, then she cocked back and rocked her jaw so hard that Jazmine farted and fell.

Stacks' young ones all stopped what they were doing and turned toward where Jazmine was on her ass, and Evelyn stood over her. They looked at Stacks, seeing him pull out a Desert Eagle.

"You just fucked up, shorty," he told Evelyn, cocking the .40 back.

"Well, go on 'n buss then, gangster," Evelyn told him, stepping around the dazed Jazmine and walking right up to Stacks. She looked right into his eyes. "You a goon. Pull the trigger. Come on."

Stacks' jaw muscles clenched, as his anger soared. He felt highly disrespected – and in front of his guys and his baby mama. But he couldn't light the girl up. He wasn't stupid. Not only was it broad daylight, and not only was he in front of his stash spot, but he knew who Evelyn was. He was smart enough to know that if she was hurt or killed, the Dominicans were going to find out, and Stacks was very sure that they would come for him and those dearest to him.

"Man, back up off me, shorty," Stacks said. "All that tough-ass shit, knock it the fuck off."

"Ain't no act with me, player. If you know like I bet you do, I was born a goon," Evelyn said, as Jazmine woozily stood up. "Now, as I was sayin', yo guys are outta order, and you 'n ya' wife ain't got shit organized. If you want my yayo, y'all finna get this shit right. There's a reason why me and my people stay clear of cop cars."

Stacks looked at his baby mama. Jazmine was grilling him, mad as hell he wasn't strangling the bitch. He looked at his guys and saw what Evelyn was talking about. If a cop rode past right now, they'd have eyes on them for the rest of the day.

"Aight." Stacks tucked his gun back into his waistline. "Say what's on yo mind, joe."

"Who out of all them young muhfuckas is ya' top dog?" Evelyn asked.

"Aye, Lil' Five. Come here, Lord," Stacks called.

Evelyn saw a young, very handsome boy step up. His long dreadlocks were freshly re-twisted. His high-yellow complected skin, his hazel eyes, and his tattooed, five-foot-eight, lean, muscular frame intrigued Evelyn. He looked like Kirko Bangs with dreadlocks. He wore a red tank top that let his inked-up arms, chest, and neck show. He wore black, leather Balenciaga shorts with a red, Louis Vuitton belt, monogrammed with LVs, and a LV belt buckle, and on his feet, he kept it thugging with black Timberlands. Gold chains were around his neck with a gold Rolex on his wrist. Evelyn could tell that the young boy was either getting money or had a gullible bitch with cake.

"What 'oun, joe?" Lil' Five shook with Stacks, making eye contact, then side glanced at Evelyn.

"This is Eve. She gots some things to say," Stacks said and stepped back to watch.

Evelyn got on boss status. She gave Lil' Five a whole truckload of game. He was amazed by all the things he and his Lord homies hadn't been up on. Everything she told him, teaching him how to be more structured and careful, he took into his head, locking it in.

Even Stacks was impressed. He started thinking to himself that with a boss chick like Evelyn on his team, he couldn't lose.

Jazmine, as her vision cleared, looked at Evelyn. She had no clue why, but she was getting aroused by the very sight of her. Even though the Dominicana was in a loose-fitting Nike shirt, sweats, with Jordans on her feet, she was still so bad. Jazmine wasn't even into women but feeling moisture between her legs had her feeling some type of way.

After Evelyn finished, Stacks walked back up to her.

"Damn. I can't 'een lie. You a boss, shorty. On Ghost, I need you on my team."

"Move right and I'm here," Evelyn replied, secretly feeling herself. "You and yo' guys tryna get rich, then we finna do it my way. Yah mean?"

Stacks nodded. "Let's eat then… Queen."

Evelyn smirked. "Queen… I like that but no. I'm Evie Fuckin' Baby, nothin' more, nothin' less. Lil' Five, have four of ya' youngins post at each end of the block to keep a look out for the jakes. Have three more post two houses down, incognito. The rest, inside the house, ready to cook, weigh, bag, and package up the yay. Let's do it."

Jazmine's pussy was so wet now. Hearing the gorgeous chick give crew of killers all these commands had her wanting to jump down too.

"What can I do?" she asked, walking up to Evelyn, ignoring her baby daddy attempting to take her hand into his.

Evelyn turned and saw his baby mama there. The glint in her eyes told Evelyn that she had the bitch ready to do anything she told her to do. Evelyn looked at Lil' Five, making her commands his own.

Hmmm... Evelyn got another idea that she planned to make a reality real soon.

"Stick with me and I'll lead you to where I want you, lil' mama," she told Jazmine.

Stacks looked at the scene in front of him. Evelyn had just taken over his crew and his bitch. He didn't even see it coming.

Ten million and I'm out the game... and I'm puttin' five hot ones in that bitch's face – after I sample that wet ass pussy I know she got. And if cuz wanna defend the bitch, his ass can catch 'em too, joe, Stacks told himself, as he watched the young girl boss up before his very eyes.

XAVIER

Xavier left his rig parked in the truck parking lot of the Pilot truck stop at Russell Road and I-94. Creeping through the mass of big rigs, he headed toward the car parking area. Rounding the corner to the building, Xavier saw the Audi's rear end sticking out slightly from in between two other vehicles.

He walked past the front entrance door, where the regular gas pumps were, approaching the A4. As soon as he got to it, Xavier saw that neither Pamela nor Keisha were inside.

Scratching his chin, Xavier entered the Pilot's building. He looked around the little restaurant inside. No sight of them. He went to the other side where the Pilot's convenience store area was. Still no sight of them. Xavier, for a second, thought about waiting to see if they'd gone to the bathroom. But it seemed creepy for him to do so, so instead, he grabbed a six-pack of Red Bulls, paid for them, then leaving out of the store, he headed back to his truck.

Xavier approached his rig and opened the driver's door. He sat his energy drinks on his seat then climbed up into the cab. The second he closed his door, he heard a noise behind him.

Quick and fast, Xavier whipped out his Glock .40 and pointed it back into his sleeper.

"Aahh! Don't shoot!"

Xavier's jaw dropped when he saw both Pamela and Keisha sitting on his bed... naked... with heels on their feet. They both held each other out of fear, not expecting a big-ass pistol to be pointed at them.

"Shit. Yo, the fuck is wrong with y'all? Are y'all tryin' to die?" he asked, lowering his gun.

"No!" the voluptuous, milk-chocolate Keisha stated. "We was just tryna surprise you, Xavier!"

"Yeah!" The caramel-brown Venezuelan girl looked at Xavier. "We just wanted to apologize for jumping yo bitch!"

Xavier sighed. "First off, Kenzie is not my bitch; she is my woman. Second, you got knocked the fuck out, so you didn't do shit." He looked at the dark-haired chocolate beauty. "Keisha and Nena did."

"Look, Xavier, I'm sorry! I was just mad yo ass ghosted me," Keisha replied. She let go of Pamela and stood her five-foot-seven, hourglass shaped frame up, letting Xavier get a good look at what he'd been missing. "We better than that, baby," she told him, taking the few steps toward him until she was inches away. "You know I'm yo' boo, no matter what." She pulled him down to her by the collar of his work shirt and kissed him.

Pamela hopped up and went to him too. "And so am I!" she said, pulling him away from Keisha and kissing him.

Keisha reached out to his pants and started undoing his jeans. Pamela pulled back. She bit her bottom lip, as she lifted his shirt up and over his head. Xavier chuckled as the sexy ladies undressed him. When he was ass naked, they both took a step back and gazed at him.

"Wow... chocolate cake delight," Pamela said with lustful eyes.

"Mm mm... goddamn, you are fine," Keisha said, looking him up and down.

Xavier smirked seductively at the horny ladies. He closed the privacy curtains to his sleeper, preventing anyone from seeing the events that were about to take place through the windshield of his cab.

"This what y'all want?" he asked, stepping toward them with ten inches of hard dick, ready to pipe them down. "Y'all feenin' for some of this dick, huh?"

"Yeesss!" Keisha replied, eyeing his thick tool, mouth watering at the sight of it.

"¡Sii, Papi!" Pamela pleaded. "¡Lo quiero tanto!"

"Both of y'all, get over here and show Daddy how much y'all want this tube-steak."

In less than a whole second, both of the ladies were on their knees; Keisha stuffed as much of Xavier's cock down her throat as she could, while Pamela took his balls into her mouth and sucked on them.

Xavier's eyes rolled to the back of his head, loving the feeling of two bad ass bitches licking and sucking his dick. He planned to fuck the shit out of them, cum all over their faces, smack them on their asses, and send them on their way. Then, he was still going to go pipe his woman down before heading to deliver his load.

STACKS

"Damn." Stacks grinned from ear to ear, as he and Jazmine and Lil' Five looked at the bricks of coke on his kitchen table. "Now this is what I like to see, joe. On the Fin, muhfuckas gon' eat." He looked at Evelyn, who leaned up against the refrigerator. "How much yo family be movin' keys fa?"

"Depends on how much you buy. These is free. Get ya' money up, then there'll be more to come. Keep structure, stay organized, and don't take no bullshit."

Stacks nodded. "Fa'sho. You gon' stick around?"

"Naw. Told you I got shit to do, playboy. Get at me when you need me."

Evelyn exited out of the house and was about to hop into her BMW when she saw it. It sat right in the middle of the street in front of the house. It was the same big, black, pickup truck she'd seen up on the overpass when she, her girls, Xavier, and ChaCha made it just in time to save Javi and Michelle from the mob of sicarios that had been assembled to murder them in cold blood.

Instinctively, she whipped out her automatic pistols and got to blowing at the dually. The young Lords posted a couple houses down were on it, hopping out of their Caddy truck and running to assist Evelyn, dumping at the back of the pickup truck.

The dually's rear wheels started smoking, as the driver mashed the gas pedal. The pickup took off, as bullets pinged right off of it, having absolutely no effect on it whatsoever. Evelyn ran into the street and led the group, all of them bucking at the fleeing vehicle as it raced up Winter Street toward Martin Luther King Jr. Drive. As soon as it reached the corner where a Domino's Pizza set, it bent the corner and disappeared just as the youngsters posted there got out to blast at it.

The young Ghosts had no clue why they were shooting at the pickup. It didn't matter though; they were riding with their plug, no questions asked.

Stacks and Jazmine ran out of the house, as the watchers posted at the ends of the street ran down to them.

"I thought you was about not attractin' the police," Stacks said to Evelyn, as she opened the door to her BMW to get in.

"Fuck the police!" she shouted angrily, slamming her door and starting her engine.

Evelyn put it in drive and mashed the gas, shooting out the driveway and swerving right, racing toward Winter, toward Martin Luther King, to go hunt down the pickup truck all by herself.

Stacks and his crew were all godsmacked by the gangstress' fearlessness. Jazmine was so turned on that she wanted to take Stacks' car, hawk Evelyn down, and beg to be her ride or die bitch.

"Lord," Lil' Five said, getting Stacks' attention. "I ain' know how nor where you found shorty, but on Ghost, we need more bitches like her, joe."

Stacks nodded. "I'm already knowin', Lord. Don't 'een trip," he said, as sirens began wailing out in the distance, like from the North Chicago Police station minutes away from the stash house. "Let's get up outta here for a while 'til it cool down."

At that, they all hopped into their whips and bounced before NOGO PD got on the block. Stacks pushed his Benz north on Green Bay Road, approaching the intersection where Argonne was. He looked over at his BM and saw her smiling like a bashful love-struck teenager.

"Fuck yo' ass smilin' like that fa?" he asked, passing through the intersection, seeing cops to his right, flying off of Dugdale Road onto Argonne to get to Winter.

Jazmine pursed her lips, shaking her head. "Bae, that girl is a muthafuckin' goon, joe. On Ghost."

Stacks chuckled. "She a thoroughbred fo'sho. And she gon' get us where we need to go, then her ass finna go meet Rambo."

Jazmine's smile faded then. At first, she wasn't feeling Evelyn at all. But she changed. Now, she saw that the Dominican beauty was an asset, not a loose end. As her baby daddy drove toward her mother's to go pick their son up, Jazmine began thinking, thinking about things she never thought she'd think of when it came to her baby daddy.

CHAPTER 9

JAVI

"The fuck?! Maan, what the fuck is she doin'?!" Javi asked, furious to hear of his baby sister wildin' out like she was.

"Can't say for sure about the mob of young dudes," said the deep male voice coming through the Pride & Class' speakers. "But the pickup was that sicario dude that mobbed them shooters up on you and Michelle."

Michelle shook her head as she sat reclined in the passenger's seat. She and Evelyn were going to have a talk whenever she and Javi got back to Illinois.

"I'm still on her tail," the man continued. "Looks like she might be heading toward your yard, fam. What you want me to do?"

"Stay wit' her, bro. Keep her from doin' somethin' crazy."

"You mean somethin' else crazy?"

"Yeah, man. Just don't let my baby sis get hurt, Tank. Please."

"You know I got chu', Javi. No question. Ride safe," the biggest guy on Javi's crew said, then the call ended.

Michelle looked over at her fiancé. "Think this has anything to do with whoever was in her car that night that she dipped off on Gold Mouth and his guys?"

Javi shrugged. "I don't know, bae," he said, pushing up the hammer lane with Yessy nowhere in sight. "But whoever the fuck it is that got my lil' sister runnin' around actin' crazy, on my dead Uncle Pedro, I'm finna take 'em myself to go meet Heavy B when I catch they ass."

Michelle's eyes went wide in shock. "Whoa... Heavy B though?"

"Muhfuckin right Heavy B. It is not a game when it comes to my baby sister," Javi declared.

Michelle fell back and started thinking of her own plans to holla at Evelyn. Javi turned the music back up, and they both fell silent, as Lil' Webbie's *You A Trip* bumped.

KENZIE

Goddamn! Why is this line so fuckin' long?! Where is the bitch that's supposed to take over?! I gotta use the fuckin' bathroom! Come on!

Kenzie scanned items as fast as she could, trying to keep from thinking about how badly she needed to use it. Her Crohn's was flaming up, despite the medication she took earlier that morning.

Pressure in her gut had her sweating, going pigeon-toed. She passed gas repeatedly, bit her bottom lip so hard that she swore it wouldn't be there when she let it go.

She managed to check out six more people before the girl that was supposed to come arrived to give her a break. Kenzie took off running in her flats toward the bathroom at the center of the front of the store.

She saw it to her left and was filled with relief that she was going to make it. But two checkout lanes away from it, an old woman rushed out with a shopping cart loaded with purchases. Kenzie screamed as she slid right into the cart, knocking it over and tumbling with it to the floor.

"Fuuuuck!" she screamed as her bowels evacuated where she laid.

The old woman started cursing her out then. An undercover loss prevention cop ran over as Kenzie attempted to get up and trash the lady. She screamed angrily, trying to get past the cop and hurt the elderly woman. The cop pulled her away, nearly dragging Kenzie.

"Ew! Mommy! Look at her butt!" a little kid laughed, pointing to the brown stain on the bottom of Kenzie's jeggings.

Kenzie snapped. "Shut the fuck up, you little future punchin' bag!"

~ ~ ~

"Kenzie, I'm gonna have to let you go," said Kenzie's boss.

"Ms. Beth! Please! I need this job! Please don't fire me! I can get the shot that'll help my system!" Kenzie begged, as she felt more coming out. "I just need to be able to work! I have a daughter!"

"Well, you must not be too broke. I see that Porsche you came in," Bethany said, wrinkling her nose in disgust. "I'm sorry, Kenzie. But I can't have an employee here that has your... uh... issue. If you could please vacate the premises. You're smelling up the place."

Bethany turned on the heels of her pumps and scampered off, leaving Kenzie embarrassed and devastated in front of the loss prevention cop.

XAVIER

"Yo' ass better call me, Xavier," Keisha said, as she hiked up her skin-tight leather pants over her phat, juicy, bubble booty.

"Me too, Papi. For real," said Pamela, putting her long, ankle-length, tank top dress back on. "Or we gon' hunt chu' down again."

"I told y'all I will," Xavier told them again, as he put his Tims back on. "I gotta ride though. Get at me."

They put their sexy pumps back on and got out of his truck, walking pigeon-toed, still feeling filled up with dick.

"Aye!" he called to them.

They turned around.

"Where's Nena?"

They both smirked, shrugged, then ran off toward Pamela's car.

Xavier sat in his seat, ready to head over to Zion. Suddenly, he heard gunshots ring out. People that were walking about the truck area took off running, not knowing where the shooting was coming from.

Xavier's heart dropped as he looked out his windshield toward the car lot. Amongst a crowd of people that had been hit, he saw Pamela and Keisha laid out on the ground... bleeding out of multiple bullet holes.

"Shit!" he cursed and jumped out of his Kenworth, running to where they laid.

Pamela was gone. The whole top of her head was off, lying in pieces scattered around her brains.

Keisha was alive, trying to crawl to safety. Gunshot wounds in her leg bled profusely. She cried in agony, screaming for help.

"Keisha! Yo, I'm right here, Ma!" Xavier said, scooping her up off the ground.

"What the fuck, man?! Why am I shot?!" she cried.

Xavier heard tires screeching just then. He swiveled his head around to the right where the truck parking area was along with the car scale. Out on Frontage Road, he saw a dark red SUV speeding off, heading north, passing the yard that used to be Javi's.

"Xavier! It hurts so bad!"

He carried her to the car lot, skipping past Pamela's body, hoping to keep Keisha from seeing her like that. But she saw the girl and sobbed, wailing loudly.

"Yo! We need an ambulance!" Xavier shouted, as he rushed Keisha into the restaurant section, sitting her down on a bench.

KENZIE

Kenzie did her best to wipe away the tears that constantly poured from her eyes, but they kept falling. With haste, Kenzie speedwalked out of the Wal-Mart. She felt the mush under her bottom squeezing out into the thighs of her jeggings. She was horrified to have had to leave up out of the crowded store with a big, wet, brown stain at her ass that everyone stared at.

Just as she got to her SUV, a car pulled up next to her. Kenzie glared at the silver Audi R8, as the driver's window rolled down. Behind the wheel, she saw a beautiful Latina. Her skin was brown like ancient Aztecs. Her long, flowing, blonde hair was luscious, styled to look wet with the mousse that ran through it.

Big Chanel shades concealed her eyes but not the smile that had her perky pink lips curled upwards.

"Hey, girl. Long time no see," the woman said, parking her exotic two-door in front of Kenzie's Porsche truck, blocking her in.

Kenzie ground her teeth in anger. She wanted to leave!

"Can you please move your car?!" Kenzie said between clenched teeth.

The woman started grinning. "Aww. What's the matter, Red? You don't remember me?"

Kenzie looked at the girl. She couldn't place her at all.

"No! Now please, I need to get home!"

The chick laughed. "I saw you waddling out of your job. You musta boo-boo'd on yoself... again. Stacks told me all about yo shitty booty ass."

Kenzie gasped, jaw dropping to the ground. "Bitch!" she screamed, grabbing her FN out of her Michael Kors bag and taking aim at the girl. "Move the fuck outta my way or I'mma pop yo ass!"

The girl laughed. "Bitch, the parking lot is full of cameras, joe. Yo ass ain't no G. You work here, and you can't be mistaken for nobody else with that hair."

Kenzie grew irate with fury. But the girl was right. She couldn't pop her ass, but… she could beat her ass.

"Yeah, you right,", Kenzie said, stuffing her gun back into her bag. "I'ma show yo ass what it is though."

The girl gasped when Kenzie dropped her handbag and rushed her with the speed of a track star not wearing flats.

Bink! Bink! Crack!

Scurr!

Kenzie rocked the girl three time before she hit the gas and peeled off. The monster V10 engine in the Audi's rear shot the little car off like it was shot out of a cannon.

"Where you goin, bitch?! Come back 'n get that ass beat some more!" Kenzie shouted, as the R8 bent the corner, nearly mowing some shoppers down.

She then grabbed her bag off the ground and fished her key fob out. Feeling eyes on her, she looked up and saw two young Hispanic guys across the way staring at her.

"Fuck is y'all lookin' at?!" she snapped, unlocking her vehicle.

The two dudes chuckled, then they walked off. Kenzie got into her Porsche, grimacing as she sat down. The mushed squeezed farther down her legs as her weight forced it all around. She hit the push-start button, slammed it into drive, then she hit the gas, and tore up out of the lot like she'd just robbed the place.

MAGALI

Magali rubbed her jaw angrily, as she parked her R8 in the lot of Westside Foods right on Loreli Drive, across from the Waterfort apartment complex buildings.

The raspy laugh that came out of her exotic car's speakers annoyed her even more.

"What the fuck is so funny?!"

The man laughed. "How does that happen, chula?"

"She got fucking lucky!" Magali saw the Porsche truck turn off of Route 173 onto Loreli and speed past her. "It's cool. She gon' lead us to Stacks, and after that, I'ma chop that bitch's head off!"

"You think it's wise for a pregnant chick to be decapitating people?"

"Diablo! I'ma gangera!" Magali said, absentmindedly putting her hand on her stomach, thinking about the life growing inside.

Having very recently found out she was six weeks along, and knowing it was Stacks' baby, had the thirty-year-old Mexican girl feeling depressed.

Magali was his ride or die bitch. She put him and his homie, Rambo, despite her hatred for Stacks' guy, onto a lot of licks. Her family consisted of a lot of gangbangers and cartel members. She knew of many stash spots, businesses around Wauk-Town and surrounding areas that were really fronts, and she even knew many of the top dogs around Lake County all the way down in Chicago. For being only five-foot-three, the Mexican chick was a big dog in her own right. And after tipping the scales in her favor by turning her snitching, homosexual little brother in to the Rojas-Gomez Cartel's head hired sicario, as they searched for the crew responsible for hitting one of their dope spots and killing everyone inside, Magali was now a made woman.

Through contacts on the street, she'd heard about the shooting involving Stacks and his homie, Rambo. She and everyone else believed them both to be dead. But hearing Stacks' body had never been found told her that he couldn't be dead. The pond that they'd crashed into was not big and didn't flow into another body of water. Rambo's corpse was found but not Stacks'. Magali was smart enough to know that he had to be alive.

"I'ma still be a G, even when my belly gets bug, and my feet can't fit into shit but slippers."

Diablo laughed. "I can't believe you're pregnant by a pinche prieto."

His words immediately pissed her off. Magali loved Black men, as many women actually did. Hardcore, resilient, strong, and historically cultured, there wasn't anything about a Black man that Magali didn't like. And she was gone over Stacks. Just thinking about seeing him again had her so desperately exploring every avenue possible.

"What about the other baby momma?" asked Diablo. "The Black girl?"

"I don't know where she lives. I only know that her name's Jazmine."

"I can find out. He's got a record of being in prison. If that's a significant bitch in his life, she was on his visit list. Her name and address will be listed. We'll start from there."

"We are not hurting him, Diablo; we're recruiting him," Magali reminded the seasoned Mexican hitman.

"I know, chula. I gave you my word. I do not double-cross."

"Good. I'm going home. Let me know when you got info on his other bitch," Magali said and ended the call.

She put her R8 into drive and pulled off, exiting the lot, en route to head back down to Chicago's Little Village area where she was head of a whole hood of Latin Kings who moved cocaine and heroin for her, supplied by a new connect she'd bumped into.

XAVIER

"I'm not gon' be able to make it to you, bae," Xavier said, as he changed out of his bloodstained clothes into clean ones while in the Pilot's bathroom. With his Bluetooth earpiece in, he'd called Kenzie, having to cancel their quickie date. "Shit just went down at the truck stop I'm at, and it pushed my schedule back."

"It's okay," Kenzie said softly.

Xavier paused. "Hey, what's wrong?"

Kenzie sighed. "I lost my job today."

"What? How?"

She told him. Then, she started crying.

"Kenzie, baby, stop cryin', Ma. You good. I know you a independent woman, but you should already know that you ain't gotta work. I do good enough for all of us to live real good," he said, keeping his real true worth to himself.

"I appreciate it, baby. I do. But I just never been the type to allow a man to take care of me. My mom came from Cuba, poor as hell. She was a bad ass chick, ass and titties; she could've easily fucked and sucked her way into money, but she worked a legit job to earn a living. She taught me that a real woman never lets a man take care of her. He'll think he owns you if you do that, and ain't nobody ever gon' own MacKenzie Cardoza."

Her confidence made him smile. He respected how Kenzie was content on making her own way in the world. A lot of people were too lazy to be self-sufficient, let alone desire to achieve success on their own. The odds were stacked against Kenzie in so many ways. Yet she was so strong and full of life. The love she had for her daughter, how she cherished and put her child first, was what made Xavier see her as a queen.

"I understand. I would never become a man that feels he owns any woman, for any weird-ass reason. I could help you find another job... or..."

Almost a minute of silence passed before Kenzie asked, "Or what?"

"Start your own business," Xavier told her.

"Um... that costs money, babe. I'm not ballin',"

"What's your dream job?"

Kenzie thought about what she'd always wanted to do with her life.

"I like home remodeling," she told him.

"Like doin' it yourself or from a realtor's aspect?"

"Both. But I'll never have time to do online classes to get certified, and then, to do home remodeling, I'd need a home to remodel."

"Do ours then. Start there." Xavier grabbed his bag and stuffed the plastic bag with his bloody jeans in it inside, heading to exit the bathroom.

The Illinois State Police officers were still around, gathering as much evidence of the shooting that they could. People were still being questioned as possible witnesses. Xavier had been questioned as well, but the second the troopers learned who he was... they backed off, all too familiar with the Valdez family.

"What?" asked Kenzie.

"Remodel our house, bae. If I like what I see, then I'll invest," he said, beyond glad that his illegal load wasn't anywhere close to the cops.

He reached his truck a minute later. The whole walk there, he'd waited for an answer. But as he climbed up into his truck, he heard Kenzie crying again.

"Kenzie, I thought we was good? Why you cryin' again?"

"Because... I don't deserve a good guy like you, Xavier! I'm broken! I'm flawed! I can't control my goddamn bowels! Why are you really doin' this?"

"I love and believe in you. That's why. If you lookin' for ten perfect reasons, then I don't have those," Xavier told her. "I just know how I feel, and I roll with my instincts. They're tellin' me that you can be even better than you already are. I'm a man. A man helps his woman if she isn't content with her professional life or vice versa. So, stop cryin'. Use my debit card for whatever. Watch some shows on remodelin', do a internet search, whatever you need to do, Ma. I'll help double and triple with Neveah, so you can do the classes. What do you say?"

It took another minute for Kenzie to speak. But when she did, it was what Xavier wanted to hear.

"Okay. I'll do it, baby."

"Good," Xavier smiled, staring up his engine. "Don't worry about bills or anything else. I got you."

"I love you, Xavier."

"I love you too. See you tonight, okay?"

"Yes, baby. Drive safe."

Xavier ended the call with a smile. He put his iPhone on the charger, then clutching into gear, releasing his brake, he slowly pulled off, tugging along his semi-heavy bulldozer, ready to get to his destination, pick up his other load, drop it off, and get home.

Dammit! I forgot about Vanessa... All these women... I feel sorry for all them guys that got five baby mamas. That'll never be me, he thought to himself, as he coasted his rig toward the truck lot's exit.

CHAPTER 10

JAVI

After an eight-hour, five hundred thirty-five-mile trip through Indiana and Ohio, Javi entered Monroeville after blazing a trail eastbound on the PA Turnpike. His escort stayed right with him, even as he'd tried to catch Yessy. She was gone, like Speedy Gonzalez.

Michelle had fallen asleep in the sleeper with the dogs on her side. Her mind and body needed rest, and being pregnant, Javi begged her to take a nap. She nearly did the same for him, but she knew that the money they were transporting had a schedule, and a setback would have them stuck on the road since there wasn't a legal extra driver.

On the exit for Mosside Boulevard, Javi got off, and at Monroeville's Business Route 22, he made a left, going away from the busy shopping areas the town was most known for. There was still no sight of Yessy nor the escorts tailing her and Macho.

It was half past one in the afternoon. Eastern time was an hour ahead of the Midwest. Javi was beyond exhausted. All the events that led from him barely being able to sleep had him so fatigued. He was glad he made it in one shot instead of having to pull over and extend time on the road when he could just tough it out, get his lady, dogs, and himself to the Murrysville yard and get settled in one of the yard's luxurious hotel suites.

After twenty odd minutes east on 22, Javi got to Murrysville. He arrived at the massive PJ&D Transport yard. The location was the first commercial property purchased by the three old heads back in the late seventies. It'd gone from just a truck yard to damn near a neighborhood. There was a gigantic service garage with an office that sat on the left as one entered. Employee parking was adequate for a large mall of customer parking spots; there was a car and truck wash for employee vehicles. There was also fueling stations that provided gas and diesel. The newest addition to the property was PJ&D's own five-star luxury hotel, built for any employee working for the company or contracted under it. Every room was a suite. They were all free, and five-star cuisine was provided at every meal, prepared by professional chefs.

~   ~   ~

Yessy was just pulling through the entrance gate's lane. A shack in between the entrance and exit housed a group of armed security guards but stationed around the perimeter were men and women, all highly trained to combat any unwelcome guests.

Javi rolled right in behind the dread heads tailing Yessy, as his own tailers entered with him. They both coasted past the garage/office and the employee lot. Passing the vehicle wash ports, fuel station, and hotel, they got to the very rear where a trio of standalone garages were.

As they approached a long and tall garage, Yessy swung her man's rig out, lining it up with the second bay door that was raising up. Javi waited until she backed up into the garage to follow. Once he was backed in, he cut off his engine, put his trip-log onto 'Off Duty', and yawned.

"Aww. My future hubby's exhausted," Michelle said, grasping his shoulders from behind, massaging them.

"Damn, that feels good, bae," Javi told her.

"I bet. Let's go get us a room, and I'll give ya' the massage of a lifetime."

"Sounds good to me."

The head diesel mechanic for the yard greeted the four and their dogs. After shaking the man's hand and being told that he'd get their rigs unloaded and uncoupled from the trailers then he'd service them, they exited out of the garage.

Jamaica was parked out front. His crew lined up behind him. Stepping out of his H2, he dapped Macho and Javi up.

"Mon, de gal drive like race car driva', yo," he chuckled, looking at Yessy. "Me need 'ta supercharge me motor 'ta keep up wit' 'er."

Yessy smiled and shrugged innocently.

Michelle laughed.

"She got her whip skills from me, Jamaica," Macho told the man.

"Maybe a little but I'm a better driver," Yessy added.

Jamaica chuckled as Macho twisted up his lips. "Okay. Me go now. We in 'de Burgh. No one comes 'ta our home 'n start no 'ting. Me got a nice gal waitin' on me downtown. Me fiya' up a spliff 'n relax wit' 'er. Ya' call me if ya' need me. Ya' 'ear me?"

"Fa sho, viejo," Javi told the old head.

Jamaica hopped back into his H2 and pulled off. A few of his guys followed, while the others parked over by the hotel. Javi and his posse saw a group of women emerge from the entrance doors, waiting for the dreads.

"Eeeee, the rude bwois 'bout to get rude pussy!" Macho joked and laughed.

"Womp womp," Yessy replied. "Not funny."

Whop!

"¡Aayy!" she screamed after Macho smacked her booty hard with an open hand then took off running. "Motherfucker!"

Javi and Michelle laughed their asses off as they watched Yessy hawk her man down… again… dive on his back, and take him down.

"You'd think he'd realize that she is waaay faster than him," Michelle said.

"Cuzzo doesn't care. He loves pissin' her off."

"I see." Michelle looked back to where her dogs were kicking it with Maliante and Dreams. "Come on, y'all. Let's go get us a room, so Mami can put Papi to sleep."

"Unless I put you to sleep first," Javi countered, pulling her into his arms and kissing her, hands gripping her juicy booty cheeks and squeezing.

Michelle melted into his arms and nearly creamed her panties at the thought of all that she was about to do to him as soon as they got into their suite.

EVELYN

Evelyn got to the yard to see that Nena was pre-tripping her new ten-car transport Peterbilt 389, preparing to head out. The pregnant beauty was a wild five-foot-six mixed girl. Black, Mexican, and Greek gave Nena all sorts of personality, not always in a good way. She was a yellow-bone with long, wavy, dark hair with the voluptuous body of a K.O.D. dancer. At twenty-four, Nena was already financially established. She had cake. Mainly because of working for Evelyn, she got big checks and big bonuses. The same went for all of Evelyn's crew.

Originally from down in Chicago, raised in the Pilsen area, the mixed belle was all street, fearless, and loyal. Her heart was made of gold, but when one pissed her off, her fists were made of bricks, and her bullets were dipped in cyanide.

Evelyn rolled over toward the yellow chick. Nena wore a gray Valdez Transport, LLC t-shirt with black leggings, black Air Max 90s, and her hair was pulled back into a ponytail. Evelyn really admired Nena, despite her ratchet ways at times. With her being pregnant by her brother, she had been developing a strong need to cradle Nena. So, that was exactly what Evelyn was going to do.

Nena looked her way as Evelyn pulled up on her. The tinted driver's window rolled down.

"I'm puttin' you in charge of this new contract my dad gave me," Evelyn told her, getting her iPhone out of her purse.

"In charge?" Nena questioned with a puzzled brow.

"Yahp. Take my 780 and my Kentucky trailer. You need to go to Jersey. Six Maybachs are on their way in right now."

"Um… okay," Nena replied, wondering why Evelyn had so suddenly given her such an opportunity.

"I'll email you the incoming schedule for the month." In her online banking app, Evelyn disbursed $125,000 into Nena's account. "My truck's good to go, fuel card on the dash. Keep my shit clean, Nena."

The Pilsen girl looked over at where Evelyn's gleaming, emerald green, 2015 Volvo 780, a big, spacious tractor with a roomy luxurious sleeper berth, was. It was coupled to a fifty-three-inch-long luxury enclosed Kentucky brand car-carrier, similar to those that transported NASCAR race cars. The trailer was painted to match Evelyn's 780 with gold letters, decaling Valdez Transport, LLC, as was the tractor. The 780 set next to Evelyn's recently bought 2006 Volvo 880, a semi tractor that was even bigger than the 780, which was huge.

The rigs that Evelyn's crew had traded up from after she got them all new rides set parked in a row, waiting to either be sold or have new drivers put in them.

"Can I… maybe introduce you to my cousins? They both drive trucks down in Chicago, but they hate the companies they're with."

Evelyn nodded. "Yep. If anything, you can build yourself a crew and put them to work."

Nena gasped. "Are you for real?"

"Yeah, bitch. Now go hop ya' pregnant ass up in the truck and go. You got six months to stack up before ya' butt gets too big to fit in most of the cars you'll have to haul."

Nena started laughing. "Bigger booty means Xavier puttin' his…"

"Aye!" Evelyn covered her ears. "¡Puta, no quiero escuchar esa mielda!"

Laughing her ass off, despite not knowing what was said, Nena closed the engine hood of her ridiculously expensive Peterbilt then headed over toward Evelyn's 780.

Evelyn brought Javi's name up in her texts and typed one. She didn't get a response right away, so she called Xavier.

"What?"

Evelyn sucked her teeth. "That's how Papa taught you to answer the phone, bro?"

"No. My bad. You aight?"

"Yeah. Why wouldn't I be?"

"I'm hearin' things. Don't get to actin' crazy. You know you got two older brothers that's gon' break Jordans off in ya' ass."

"Is that why Tank's following me? You and Javi put him to tail me?"

"I don't know shit about that, but if he's followin' you, then you might want to remember what he's capable of."

Evelyn shuddered at the thoughts. She'd seen the enormous Samoan bone-crusher bash a man's head in… with his bare hands.

"So… where are you?"

"Almost in Chicago."

"Nena needs to talk to you, Xavier. She's carrying your seed… my niece or nephew, and I know Grandma talked to you about that."

Xavier sighed. "Yeah. Grandma holla'd at me. I'ma call her right now, sis."

It was at that moment that Evelyn heard something in his tone that told her he was stressing over more than one pregnant honey dip.

"¿Que tienes, 'mano?" Evelyn asked.

She listened as Xavier told her about the shooting at the truck stop he was just at that took one of his girl's lives and left the other with bullet holes in her leg.

"Oh, damn… who was shooting?"

"I don't know. I saw a SUV dip off afterwards, but that's it."

Evelyn shook her head. "That's crazy. Are you okay?"

"Soy un tiguere. I'm always good."

She smiled. "Okay then, gangster. Well, call Nena, bro," she again said, looking over and seeing Nena doing a pre-trip inspection on her 780 and the trailer. "I put her in charge of a contract Papa sent me, and I sent her some gwap. I'm about to help her get her stacks way up."

"Aight. I'ma hit her now. Love you."

"Love you too, tiguere. Cuidate," Evelyn told him then ended the call.

She then went into her recent calls and selected a random number she'd gotten but hadn't saved yet. Pressing 'call', Evelyn waited for an answer.

"Who dis, joe?" answered Lil' Five.

"This Eve."

"Eve? How you get my number?"

"The same way anybody on my level makes things happen, youngster. Anyways, meet me somewhere."

"Where?"

Evelyn told the young Ghost the location. He agreed to meet her then ended the call.

Evelyn put her Alpina in drive and pulled off, beeping at Nena as she banged a U-turn, heading to the exit yard.

STACKS

Stacks carried his one-year-old son, Dontae Jr., out of Jazmine's mother's house with his baby mama behind him. She carried a baby seat in her hands. She fastened it into the rear seat of the Benz, then Stacks strapped his sleeping son in.

As he and Jazmine were about to get in, a silver Audi R8 pulled up alongside of the Benz. Stacks' eyebrows furrowed up, wondering who the hell was inside. The windows were too dark to see inside.

The driver started revving the engine up. Jazmine went into the car, grabbed her big Chanel tote bag, and got her Glock 9 out, cocking it back. Stacks upped his Desert Eagle and pointed it at the driver's window.

MAGALI

"They're pointing guns at me," she said, as she kept hitting the gas pedal. "Why do people think they're gangster enough to get to poppin' in broad daylight?"

"Nobody's scared to shoot your ass, chula. Stop playing with people," came Diablo's voice.

"Where are you?" Magali asked, looking at Stacks, letting go of the gas pedal.

"Right behind you."

Magali looked in her mirror and saw the maroon-colored PT Cruiser turn onto Johanna from off of 18th. She laughed.

"Wow. Big bad sicario in a girlie ass car, eh?"

"Nobody would expect it, chula. Now move your ass. We know where the bitch's mother lives; that's all we need."

Stacks and Jazmine saw the PT Cruiser turn onto the street and ride up behind the R8. Fingers wrapped around the triggers, they were ready to get to shooting. The PT Cruiser came up on them, slowing enough that when the driver's window rolled down, they both saw the rough-faced Hispanic man behind the wheel.

He winked at Stacks, smirking evilly, before skipping by them.

"Who the fuck was that?" Jazmine asked.

Stacks shrugged. "Don't know but let's get up outta here."

They got in the Benz, and Stacks pulled off. He called Lil'
Five as he bent the corner, reaching 21st Street.

"What's up, Lord?" he asked.

"You tell me," Stacks said.

"The birds have flown south."

Stacks nodded. "Good. Make sure all of them disappear
before the weekend, joe."

"Yup."

"Where you at?" Stacks asked.

"Ridin'. Bouta meet this bitch."

"Maan, get pussy later. Money first."

"She is money, Lord. You know how I am," Lil' Five
chuckled.

"Aight. Hit me, joe."

"Almighty, Lord."

"Mighty," Stacks replied back then ended the call.

CHAPTER 11

NENA

Nena gasped when she saw Xavier's name and number pop up on the touchscreen Kenwood, as she maneuvered Evelyn's big rig down Russell Road, heading toward I-94.

She reached out and pressed 'Answer'.

"Hello?"

"What's up?" his deep voice came.

Just the sound of it brought glee to her heart.

"Hey… you called me," Nena said, shocked as she hit the switch on the dashboard to turn on the jake-brake, as a curving down-grade came up.

"Yeah. I did. It's time we talked. I hear a jake, so I guess you on the way to Jersey?"

Nena rolled on after the road levelled and straightened out. She shifted up a gear and got back to the speed limit.

"How you know where I'm goin'?" she asked, passing a small fishing area on her left.

"I'm smart," he chuckled.

Nena smiled. "Shut 'cho ass up, joe. You ain't smart or else you wouldn't have left me, nigga."

Xavier groaned. "Nena, I did not call you to get into it. I called you to tell you that I love yo' crazy ass. I'm sorry I left you hangin', and I promise you that I'ma be there for you for it all."

Nena ascended an upgrade just then, cresting the top seconds later. Her eyes filled with tears as signs for I-94

North and South came up. She wiped them, going over the overpass of the interstate, coming to another hill where a big TA and a Pilot set at the end of Russell Road at Frontage.

"I love you too, Xavier," she told him, trying to keep her voice from breaking, as she down-shifted gears to come to a stop at the stop sign at the crossroad.

"How 'bout we link up when you get back? We can sit down and talk? See what we can do for each other?"

Nena came to a stop in the left turn lane with her turn signal on. She waited for traffic on Frontage to cease, so she could turn. A quick glance to her right, and she saw where they all used to park just minutes up.

"Okay. But Eve put me in charge; it's gon' be a real busy month."

Nena pulled off again, making her left turn wide, watching her trailer's wheels in the driver's side mirror.

"We'll find a way, Ma. Drive safe, aight?"

"You too, baby."

The call ended. Nena wiped more tears away, as she passed up the entrance to the TA, gliding along in the left lane. Coming up on a Peterbilt dealership, Nena merged on a ramp to U.S. Route 41, having to stop at the southbound weight station just a couple minutes away before getting onto the road and making her way out to Elizabeth, New Jersey.

Nena smiled at the thoughts of getting Xavier back with her.

Time to turn up my game on his ass. I needs me a ring, joe, and bae is definitely finna give me one, she thought to herself, as she reached the merge-on to 41 and got onto the highway for the two-minute-long ride to the weight station on her right.

EVELYN

Evelyn sat parked and waiting in the customer parking area. She looked at the time on her dash, as Ivy Queen's *Te*

TIPPIN' THE SCALES 4 | DIESEL

Voy A Recodar bumped. It was half past seven in the evening. Lil' Five was late.

"This muhfucka ain't gon' make it," she told herself, stroking behind her piglet's ears. She'd swung past her house to pick Oinky up since Gloria was out working. "Bosses are never late, right, Oinky? Real bosses, I should say."

Sitting on her lap, the bay pig looked up at her, wiggling his snout. He gave a snort, then he laid on his side, stretching out across her lap.

Minutes later, Evelyn saw a white Cadillac truck enter the lot. It paused for a second then started rolling toward her. It pulled up next to her and parked. As she sat waiting, Lil' Five got out of the passenger's side and walked up to her window. Evelyn rolled it down and saw the look of surprise on his face.

"Why do you have a pig?" he asked.

"He's my baby, muhfucka."

"Okay. Why are you havin' me meet you at this dealership?" Lil' Five asked, looking up at the Land Rover Range Rover sign that was there for all north and south bound travelers on Route 41 by Lake Forest to see along with the impressive dealership building and the big off-road hill for customers to test drive Land Rovers and Range Rovers.

Evelyn nodded her head in the direction of where a brand new, sparkling red Range Rover Supercharged set. Lil' Five's eyes went to it then back to her, confusion wrinkling his forehead.

"That's yours, Lil' Daddy; the key's inside waitin' on you."

"Never. Shorty, quit cappin'," he said. "Yo' ass ain't never buy a nigga a Range Rover."

Evelyn shrugged. "Then don't go get it. I'm sure someone else would love to push around in that."

She put her BMW in drive and pulled off on him, Oinky still in her lap, a smirk on her face, and Lil' Five's mind all the way fucked up.

XAVIER

Out in Wisconsin's West Allis area, Xavier took the rock truck to his grandfather's longtime friend and client. He got unloaded as fast as he could, then the owner came out to greet him. Seeing that both loads were finally there, he pulled out his phone and electronically sent Xavier his cut for the safe delivery of his cocaine.

Xavier got the notification of the deposit into his non-traceable offshore account in the amount of six hundred thousand dollars.

Thanking him, Xavier shook his hand then hopped back into his ICON and headed back south to Illinois.

~   ~   ~

"Dammit," he cursed when he saw that Vanessa was still there.

All of his heavy-hauler trucks were back and parked, clean and shiny from being washed after their trips, just like Xavier wanted.

Many of Javi's guys were gone still as were the ladies in Evelyn's crew.

Xavier wanted to turn around and just take his truck home, but without a doubt, Vanessa had already seen him pull in.

Passing by the office building, Xavier caught a glimpse of Vanessa stepping out. With the bright lights around the yard, he could see her as clearly as if it was still daylight.

Goddamn, 'Nessa so bad, he thought, as she watched him roll by with a smile on her face.

"Hey, Zay," she said, walking up as he climbed out of his W9. "How was your day, Pa?"

"Very long. Yours?" he replied back, closing his door then stepping back to manually drain the air out of the tractor's air tank.

"It was so dope, yo! I love how this place makes me feel! I got my own system in place already too! I got a load-manager application uploaded on the computer Javi designated for me, and I got the fleet all entered in with the schedule for maintenance and inspections; I got the driver hours tracking installed and payroll, plus I got a guy scheduled to come re-decal all the trucks with Valdez Transport. I even got permission from ChaCha to contact the connections I made at PJ&D's yard out Jackson Heights to use them for y'all, and," Vanessa paused, and her smile got bigger, "my cousin will still supply loads to us whenever we'll want them!"

Xavier was wowed by all of it. It was her first day working for Valdez Transport, and she had already done a week's worth of work. He had always known Vanessa to be very thorough about everything she did. She was as tenacious and as driven as a woman with true ambition could be.

"Damn, 'Nessa! You did all of that in just one day? It's…" he looked at his Rolex, "ten-thirty-three at night, and you started at what, six-thirty?"

Vanessa smiled confidently. The sound of his amazement was music to her ears. Since they were kids, Vanessa had loved impressing Xavier. Now, as a grown woman, she planned to do a whole lot more.

"I started officially at seven and worked my ass off," she said, then she took a step toward him, closing the gap, making sure that her big, succulent, DD breasts touched his sternum. "I wanted to get what I scheduled my workload for the day to be done because I didn't want anything getting in the way of our time tonight."

Xavier gazed down into her glistening brown eyes, as Vanessa gazed up into his. The next thing he knew, his arms were around her waist, and their lips met in the sweetest reunion that he ever remembered having.

He could feel her pushing him back to his truck. Their kiss deepened. Sparks seemed to go off. Xavier stuck his tongue in her mouth. Vanessa's moaned as he heated her up like coal in the firebox of an old locomotive that could not be stopped.

Xavier felt a rush shoot through his whole body. His dick got hard as steel, throbbing in his True Religion boxers. It poked Vanessa in her stomach, which seemed to make her want to climb the tree.

The kiss deepened before they pulled back. Vanessa started sweating, and it wasn't because of the eighty-nine-degree weather that had it hot and humid that night.

"Um… wow… that was…" Vanessa couldn't stop herself from cheesing up and blushing.

"Crazy," Xavier finished for her, chuckling, with his arms still around her.

"Yeah." Vanessa laid her head against his chest. "I missed you, Zay."

He rested his chin on her head. "I missed you too, 'Nessa. That shit's crazy that you here."

"Destiny," she told him then lifted her face off of his pecs. "You ready to go eat?"

"Uh… look, Ma, I gotta be real… I'm in a relationship."

Vanessa nodded her head. "Thanks for being honest, but I didn't ask you that. I asked if you were ready to go eat?"

Xavier chuckled. "I could eat a cow right now, lil' mama."

I got a pussy you could eat… dammit! Stop, Vanessa! Bad girl! she thought to herself, though she wanted to feel his erection somewhere else other than poking her stomach.

"You look like you're thinkin' something crazy right now," Xavier said, knowing that the big cheesy ass grin Vanessa had on meant something was on her mind.

"Who? Me? Naw, yo," Vanessa capped, still smiling her ass off.

"Uh huh. So, where you takin' me to eat?" he asked.

Between my legs... shit! Vanessa! She scolded her thoughts then said, "I have the perfect place in mind. Come on. I'll drive."

JAVI

"Shit! Goddammit, this pussy so good, baby!" groaned Javi, as he went deep up in his woman, filling her up with all nine inches. "¡Diablos, mamita!"

Michelle cried out in bliss as her future husband satisfied her urgent need. She moaned his name, repeatedly screaming how much she loved him. He held her hands with his, fingers intertwined, hearts beating as one. Their heart and passion made their hotel suite swelter.

Avant's *Makin' Good Love* crooned from the music system, serenading the two love birds, as they made good love to each other.

Javi woke up and got right on it. Full of energy, he put it on his fiancée, giving her the love she'd been craving. Michelle felt like she'd blasted off, heading to a whole new world of pleasure. After her third orgasm, she took over, putting Javi on his back and climbing aboard to ride him all the way to nutville.

Javi was so entranced by her on top of him. Coincidentally, Tyrese's *On Top Of Me* came on just then.

Michelle placed her hands on his chest, gripping his pecs. She gyrated her hips, moving to the beat of the song. Javi held onto her hips, gazing up into her eyes, as she gazed down into his dreamy greens.

Suddenly, Michelle burped. She gasped, closing a hand over her mouth. Javi's eyebrows furrowed, then a second later, he was covered in vomit.

"Oh, my God! I am so…" Michelle tried to apologize, but her not-exactly morning sickness threatened to act up again.

She jumped up of Javi and ran full speed to the bathroom. Making it to the toilet just in time, Michelle dropped to her knees and puked her brains out.

Back in the bed, Javi laid there, still shocked that his future wife had just thrown up on him while she was riding his dick.

Diamond jumped up onto the bed, crawling up to him. She sniffed at his face, grunted, then jumped back off, running toward the sound of Michelle's retching.

~   ~   ~

Close to eight-forty that night, Michelle washed all of her throw-up out of Javi's hair after taking out his zig-zag braids. They both got into the shower and got it in again. This time, all orgasms, no vomiting.

With plans to meet up with Macho and Yessy, Javi and Michelle called a clothing service ran by a friend of theirs' girlfriend, who was an aspiring designer.

While they waited, Michelle re-braided Javi's hair out on the balcony of their tenth-floor suite. She gave him four very neat triangular cornrows to the back, but she'd did his parts in zig-zag patterns.

Javi received a text from Macho that he and Yessy were at the door. Michelle let them in. With them was the youngest member of the Steel City Mafia, who was joined by his beautiful lady.

Perry Royce was a light brown-skinned man with a physique that bordered in between athlete and bodybuilder. He stood six-feet-five inches tall and was rocking a fresh ball-fade haircut with waves up top. The twenty-year-old wasn't even old enough to drink alcohol but was already touching a few million. He was part owner of a rapidly growing dog breeding and training business; he had also just gotten his Class B CDLs and had started his own dump truck company.

Perry had legit paper flowing in easily. But his true love was pretending to be Robin Hood; he and his own crew of goons religiously kicked in doors belonging to the opposition, snatched up everything, and sold it all, one hundred percent profit.

Add that with the cocaine Macho supplied him with, and Perry was touching Ms… more than an average twenty-year-old ever would.

His honey-mustard-colored woman, Felicia, was an entrepreneur by very definition. The ravishing African American belle radiated a flawless perfection. Her long chestnut-colored hair flowed down to the middle of her back. Her model-like face had the defined cheekbones of a goddess with slightly slanted eyes. She was five-feet-seven inches tall with a physique a little more than petite, but she was not bubble-booty thick. At twenty-three years old, the Wilkinsburg raised chick was both brains and beauty with an ambition that many women wished they could have. She'd gone from selling high-grade weed to cocaine and dope, and now, she was designing fashionable clothing.

Both Perry and Felicia rocked denim outfits that she'd designed recently with custom, low-top Air Forces on their feet. Flicking on their wrists were yellow-gold Audemar Piguets embedded with baby diamonds as was the matching Cuban link chains around their necks.

"Whaz good, cutty?!" exclaimed Perry, happy as hell to see Javi.

Javi got up and emphatically dapped Perry up. "My fucking boy, Pdub! What's happenin', bro?"

"Man, it's all good, cuz. I'm happy to see you, yo. Homies, cuz, y'all ass out there wild'n, I hear."

Javi laughed. "Muhfuckas keep fuckin' with me, P. Ain't no bitch in my blood, yah mean?"

"I dig it, cutty. What up, Little Miss Michelle, a.k.a. Miss Future Wife and mother of my unborn nephew?"

Michelle chuckled at the long greeting, hugging Perry, then she gave Felicia a sisterly hug. Demon and Diamond got love from Perry, remembering him from many times in the past, and they remembered his dogs.

"I brought y'all some of my newest numbers, yo. Boyz," Felicia said, swearing her word like those from Wilkinsburg did, "y'all gone love these joints."

She extended the gift boxes to them then.

"Go get fresh, y'all," Macho said. He was fresh in one of Felicia's custom-made fits, a design similar to the old Coogi line mixed with a little Prada flare with custom-painted Timberlands on his feet, and his hair was freshly re-braided in just two cornrows to the back.

Yessy was in a leather dress that fit her body like a second skin. She had a waistline tie, ribbed wool turtleneck top, and a mid-thigh length hem. She wore sexy pantyhose that had star-patterns, and going from her feet up to just below her knees were leather stiletto boots with spikes all over them. Felicia had gone crazy designing her outfit. And it showed.

"Yeah, yo. We about to slide downtown," said Yessy, looking like a sophisticated hood chick with her long hair pulled up into a high ponytail and her baby hairs gelled down around her beautiful face. "Let's go. Time is money."

"Give us twenty minutes," Javi told them, then after the four left out, he and his woman opened the boxes and were wowed by what they saw.

CHAPTER 12

XAVIER

"Damn, 'Nessa. This you?" Xavier asked, as Vanessa turned her Porsche into the freshly seal-coated driveway of a big, six thousand six hundred square-foot, two-story home out in North Brook.

"Yes, indeed it is. Cuz bought it for me as one of my conditions to move out here and work for Javi."

"Hold on... ChaCha asked you to come out here?"

She cut the engine and nodded her head. Xavier's phone rang right before he could ask her why. It was Kenzie.

"Hey, gorgeous," he answered.

Vanessa kept a straight face, but inside, she cringed at the fact of her dude talking to another female while he was with her. She just knew it had to be a red head.

"Hey, babe. Where are you? It's late. Neveah and I been waitin' for you," Kenzie told him.

"I'm sorry, bae. I'm stuck down in Peoria," he lied, which made Vanessa smile to herself. "My load wasn't ready when I got here, and now I can't be on the road 'cause of the drive-time limits on my heavy haul permit."

"Oh. So, you won't be back at all tonight?"

Xavier paused, glanced over at Vanessa, who was looking out of her window, patiently waiting on him.

"I'm not sure. All I can say is I'll try. Okay?"

He heard her sigh.

"Okay, baby. I love you."

"I love you, Daddy!"

Xavier smiled, hearing both Kenzie and Neveah express their love for him. He felt like a straight asshole now. But glancing over at his thick, sexy, ex-Persian-Rican girlfriend's thighs... he got over it real fast.

"I love y'all too. I'll see you two beautiful ladies when I make it back."

"Be careful," he heard Kenzie say, then the call ended.

Vanessa turned and looked at him tucking his iPhone into his pocket.

"All good?" she asked.

He nodded.

"Good. Let's go inside," Vanessa suggested, then pressing a button in her overhead visor to open the garage and grabbing her tote bag from the backseat, she got out.

Xavier took a deep breath, stilling his nerves, then got out, following her into the garage to a door that led into her plush home. He did everything he could to keep his eyes off of her round K.O.D. booty, but it was just not possible.

JAVI

Dressed to impress in one-of-a-kind fits, Javi and Michelle looked and felt like they were stars. Javi rocked a leather, biker-style jacket, with leather biker-style pants, and custom-painted Retro Air Jordan 5s, matching the all-white fit. The V-collar t-shirt that emphasized his athletic physique had EL MATATAN in silver letters. Around his neck, a diamond-encrusted, white-gold Cuban link chain hung low to his chest, and the Patek on his wrist matched, flicking as hard as the diamond studs in his ears.

Michelle had a matching biker jacket, V-collar, belly shirt, with a tight, leather, mini skirt held together by leather straps woven in on the sides. The pointed-toe stilettos on her feet had diamond-encrusted Cuban link chains as ankle-straps, emphasizing her oiled-up legs. Her hoop earrings, necklace, and her new Rolex were all iced out as well.

Javi couldn't stop gazing at his beautiful future wife. She was so goddamn bad! Her little skirt hugged her hips and thighs, making her ass look so much phatter. The heels on her feet, the tight ass top, her free flowing hair, and no makeup – letting her natural beauty show – had him mesmerized.

The same went for Michelle. Javi was the most handsome man in the world to her. His Tom Ford cologne made her mouth water for him.

"¡Diablos, mamita!" Javi said, taking his woman's hand into his. "¡Tu 'ta buena!"

Michelle blushed from his enthusiastic compliment. "Thank you, baby. And you look good too. Como EL Matatan."

Javi's iPhone rang at that second. He saw it was Jamaica calling, so he had to cut the conversation short and see what the O.G. had for him.

"Talk to me, viejo," Javi answered, putting it on speakerphone.

"Tiguere. Me 'gean send ya' a clip ta watch," Jamaica told him.

"Aight." Javi ended the call and waited.

Michelle went to open the door when a knock came. Macho, Yessy, Perry, and Felicia entered just as Javi got the video notification.

"Yo, check this out," he called to them all, pressing on the clip to watch it.

They all joined and saw Detective Barrera tied to a chair, ass naked, face swollen, nose broken, jaw sagging to the side.

"They beat his ass! Ha!" Macho laughed. "That's for my Bentley, fuckin' pig!"

They saw a masked dread head walk to the detective with a razor-sharp blade.

"Aaaaghhh! Aaaghhh! Aaaaagghhhh!"

The detective howled in pain as the goon started slicing him all over, opening him up like he was in for surgery.

Another masked goon appeared. This one had a cylinder-shaped plastic jug fitted with a hose tipped with a nozzle. The man with the blade stepped back, out of view of the camera.

The dread with the jug began pumping the pressure handle that was at the top of the jug.

"Please... pleeaase!" Barrera begged, eyes wide in fear, looking at the man with the jug.

Another dread walked over to him and socked the detective hard in his face, making the cop yelp.

"Shut de fuck up, beetch!" the dread shouted then spit in Barrera's face.

He stepped out of view just as the goon with the jug pointed the nozzle at Barrera and squeezed the handle.

The detective screamed like a banshee as the liquid fire doused him, hitting his cuts.

"What are they sprayin' him with?" Javi asked.

"By the way he's screaming," Yessy spoke up, "and how we can hear him sizzling like bacon... I'd say acid."

"Piranha solution," Macho corrected. "Hydrogen Peroxide and Sulfuric Acid put together... destroys everything... eats through anything."

They all continued watching. Barrera melted before their very eyes. Skin and blood and remnants of his body were reduced to puddles. The dread emptied the whole jug. Barrera looked like bloody vomit on the floor.

A voice then spoke. "Na, na, na, naaa... na, na, na, naaa... Fuck yoouu, pig! Yoouu diiieeed!"

Javi and his people all laughed their asses off at the dread, then the video ended, deleting itself completely from existence.

"Well," said Javi, tucking his phone into his jacket pocket. "Now we just gotta find out who it is that Eve's givin' coke to and why."

Macho nodded. "I have a feeling that we are not gonna like the answer, lil' cutty."

"All I know is," Perry chimed in, "I better be included in on this, yo. Homies, I want some action, cuz."

"You will definitely get it," Yessy told Perry. "Nothin' is ever simple when it comes to a problem needing solved."

EVELYN

Evelyn entered her house with Oinky in her arms. Right away, the aroma of something delicious cooking wafted into her nostrils. She set her piglet on his hooves and nearly floated toward the kitchen. Oinky trotted right behind her, hot on her heels.

Entering the chef-style kitchen, Evelyn saw her thick, cocoa-colored Dominicana frying up some catfish and crinkle cut fries… ass naked with sexy, neon yellow, *fuck me* pumps on her feet.

Gloria turned and looked at her girlfriend. She smiled so seductively that Evelyn found herself rushing over to her, pulling her to her by her waist and kissing her.

Gloria wrapped her arms around Evelyn's neck, as Evelyn's hands slid down Gloria's sides, to her waist, then to her ass. The two ladies tongue-kissed each other like hot, horny, French sex workers.

Moaning, Gloria felt her juices running down the insides of her thighs. Evelyn slid one hand into Gloria's ass crack and played with the pussy, making it wetter.

"Ay, dios mio, mi amor," Gloria moaned, as Evelyn started kissing on her neck. "Hazme el amor, Eve. Por favor. Yo quiero sentir tu cuerpo en todo mi cuerpo. Tu lengua, adentro de mi piernas. Damelo, mami." Her sex language matched the pleasure she felt.

"Te tengo, bebe," Evelyn whispered into her ear then started kissing down Gloria's body until she was on her knees in front of her.

She made her lady put her left foot up on her shoulder, then she put her face in between Gloria's legs. Gloria bit her bottom lip, closed her eyes, threw her head back, and enjoyed the bliss of Evelyn's lips and tongue pleasuring her swollen clit.

"Shit! ¡Ay, mami! ¡Siii! ¡Mamame el toto!"

Evelyn stuck two fingers inside of Gloria as she kept on sucking.

Gloria's whole body began to tremble minutes later, as she got close to cumming. Evelyn could tell she was seconds away. She started finger-fucking Gloria's pussy faster, sucking her clit harder. Gloria cried out, then she came all in Evelyn's face, drenching her.

"¡Maldita sea!" Gloria cursed, breathing hard, as Evelyn licked her clean.

She stood up then, planting a wet kiss on Gloria's lips. "Feed me then I got some shit to holla at you about."

Gloria nodded, legs still feeling shaky. "Okay, mi amor. Go to shower. I'll make you a plate."

"Good girl." Evelyn kissed her woman again then left out of the kitchen.

Gloria looked at Oinky. He was laid out on his side in the middle of the marble floor. She giggled at his snoring then got back to the food, anxious to get done and see what Evelyn had to rap with her about.

XAVIER

Xavier sat on the big, comfy, leather, reclining chair in Vanessa's spacious living room. Across from him, the big seventy-two-inch HDTV was on; *Wild 'N Out* was on the screen, and the red head, white girl was currently frying D.C.

Young Fly with her bars after trying her with his whack-ass lines.

Laughing his ass off after Justina Valentine completely shitted on the crack-fiend looking guy, Xavier started picturing it being Kenzie up on the stage, fucking up everybody that tried to get down on her. It brought a smile to his face and memories of how fearless and nice with her fists she was.

Delicious smells came from the kitchen, as he watched Remy Ma come out and do her thing. Vanessa then entered.

"Hey. About twenty minutes, the food'll be done. I'm gonna go shower. Do you want another beer?"

Xavier looked over at his half-drunk Presidente. "Naw. I'm good, 'Nessa. Thanks though."

She smiled then walked off. Xavier's eyes landed on her jiggling ass cheeks, following her, until Vanessa disappeared up the stairs. He groaned, wanting so badly to go with her and get it in in her shower. But he again resisted the urge. The problem was that Xavier wasn't sure how much longer he could hold out. All that ass, them tig ol' bitties, her beautiful face, and not to mention, the sex they had when they were young had to be bomb.com now.

Xavier grabbed the remote and turned up the volume, as another episode came on. He focused his eyes on the red head beauty and tried his damnedest to get his mind off of fucking Vanessa.

It did not work good.

STACKS

"Man, where the fuck you at, joe?!" snapped an angry Stacks, sitting in his Benz, looking around the parking lot of Travel rest stop in Pleasant Prairie, Wisconsin, off to the side of I-94 and Route 60.

Waiting to pop off kilos for a quick $30K, Stacks was anxious for the last of what he had to be sold. His young

Lords were making it all disappear down in the city. He'd had them leave him ten kilos, and they were already gone, except for the last three.

Stacks was up in front with Arab, a bronze-colored youngin with a thick beard, bald head, and dark eyes. He was heavy set; he got his name because of how he resembled a man of Arabic descent, though a few said he looked like Suge Knight.

In the rear seat was Dre and Wax. Dre was a former football running back that got lost in the streets. He was tall, thin, dark as charcoal, with a faded haircut.

Wax was brown like coffee with creamer in it. His hair was in braids that barely reached his neck. He was of average height and weight, tattooed, and always ready to get it cracking.

"I finna pull in right now, my boy. I ain't from down this way. I'm from the MiL, dog."

Stacks hated how the people up in Milwaukee talked. To him, they sounded retarded or like they watched too many New York slum movies. He especially hated how many of them talked crazy about Chicago, yet, in his eyes, it was Chicago that made Milwaukee what it was.

"Man, hurry up, joe! Muhfuckas is dirty as hell! Bring yo' Milwaukee ass on, fam!"

Stacks ended the call and grinded his teeth.

"Why is we fuckin' with this dude, Lord?" asked Arab, as he pearled up a blunt of some Sour Diesel loud pack.

"He was one of Rambo's homies," Stacks told him. "I never liked dude, but his GD-ass got that chop."

"Don't you mean 'chicken'?" Wax joked, making them all laugh.

"Love too, foo'," Dre joined in, clowning how he always heard that said by Milwaukee cats while he did time in a prison in Racine, Wisconsin.

They all laughed again, each one of them quoting things they'd heard the homies up in the MIL say.

Backed into a parking spot close to the exit, Stacks had a clear view of the building that was centered inside the area. Semi-truck parking was on the other side, while the non-commercial vehicle parking spaces were half filled, mostly with people passing through, stopping to use the bathroom, or taking a nap to kill fatigue during their travels.

Arab sparked up the loud and put it in rotation. Lil' Durk filled the Benz with tunes perfect for blazing. Stacks took a few puffs then passed it to the left, which was really in back of him. Headlights turning into the rest stop a minute later caught his attention. He and his young Lords all saw four vehicles enter. Only one rolled toward them, while others parked on the opposite side of the building.

Arab, Dre, and Wax all grabbed their Dracos, each one equipped with drums that held a hundred rounds of 7.62s. Stacks' Desert Eagle was on his lap, and his own Draco set at his side.

The older BMW 745iL pulled up and backed in next to him. The tinted passenger's side window rolled down. Stacks saw a bad redbone in the driver's seat. On the passenger's side was Rambo's former client, Lil' G.

The light brown skinned dread head had tattoos on his face, big eyes, and big diamonds in his ears. He grinned at Stacks, revealing a gold grill.

"What up?" Lil' G asked, as Stacks rolled down his window. "We right here, bro?"

"Yup." Stacks popped the trunk and got out of the car.

Lil' G got out to follow; Dre's and Wax's eyes were on him, while Arab's eyes were on the girl.

"Okay then!" Lil' G's eyes lit up with excitement when Stacks revealed a box of cereal boxes, three of them, with a brick in each one. "Feedin' the needy, huh, bro?"

"Where my money at, dog?" Stacks asked in a taunting way.

"In my trunk." Lil' G stepped to the back of the BMW. "Bae!" he hollered out, tapping the trunk.

Stacks heard the trunk pop. Lil' G opened it up, then suddenly, a female hopped out with twin Glocks in her hands and started popping at Stacks.

"Shit!" He panicked and dove out the way just in the nick of time, landing on his back.

Brrrrrrrrrrr!

Brrrrrrrrrrrrr!

Dre and Wax immediately hopped out and got to dumping, hitting the girl up so many times, as she tried to get Stacks.

Brrrrrrrrrrrrr!

Arab aimed his Draco at the girl behind the wheel and fired, but she'd jumped out the car.

Boom! Boom! Boom! Boom! Bom! Boom!

Stacks popped Lil' G multiple times just as he'd tried to up his own pistols and blast him. Lil' G's body flew backwards, landing on top of the dead girl.

Bocka! Bocka! Bocka! Bocka! Bocka!

Brrrrrr! Brrrrrrr!

Pow! Pow! Pow! Pow! Pow! Pow!

Boom! Boom! Boom! Boom! Boom!

In seconds, a bad situation turned even worse, as a mob of shooters came running from around the building, appearing from seemingly out of nowhere. They were deep as hell, firing so many different types of guns.

Bullets slammed into Stacks' car, exploding the windshield. Arab caught a face full of hot ones that exploded his whole head, coating the Benz's entire interior with his brains.

Stacks hopped up and took cover with Dre and Wax. They got to bucking back, going at it like Crips and Bloods in the heated gangbanging days.

Bocka! Bocka!

"Aaagghhh!" Dre howled out, as pain exploded in his back.

Stacks and Wax whipped around and saw the girl that had driven the BMW behind them. She screamed as she pointed both Glocks at each of them. Before she could get a shot off, Stacks rushed her, smacking her hand away hard enough to knock the gun out of her hand. She squeezed the trigger of the gun in her right hand, hitting Wax in his knee.

"Aaghh, shit!" he shouted in agony then lit her ass up with his AK-47 pistol, sending her backwards into the tall weeds. Brrrrrrr! Brrrrrrr!

Stacks felt liquid splash him just then. Time seemed to freeze, as he saw Wax's body jump and flip, as slugs slammed into him. One of the shooters had snuck up on them, as the girl distracted them. He caught Wax unaware and took him out with ease.

Boom! Boom! Boom! Boom! Boom!

Stacks returned fire before the shooter could hit him up. But gunfire continued flying at him, even after he'd put the sneak down. His Benz was out of the question as a means for escape. He was overwhelmed.

I gotta get the fuck up outta here, joe! he told himself, then, throwing caution to the wind, he jumped up and ran, disappearing into the tall weeds behind his vehicle, leaving his fallen homie bleeding on the ground next to his shot up Benz.

CHAPTER 13

KENZIE

"Mommy?" Neveah whimpered, as Kenzie whipped her Porsche truck into the BP gas station on Route 60 in Pleasant Prairie, close to the outlet mall and I-94, after taking her daughter out for some ice cream.

Kenzie's bowels were about to burst. "Sorry! Sorry, baby! Mommy needs the bathroom!" She panicked, as her body got ready to betray her.

She screeched to a stop in the parking spot right at the store's front door and slammed it into park.

"Hold on, baby! I'll be right back!" Kenzie squealed, flinging the door open and jumping out, just as a turd slipped out of her and into her panties.

"Shit!" she cursed, cupping her ass as she ran toward the sliding entrance doors.

Kenzie heard gun fire erupt as she ran into the gas station but didn't pay any attention to it. She saw the signs for the bathrooms to the rear and ran like the wind in her flats, making it to the ladies' room right before exploding.

~   ~   ~

After relieving herself and tossing her slightly soiled panties away, Kenzie cleaned herself, then washed her hands, and hurried out to get back to her daughter.

But as she speedwalked out, through the windows lining the front of the store, Kenzie saw her Cayenne was gone... and so was her daughter.

"Oh, my God! Neveaaaah!" she screamed, which got the attention of the clerk and the few people inside. "My baby!"

Kenzie ran outside just in time to see her SUV speeding off out of the gas station's exit.

"Neveeaaah!"

STACKS

Stacks floored it up Route 60; the powerful twin-turbo V8 roared out of the pipes, as the Porsche Cayenne rocketed toward the Rec Plex. He couldn't believe his luck. When he escaped the mob of shooters, he'd ran to the BP, knowing he'd catch someone pulling in or about to leave out, take their whip, and hightail it out of there. He thought he was high off of something when he found the Porsche truck idling at the gas station, the driver's side door unlocked. He jumped right in and smashed out.

Stacks got his iPhone out and called Lil' Five.

"What 'oun, Lord?" Lil' Five answered.

"Joe! Them Milwaukee clowns just got down on us, fam!" Stacks told him. "Dre, Wax, and Arab are dead!"

"What?! How?!"

Stacks filled him in then told the young dude to meet him at his baby mama's house... and to get the squad on point.

"I got chu', Lord! We on the way, joe!" Lil' Five told him then ended the call.

Passing the Rec Plex, Stacks continued blazing a trail, heading into an industrial warehouse area. He blew through a red light, but as he came up on Green Bay Road, where the Jelly Belly factory set on his left, he saw two Pleasant Prairie Police cars sitting in the parking lot, posted under the cover of darkness.

At the intersection of 104th and Green Bay Road, Stacks came to a stop as the light turned red. He kept his eyes on the cop cars. Suddenly, both cop cars' lights lit up, and they shot off, heading toward the exit, right by where Stacks sat at the red light.

Shit… if they turn this way, I'm takin' off, joe! On Fin! he swore to himself, as his foot inched toward the gas pedal.

The two cop cars hit a right onto 104th instead of left. Stacks sighed in relief, as they raced in the direction of the shootout and the BP.

The light turned green then. He rolled onwards, crossing over Green Bay Road. Doing the speed limit, Stacks navigated to Old Green Bay Road and made a right onto the small dark two-way street. But just as he turned, he heard whimpering behind him.

Startled by the sound, Stacks turned his head and saw the silhouette of a young child in a car seat.

"Oh, shit," he cursed, as the child started crying.

He hit the brakes and managed to find the button to turn on the interior lights. Stacks' eyes went as wide as dinner plates when he saw that it was not just some little girl in the car seat… it was his four-year-old daughter.

"Neveah?!" he gasped in utter shock.

JAVI

From one of the garages, Javi pulled out a one-of-a-kind Mansory edition Rolls-Royce Phantom. The sleek exterior stylings and the custom forged twenty-four-inch Mansory rims made the big foreign luxury automobile stand out like a Gulfstream sitting on the tarmac next to a Lear jet.

Parked out front of the hotel was Perry's matte-blue Mercedes G63 AMG truck, sitting on black, factory twenty-two-inch AMG wheels. Macho had also pulled out a whip from the garage that Javi pulled the Rolls out of. He pulled up next to the Phantom in a big, green Bentley Mulsanne

Mulliner spec squatting on chromed twenty-four-inch Forgiatos.

The cousins hopped out and assisted their ladies to the cars. Perry hollered for them all to hold up, then grabbing the attention of a PJ&D employee, he requested the woman snap a flick of them.

The Mercedes truck, Phantom, and Bentley were in the background, headlights on, paint gleaming like they just came off the showroom floor.

The men leaned against the grilles of their whips. The women leaned against them with their man's arms wrapped around their waists. The woman took two pictures and nodded her head.

"Yo, y'all should make a poster or a shirt outta this," she said, handing the phone back to Perry. "This what rap videos should look like."

"Thank you, gorgeous," said Macho, pulling out a wad of cash and tossing it to the girl.

She went wide-eyed when she saw all the c-notes in it. Thanking Macho graciously, she hurried off into the hotel.

"Let's go to Grandma Kingston's, yo," Perry suggested. "You know she got that bomb-ass jerk chicken, curried lamb, and that roasted pork calypso."

"Oooweee! Let's go!" Macho shouted, already tasting the Jamaican cooking.

"May be a little too spicy for me," Michelle said. "I want gyro."

"Me too," Javi said.

"Meet us up top then," Yessy said, solving the issue with a shrug.

"Period. We'll see y'all there," Javi agreed then escorted his fiancée to the Phantom's passenger's side, helping her into his Rolls Royce, as Perry got his woman up into the G-Wagen. They all headed off toward the exit, leaving out of the yard without any dread heads following. The Steel City was theirs; their opps weren't crazy enough to leave the Midwest to try them on their own turf.

Javi put the tunes on and cruised with Ready For The World's *Love You Down* playing. Michelle looked over at him, smiling at how good he looked to her. She could feel her nipples getting hard and her pussy getting wet. With naughty thoughts on her mind, the nymphomaniac Dominicana reached over and started massaging Javi's dick through his pants.

He grinned. "Freaks come out at night, they say."

"Sho' do, guapo," she told him, as she worked his cock out.

Michelle got up on her knees in her seat. Gripping his joint in her hand, smiling mischievously at her cheesy future husband, she lowered her head down into his lap, kissing the tip of his dick. She swirled her tongue around it then licked down the shaft to his nuts.

"Ooooo, shhhit!" Javi groaned, as she took his balls into her mouth and sucked on them while using a hand to jerk his dick.

It made his toes go crazy in his sneakers.

Michelle deep-throated him, going balls deep, taking him to the back of her throat every time she inhaled him in. She felt his cock spasm in her mouth; his hand reached around and lifted up her skirt. Javi palmed her phat, juicy ass, rubbing and smacking on it, as she snacked on him. He ripped her G-string right off, then he put his hand by her mouth. Michelle spit his dick out and took his middle finger in, sucking on it, then she spit on it, lubing it up. Javi reached back behind her and stuck his finger into Michelle's asshole, making her turn up her super freak mode just as Jodeci's *Freek 'N You* came on.

Michelle moaned as she went back in on Javi, sucking him wildly. His finger fucked her butthole, making her toot it up higher, wanting his whole hand in it.

She kept sucking Javi until he started groaning and cursing at the top of his lungs. Michelle then lowered down until the tip of his dick touched the dangling thing at the back of her throat and started humming.

"Oohh, sh-shit!" Javi shouted, as the vibration in his balls made him jump and nearly swerve into the left lane.

He busted his nut seconds later. Michelle drank him all up, licking him all the way clean. Javi pulled his finger out of her ass. Michelle took his hand and sucked his finger clean of her, then she sat back in her seat, fixing her skirt.

"You are amazing," Javi told her, as he and the two other whips entered the Monroeville area.

Michelle smiled. "I know. Wait until we get up top. I'ma make you feel like we dun' went to Mars, Papi."

XAVIER

"Vanessa... Hold up, Ma... Hold on."

"Whyyyy, Zay?" she whined, as she straddled his lap, kissing and licking on his neck, while her hands were under her, trying to free his bone-hard cock. "Stop trying to fight it. You know you want me, and you know I want you."

"I do," he admitted, as he felt her hands enter his pants and grip around his dick. "Fuuck... Come on, 'Nessa. I got a girl, Ma."

"So, whaaat?! She's not here! It's you and me! Let it happen, Zay," Vanessa begged.

"I can't! I love her, Vanessa!"

She stopped and looked at him. Pulling her hands out of his pants, Vanessa nodded her head. She stood up, halting right in front of him.

"How about now?" she asked, untying her robe and letting it fall to her feet.

Xavier's jaw dropped. Her body instantly hypnotized him. Her succulent 36 DDs made his mouth water. Her slim twenty-five-inch waist made him think of Shakira and her enticing dances. Her thick thighs and the gap between them, her trimmed womanhood, leaking in anticipation down her thighs, had Xavier stuck.

Fuck it... She wants it... I'ma go on 'n give it to her, he thought to himself and let go of all of his thoughts of Kenzie, now completely focused on the sexy Persian-Rican dying for him to bone her brains out. The tattoos she had made him desire her even more – sexy, nerdy, and horny all together.

Xavier got up and stepped to her. Vanessa felt a rush of excitement, as he eyed her with hunger. He pulled her to him by her hand. He pressed his lips to hers and kissed her softly, hungrily. Vanessa's hands found the hem of his shirt. She raised it up, making them have to pause their lip-locking, until she'd pulled it over his head.

She tossed it over her shoulder, then she marveled at his body. His cocoa skin and muscular, tattooed physique had her clit throbbing. His handsome face was of GQ model status. She had to see how the rest of her ex-boyfriend changed.

Vanessa reached down to his crotch. Xavier kicked his Timbs off as she undid his pants. She yanked them down and gasped at the big bulge in his True Religion boxers.

Xavier smirked to himself, watching her face. The second she pulled them down, exposing his throbbing cock, Vanessa nearly climaxed off of the sight of it.

"W-Wow... that is... wow."

He chuckled. "Too much for you?" he asked, taunting her.

Vanessa looked up at him, then she took his dick in her hands, slowly jerking it. Xavier groaned from how good her hand felt. She was just about to drop down to her knees when Xavier stopped her.

"Naw, baby. It's all about you tonight, Ma," he told her. "I'ma show you some grown Zay that's gon' have you tryna run from me."

Vanessa shook her head. "I'll never run from you, Zay. I'm gonna run to you, baby."

Xavier then scooped her up and took her over to the couch, sitting her down on it.

Vanessa's heart raced as the naked hunk sank down to his knees in front of her. He buried his face in between her breasts, motor-boating them. She shrieked, laughing at him. Then, she hissed as he took her right breast into his mouth, suckling her nipple.

Her back arched up, as his tongue swirled around it, heating her up. He kneed his way in between her thighs and cupped her left breast, massaging it.

"Mmmmm, yeeeaaah, Zay! That feels so good, baby!" she moaned, as her pussy got even wetter.

Xavier sucked her left breast then started slowly kissing her stomach, making his way down to her goodie box. He pushed her thighs open as far as they'd go. He lowered his face in between them. He planted kisses on her inner thighs. They made Vanessa yearn for him to taste her.

Xavier kissed and licked down her legs, to her toes, fucking her head all the way up, then he made his way up to her center. He ran his tongue up her swollen slit, lapping up her juices. French kissing her southern lips, Xavier made Vanessa's temperature skyrocket. She called out his name when she felt him part her and take her clit into his mouth.

"Oh! Oh! Ooohh, God! Zay! Oh, my God! Oooooo!"

Her body arched up. He made her sweat. Her toes curled up, and her asshole puckered. Vanessa's head spun around in circles from the pleasure of Xavier's crazy pussy-eating skills. He snacked and munched on her like there was no tomorrow. Minutes later, Vanessa started shaking, like she was having a seizure. She cried at the top of her lungs, then she exploded in his face, squirting all over it.

"Fuuck!" she shouted, feeling like everything she'd done with other men after Xavier left was less than mediocre and that she just could not allow him to ever leave her again. "Oh, my God, Xavier!" Vanessa panted. "That was so good!"

Xavier rose up from between her thighs. "I'm glad you liked it, but you dun' got me started. It's not over," he told her, holding his dick in his hands.

Vanessa pulled her legs up until her knees touched her breasts. She waited just two seconds for Xavier to slide inside of her. Her eyes rolled to the back of her head, as he filled her up.

"I'm 'bout to make you cum harder than you ever have before, baby," Xavier told her in a low, deep tone of voice that aroused her even more than she already was.

"M-M-Make m-me cum, baby! I wanna cum all over your dick! Then I wanna suck my cum off of it!" Vanessa begged, as he slow-stroked the pussy. "Ohh, shhhit, Zay! Yess! Fuck me! Hit this pussy, baby!"

He obeyed and started pounding her. It took just minutes for Vanessa to climax again. She drenched him.

Xavier put her on her side and hit it hard and fast, murdering her soaking wet toto. He stretched her out like Laffy Taffy until she came again. He repositioned her onto his lap. Vanessa slid down on his pole and started riding him. He suckled her breasts, as she bounced up and down on his dick. She screamed out at the top of her lungs. The pleasure overwhelmed her more than ever before. She orgasmed again, cumming all over his lap.

Vanessa turned around, getting into the reverse cowgirl position. Xavier's pleasure was amplified by the sight of her juicy ass cheeks bouncing on his dick, as she faced away from him. He let her fuck herself with his dick for a while before he wrestled her to the floor, making her get on all fours. He entered her from the back and clapped her hard, fast, powerfully. Vanessa felt it up in her chest, as he went in so deep. He smacked her ass multiple times, demanding her to tell him how the dick felt. She screamed her satisfaction to him before she came again. Xavier's dick swelled up inside of her. His nut threatened to bust. She felt him spasming and heard his grunts.

As fast as she could, Vanessa snatched him out of her, pushed him back onto her couch, then got on her knees in between his legs. She took his wet dick in her hand and opened her mouth wide. She engulfed his thick tool, sucking her juices off of it. Xavier cursed, loving how her mouth was so hot and delicious.

"Aarghhh, ffffuuuuuuuck!" he roared, then he came hard in her mouth.

Vanessa kept on sucking until he was empty, and her mouth was full of cum.

"Mmmm," she purred, swallowing it all. "Tastes just like I remember."

Xavier was stunned. "Wow... you are not the same Vanessa I left eight years ago."

"Nope." She scooted up then. "I'm a woman now, baby. A woman with needs. And what I need is for you to bring that dick, that tongue, and those lips up to my bedroom right motherfucking now. Because like you said... it is not over."

She grabbed his hand, pulled him up, and yanked him toward her bedroom, anxious to put the pussy on him again, and again, and again until he was hers again.

Xavier heard his phone start ringing as they left out of the living room, heading up the stairs.

Whoever it is, they gon' have to wait 'til tomorrow... I'm knockin' boots tonight, and ain't shit more important than this phat-ass booty that I'm 'bout to rub and smack on again, Xavier thought to himself, as he followed Vanessa to her bedroom.

CHAPTER 14

KENZIE

"Goddammit, Xavier! Pick the fuckin' phone up! Neveah's been kidnapped!" Kenzie yelled, leaving the eighth voicemail in thirty minutes.

She'd called over thirty times, leaving numerous texts. As the cops did their investigation, she tried so desperately to get in touch with her man.

Kenzie was torn apart by losing her daughter. The way the cops looked at her, as if they despised her for how she'd left her daughter in the vehicle, even though she told them about her Crohn's, they didn't have to state the obvious. Kenzie knew she was at fault, and now, her little angel was in the hands of a stranger.

"Ma'am?"

One of the detectives approached her. Kenzie turned to him, praying he was about to tell her some good news.

"We've got officers all over the area searching for your daughter. Unfortunately, your vehicle's GPS was never activated, so we can't track it the conventional way. However, traffic cameras can pick out the plates and give us a hit. That's if the suspect doesn't take the backroads and side cuts."

Kenzie's eyes filled with tears as she listened.

"We were able to obtain security footage. We'll need to review it at our office. I give you my word, we'll get who did this. We believe the person was involved in a shootout over at the rest stop across the street. Our crime scene techs are hard at work now." The detective gave Kenzie his card. "I will be contacting you very soon. Can I get you a ride home?"

She shook her head. "I-I'm gonna call m-my friend."

The cop nodded then went to his unmarked Ford Explorer.

Kenzie tried Xavier once more. Voicemail again.

"Fuck!"

She didn't want to call Javi nor Macho nor their ladies; they had enough drama. Kenzie had one other person she could call, and as she thought about it, this person was the best person. She loved Neveah like she was her mother.

Kenzie found her number and pressed 'call'. After four rings, the call was answered. As soon as Kenzie heard, "Yeeeoooo! What up, Rojita!" she burst into tears.

"I need your help... please!"

MICHELLE

"Oh, my frickin' God, this is so damn gooood!" Michelle exclaimed after taking a bite of her fresh Greek gyro.

"That's your pregnancy talkin'," Felicia chuckled. "I hear everything is better when you got one in the oven." She took a bite of her jerk chicken.

"Or worse," Yessy said with her curry chicken.

Up on a big, round, concrete viewing pad, the ladies and their men all chowed down on their Jamaican cuisine, save for Javi and Michelle, while taking in the breathtaking view of downtown Pittsburgh all lit up in the lateness of night.

It was called the Overlook. High up in Mount Washington, people came to get a relaxing look at the Steel City from high above it. The long, wide Monongahela River was first, then I-376 east and westbound parkway lanes, and then, Pittsburgh.

From where they were, they could see down to where the Monongahela connected with the Ohio and Allegheny Rivers, which was also where the Carnegie Science Museum set, across from Point Park. Heinz Field was close by with the Pirates' stadium neighboring it.

For Macho, Yessy, Perry, and Felcia, the Overlook had been their favorite spot to go visit in Pittsburgh since they were kids. Though Javi wasn't born or raised in Pittsburgh, his first time there, he'd felt the magical elements of serenity. He was instantly hooked. When he brought his Nuyominicana there for the first time, Michelle was thunderstruck with amazement. Yessy, being from the Bronx, called Pittsburg her home and the Overlook her spot.

Not many people could go to Mount Washington and leave unaffected by the sense of peace it instilled. Being on top of the world, as the six called it, was what everybody wanted to do.

For a little over an hour, the guys and their ladies enjoyed the Overlook and kicked it. Javi brought up a few things to his woman as they talked about their future.

"I sold the MC and my Escalade; cuzzo got his Flyin' Spur sold off too," Javi told her. "And your new business is ready for you."

Michelle gasped. "You mean…?"

He nodded. "Ten million in precious stones await you, along with precious metals: rose gold, yellow gold, pink gold, white gold, and even platinum. All the equipment you need to melt, mold, and craft custom pieces of jewelry are also at your disposal. You even have a few clients ready to place orders."

She couldn't believe it. Once again, her man truly surprised her. It was normal for him to go hard for her like that, but it still astounded Michelle.

"Dios mio, Papi." She threw her arms around him. "Thank you so much!"

"Seguro, mi amor. You deserve it."

"Who are the clients though? How do they know about me?"

"Me!" Macho shouted. "Another Steel City Mafia chain, cuz-in-law!"

"Me too, yo!" Perry said. "And I need one with my dogs as a charm!"

"I need a Bad Rican chain, Michelle," said Yessy. "And I want one for my little brother."

"You want your brother wearin' a chain that says, 'Bad Rican'?" Macho asked with a goofy grin.

"¡Callate, Antonio!" Yessy looked back at Michelle. "I want Romeo's to say 'El Charlatan'. With his Romeo Santos fat-head ass."

Michelle nodded her head, trying not to laugh.

"I need a chain and charm too, sis," said Felicia.

"I got you, Ma. What do you want yours to say?"

"The name I chose for my fashion line," Felicia told her. "I want it to say FeFe in white gold with blue diamonds."

"Eeeeee, I like that, yo!" Macho said. "What about you, cuzzo?"

Everyone looked at Javi. He grinned then gave his reply. "I want mines to sat 'El Matatan' in blue diamonds, on a white gold background, fitted with red and white rocks. Esa 'mielda dominica, yah mean?"

Michelle smiled and nodded. "Indeed, I do, my love. I'm gonna make yours with love, Papi. I can't wait to see it around your neck."

~ ~ ~

Around one in the morning, Javi and Michelle arrived back to their suite. Neither of them wasted any time in undressing each other. Their dogs were with Macho and Yessy's dogs, who were with the hotel's dog sitter, so the two horny love birds had no distractions.

Putting some Merengue music on, Javi set the mood. He made sweet love to his woman, pleasing her to no end. She felt his love envelope her completely. By the time they both reached the end of their multiple orgasmic bliss, Michelle's eyes had filled with tears.

"Bae, why are you cryin'?" Javi asked, as she laid on top of him.

"I love you so much, Javier," she told him as her cheek rested on the knife wound on his chest. "You fill me with so much joy. I don't know what I would do without you."

"You would live on, amor. You don't need me to live," Javi told her. "You are a soldier. You only need you."

"No. I need you. Just like I know you say you need me, Javi," Michelle replied, as her tears dropped onto his chest.

He chuckled. "This is one of those conversations where nobody wins."

"Right. So shut your ass up and hold me until I fall asleep. When we wake up, we're gonna start planning our wedding."

Javi smiled and kissed the top of her head. "Lo me suenas bien, mi amor."

XAVIER

Xavier and Vanessa jumped out of their sleep when they heard pounding on the front door. It was loud enough to hear all the way up in Vanessa's big bedroom.

The sunlight peeked through the closed blinds. Xavier looked at the digital clock on Vanessa's nightstand and saw it was nine a.m.

Bam! Bam! Bam! Bam! Bam!

"Who the fuck is that?" Vanessa wondered, throwing the covers off of her naked body to get her robe.

"Hold up, hold up." Xavier got out of her bed and grabbed his boxers that he had retrieved from downstairs in the middle of the night. "Let me go see who it is," he stated as his protective instincts kicked in.

He put his boxers on and left out. Vanessa tied her robe and followed after she grabbed her semi-automatic .357 DE out of her underwear drawer.

Bam! Bam! Bam! Bam! Bam! Bam!

Vanessa was right behind him. He told her to hold up when she got down to the third step. She obeyed, and cocking her cannon, she gripped it with both hands, ready to take aim and fire if whoever was pounding on her door meant either of them harm.

Xavier unlocked the door and snatched it open, ready to snap.

Crack!

A fist came flying at him, rocking his jaw hard enough to knock him on his ass. Vanessa froze when she saw who it was. She nearly peed on herself.

"¡Cabrón!" yelled ChaCha, angry as a bull being teased by a red flag.

Xavier was dazed by the blow. Double vision hit him, but he could still see ChaCha, dressed in a Wack tank top, sweats, and Nikes, hair pulled back into a ponytail with MMA gloves on her hands.

"Cuz, what the fuck?!" Vanessa asked, stepping down to the landing.

ChaCha shot her a look that made Vanessa step right back up on the third step.

"ChaCha?! The hell you just hit me for, yo?!" Xavier asked, still unable to get up after the furious Columborriqueria rung his bell.

ChaCha stepped up and stood over him. With red eyes that glistened with tears, she looked down at Xavier.

"While you over here fucking my baby cousin…"

"Ximena, we…"

"Shut up, Vanessa!" ChaCha screamed, silencing her baby cuz. "While you two were here screwin' around,

Kenzie's Porsche truck was stolen from a gas station... with Neveah inside of it!"

Xavier's jaw dropped. Vanessa gasped, clapping a hand over her mouth.

"Oh, my God!" she panicked, filled with dread and guilt. Xavier was speechless.

"Yeah! Neveah has been kidnapped! There is no trace of her! The cops did, however, find Kenzie's Cayenne... burned up in Zion! But the little one is gone!"

Tears ran down ChaCha's face. She pulled out a folded piece of paper from her pocket. She dropped it in Xavier's lap, demanding he open it. He did and saw the image of a man opening the door to Kenzie's SUV. "What the fuck?!" he gasped, beyond floored. "Naw! Naw, yo! It can't be!"

ChaCha grinded her teeth. "It is, Xavier! The fucking mama-bicho is *still alive!*"

Xavier looked at the picture of Kenzie's baby daddy. He saw red. ChaCha saw the goon in him coming out.

"Yes. Get mad. Your little girl has been taken by her bitch ass daddy. ¿Que vas hacer, tiguere?" she asked him, hyping him up.

Xavier handed her the picture back and stood up. Vanessa watched him stand tall. She could damn near see heat radiating off of him.

"¡Voy a encontrar a ese mamahuevo, y lo voy a matar con mis propias manos!" Xavier told ChaCha, ready to kill and cry at the same time.

"Can't do it in your boxers. Go get your clothes on and get your ass out to my whip. Now!" ChaCha demanded, then as he went to the living room, past the still stupefied Vanessa, ChaCha looked at her cousin.

"I... I'm sorry, Ximena," she wept.

ChaCha curled her lip up at her. "When we catch this hijo de la gran puta and chop his fucking head off, I'm going to kick your ass up and down this street," she swore, then she stormed out of the house, marching out to where an all-black

Chevy Trailblazer SS sat idling at the curb with ten black Hummers and Tahoes filled with armed dread heads waited for Xavier to join them.

EVELYN

Dressed in a tight, pink, Balenciaga dress with white Red Bottom pumps on her feet, her luscious golden mane loose with bouncing curled ends, and a little makeup, Evelyn arrived at the hospital where her charming Prince was. Coming to his ICU room, she entered and was hit with a sudden surprise to see her dark, handsome knight was no longer in a coma.

"Baby!" she squealed excitedly, running over to him. "Dios mio, Papi! You're awake!"

Prince managed to smile, though it hurt to do so. "Yeah," he said hoarsely.

Evelyn rushed to the door and called for a nurse. Two rushed in and saw their patient was up. Evelyn stepped to the side and let them do a thorough check on Prince. After fifteen minutes, the head RN deemed that he was able to leave out of ICU to go to Critical Care. His bullet wounds were healing up as they should, but Prince was still in so much pain. The morphine he was on helped, but he wasn't trying to become addicted.

After Prince was given some cranberry juice and ice chips, he was able to talk without being so hoarse.

"I'm happy you're here, beautiful," Prince told Evelyn, as she pulled up a chair next to him.

She smiled. "I'm happy you came back to me, bae. I was terrified."

"I'm a Ghost. Nothin' can kill a Ghost, lil mama," he chuckled, feeling high as hell off the morphine drip.

Evelyn couldn't help but to laugh with him. Then, she sighed. Prince saw something in her eyes that told him he'd missed a few things since he'd been in a coma.

"Talk to me. What you been doin' since I was laid out? Workin' hard?"

"Sort of," she replied, unable to look him in his eyes.

Prince saw her hands and fingers were constantly moving. She was nervous about something.

"Eve? What's wrong, baby?"

Evelyn took a deep breath and exhaled. She finally got the strength to look up into his eyes. Then, she told him. She told him everything.

Prince's jaw muscles clenched as he grew irate with anger. To hear that his cousin was blackmailing his chick had him ready to send his young wolves to rip Stacks apart. But as Evelyn continued on, Prince was floored when she told him that she was lesbian with a girlfriend.

"Wow..." Prince chuckled again. "Why you hide that from me?"

Evelyn shrugged. "I don't know. Maybe I thought maybe you'd be the type to try to ask me for a threesome."

Prince laughed. "I mean... if she bad like you... then I probably would've to keep it a buck, joe."

She giggled. "My bitch is bad. And guess what?"

"What?"

Evelyn got up and went to the door. She opened it and gestured to someone to come in. A second later, Prince saw the thick, ridiculously gorgeous, milk chocolate beauty. She had an auburn, spiral afro and was wearing a tiny red shoulder-less dress with red, spike toed Louboutins on her feet.

His jaw dropped as the girl strutted into his room. Evelyn shut the door.

"Prince, this is my girlfriend, Gloria, and she wants to suck and fuck you while I suck and fuck you."

Prince thought for a second that his morphine had been switched with some sort of hallucinogenic drug.

No way this is happenin', joe! he thought to himself, as his dick grew as hard as a steel pipe.

Evelyn and Gloria then undid their dresses, letting them fall to their feet. They stood ass naked before him in their sexy heels.

"Papi," Evelyn purred. "Espero que la morfina dure mucho tiempo, porque mi puta y yo, vamos a singarte hasta que nos pides a parar."

"Yeah," said Gloria. "We gonna fuck you so good, sexy hot chocolate."

All Prince could do was smile, as his hard, ten-inch dick created a tent in his hospital gown.

CHAPTER 15

MICHELLE

Michelle bit her bottom lip and closed her eyes. She focused solely on the feeling of Javi's tongue swirling around the rim of her asshole.

She moaned as his tongue made her toes try to curl up in her banana yellow Jimmy Choo pumps. On his knees behind her in their big, luxurious, marble bathroom, he had her custom-made, cobalt blue, shoulder-less mini dress hiked up around her waist, her banana yellow lace front thong to the side, and his face buried in the crack of her phat, juicy ass.

"¡Coño, Javi! Ayy, dios miiiooo! Me voy a venir!" she trembled.

Javi ran his tongue down to the space between her asshole and vagina, licking and kissing on it. Michelle gripped the swirled, Italian, marble, vanity sink top as she felt a powerful wave building up inside of her. Her knees shook and grew weak. She went pigeon-toed trying to hold herself up. He kept pleasing her. Making his way to her dripping wet pussy, Javi sucked on her swollen lips, drinking her juices. He opened her up and went for her clit. Michelle's legs began shaking, as she neared her orgasm. Then, she exploded, all in his face.

"Goddammit!" Michelle shouted, feeling Javi licking her clean. "Why are you such a booty-freak?"

Javi stood up and gave her right cheek a smack. "Because you got such a big booty. I gots to make sure this juicy muhfucka gets all the attention needed."

Michelle started laughing at him. Javi fixed her thong, letting it again be swallowed up by all that brown ass Michelle had. He fixed her dress where the hem barely covered the bottoms of her cheeks.

She turned around and faced him. He was looking good as hell to her. His blue t-shirt had a Dominican flag on his chest, as did the blue snapback on his braided head. He wore red Balmain jeans with blue zippers on the fronts of his thighs and blue Timberlands with red distressed denim tongues.

The diamond chain around his neck and his Patek gleamed. She'd given him a fresh beard and hairline trim and lining after they'd showered together. He was such a sharp, young boss. Michelle was hypnotized by him.

"You are so damn fine, Javier," she told him, wrapping both arms around his waist.

"Am I fine enough that you ain't mad at me anymore about Angela?" he asked.

Hearing the bitch's name made a tick in her eye. Javi mentally kicked himself for bringing his pregnant honey dip up, but after checking his iPhone when he woke up, he saw an update from a dread head that was taking care of Angela. She had been taken to the doctor recently for a check-up and to re-dress the gunshot wound in her right shoulder given to her by Evelyn during a heated chase, as the Boricua tried to make it to the airport and get gone.

Angela was nine weeks pregnant now. Javi dreaded when she gave birth to his child. He knew that Michelle would have the absolute hardest time ever accepting the illegitimate baby.

"Why did you have to bring her up, Javier?" Michelle asked, sulking.

"I'm sorry, amor. I just…" Javi couldn't even think of what to say.

"Javi, let's just not think about her until we have to. Please?"

He nodded. "Yeah. Let's get ready to go. We all riding down to the hood for a barbecue at cuzzo's g-ma's crib."

"Okay. Barbecue sounds good. The dogs ain't been to Homewood since they was both puppies."

Javi kissed his fiancée's lips. "Te amo, bonita."

Michelle started smiling. "I love you too, guapo. Vamos"

KENZIE

Kenzie's eyes were so red and puffy from crying all night. She couldn't eat nor sleep. She couldn't even think. She was completely flabbergasted by what ChaCha had found out.

How the hell is he alive?! How?! she asked herself again, sitting in the bedroom on the bed. She was rocking back-and-forth with her knees pulled up to her chest.

Precious sat in front of her. She whimpered, sensing Kenzie's anguish.

"Kenzie."

She looked up when she heard his voice. Looking toward the doorway, she saw him. Xavier looked like she felt… Broken.

Precious stayed where she was as Kenzie jumped up and ran to him. He opened his arms and wrapped her up tightly. She sobbed, squeezing him. Xavier's tears fell down his face, as her cries broke his heart.

"Baby, I am so sorry… I swear to you," he said. "We are gonna bring lil' mama home. On my dead Uncle Pedro. And I'ma put dude's ho-ass in the dirt with my own hands. I promise."

"I just want my baby! Please, Xavier! Please! I need my daughter!" Kenzie cried.

146

Xavier picked her up and carried her over to his bed. He laid her down and held her until Kenzie was so overcome by exhaustion that she passed out.

He looked at his dog. Precious stood at attention, grunting, ready to work.

"Stay. Protect her, Precious. I'll be back," he told her, then he left back out of the house, back to the motorcade of angry killers outside.

He hopped into the SS Trailblazer with ChaCha.

"Anything yet?" Xavier asked her, praying her connections had located Neveah... and Stacks.

Sadly, she shook her head. "He's in the wind, Papi. But everyone is looking for him. His picture is everywhere. It's only a matter of time before you get to wrap your hands around his neck and squeeze the life out of him." Xavier nodded. ChaCha started her engine up and pulled off with the Killer Caribbeans right behind her.

GLORIA

"You okay?"

Prince smiled from ear to ear. "Am I? Maaaan, I feel ggrr-rreat!"

Evelyn and Gloria laughed as they put their dresses back on. Prince was still naked, sweaty, covered in pussy juice. The two Dominicanas sucked his dick and licked his balls. Gloria went as far as licking Prince's ass, which made Evelyn's eyebrow raise up, as some crazy thoughts went through her head.

They both rode his dick, taking turns. A Horny Goat pill kept him nice and hard for them.

The threesome lasted for nearly an hour until Prince couldn't go anymore. For their grand finale, they both dropped down before him and let him skeet all over their faces. Then, they licked each other clean of his jizz.

"Alright now, tiger," Evelyn replied. "Get better and we gon' do this again. Right, bae?"

Gloria nodded, smiling at him. "Indeed."

"I need to tinkle. Be right back," Evelyn said and made her way to the bathroom, closing the door.

Gloria looked at Prince, as he attempted to get back into his hospital gown.

"Let me help you, Papi."

She went to him and assisted him. Looking at the top of the back of his head, Gloria envisioned herself putting a bullet in his dome, like she'd tried to do when she caught him and Evelyn coming out of the hotel. She burned with rage inside. Multiple times while his dick was in her mouth, Gloria had come sooo close to biting his dick off and spitting it out in his face.

"Soooo... Prince... Did the cops ever catch who shot you?" she asked.

"Hell naw. I'm Black," he chuckled. "Them punk ass cops probably mad that the goofy muhfucka didn't kill me."

Gloria smirked to herself. "That might be true, Papi. Pero la proxima vez, poneré una bala en tu cabeza. Tu vas a morir para jodiendo con mi jeba."

Prince looked at her with confusion etched into his face. "What did you just say?"

Gloria smiled then leaned in and kissed his lips. "I said I can't wait to do this to you again. Next time, it's to die for."

"Eeeeee, Jeeee ooooo eee! I gots me two bad Spanish-speakin' Latinas with thee phattest booties!"

Gloria giggled. "Uh huh."

JAVI

Outside of the hotel, Javi saw his sister's 780 Volvo rolling into the yard. He instantly started grinding his teeth. Michelle saw his jaw muscles flexing.

"Tranquilo, Papi," Michelle said to him, as Demon and Diamond were brought out on their spiked leather collars and leashes by the hotel's dog sitter.

Javi's eyes stayed on the rig as Michelle tipped the sitter $50. When the Volvo got close enough, Javi stepped out into its path, forcing it to stop.

At the same exact moment that Javi did, Michelle saw that it wasn't Evelyn behind the wheel. It was Nena.

Javi walked around to the driver's side. Nena rolled the window down and looked down at him just as Michelle and their dogs came around and joined him.

"Don't tell me your second new truck is broke, Nena," Javi pleaded.

She shook her head. "No, Eve told me to use this one; she put me in charge of this new contract y'all dad gave her."

Javi knew exactly what Nena was talking about. His pops had reached out a little while back, after his twenty-fifth b-day bash, and expressed that he wanted his princess to elevate. Javi was all for it. The plans for Xavier to grow his heavy-haul team and fleet were also in the works.

"That's good then," Javi told her. "That's gon' come with a very big and demanding responsibility. Think you can handle it?"

"I need to make as much money as I can, so when my baby comes, we straight."

"You're already straight, Nena," Michelle chimed in. "Family takes care of family, yo."

"You hungry?" asked Javi.

"Dude, I am starving!" Nena exclaimed. "I drove all night, stopped only for fuel. I was tryin' to wait until I got here, then I's gon' grub at the eatery."

"Naw. You with us today, Nena," Javi declared. "We finna ride down to my cousin's hood for a barbecue. Go park and we'll swing somewhere to get you somethin' fly to rock before we go to Homewood."

Nena nodded her head, extremely grateful for the invitation. It made her feel even more welcomed into the family.

She rolled onwards to go park, seeing Javi's Pride and Class parked next to Macho's Legacy Class, which were no longer coupled to the step deck trailers they'd pulled down.

Javi made a call to Felicia, seeing if she had a fit that was the right size for a voluptuous, five-foot six-inch-tall chick. Felicia said she had just the thing and would be right over.

Twenty minutes later, Felicia pulled up in a BMW M6 with an outfit box and a shoe box with a gift bag.

Nena was introduced to the future, big time clothing designer then hurried inside to get showered and dressed.

Michelle went in with Nena to help her out. Javi stayed outside with Demon and Diamond. Macho pulled up in his Mulsanne with Yessy riding shotgun, and the Gangsta Boo was in the back.

They all hopped out in Gucci fits. Macho was in a monogrammed shirt and shorts set with white, mid-top Air Forces that had Gucci toes, Nike swooshes, and backs. All of his jewelry had diamonds, flicking so hard as he hopped out into the sun.

Yessy and G-Baby were in skin-tight, backless, monogrammed bodysuits, with neck straps, openings over the tops of their breasts, and nude Red Bottom pumps on their feet. Their hair was done up, and they wore minimal makeup, still allowing their natural beauty to show. Their jewelry shined so hard that it looked like they were wearing bright lights.

Wooow... G-Baby so damn bad! Javi thought to himself, unable to help but gaze at the crazy thick maple-syrup toned Chicagorilla Boricua.

She was five-foot-eight, amazingly beautiful, and gangster like it was legal. The twenty-four-year-old was from Chicago's Humboldt Park neighborhood. She was as street as one could be and was currently in the military as a lieutenant. She and Yessy were in the same Motor Transport unit and had been in the service since Yessy and G-Baby were eighteen. They were like sisters to each other. They were down to ride – not only for each other but for Macho – and for them, he had killed many.

"Ooyee, tiguerassoooo! Paasoooo!" shouted G-Baby emphatically, geeked to see Javi. "Bring ya' green-eyed ass over here and gimme a hug, joe! Fo I 'fi yo' ass up!"

Javi chuckled and went to hug her then hugged Yessy. As he dapped Macho up, the ladies patted and belly-rubbed Demon and Diamond, hyping them up.

"Where cuz-in-law?" asked Macho, looking around for Michelle.

"Helpin' Nena get fly."

"She's comin'?" Macho asked, somewhat surprised by her even being there.

Javi nodded. "I invited her, cuz. She family. You remember how we met her."

Macho did indeed. Nena was a truck driver before she came to Javi's company. He and Javi had met her out in the Port of Elizabeth docks while they were picking up in-coming containers loaded with fresh cocaine from the D.R. She had sone trouble with her rig, which she owned after her truck-driving father passed on, leaving her his business.

Javi and Macho helped her out in ways the Pilsen girl didn't expect people on Earth to do. They bought her another engine to replace her blown one with no strings attached. They exchanged numbers and kept in contact.

Months later, Nena reached out to Javi, seeking his help. But it wasn't mechanical or electrical troubles. At a lot she parked at, out south in Chicago, the owner got on some fuckboy shit with her, trying to over tax her on her monthly parking dues. Nena was struggling to make ends meet as it was. Her mother was in assisted living; her house, truck insurance, and life period steadily grew more and more expensive by the day. So, she'd been unable to keep up.

Then the guy propositioned her in order to get her truck back. Nena refused. But the lot owner wasn't going for that... and neither were the others. Nena had lost more than her truck that day. The call she placed to Javi, crying her eyes out, pleading for him to get her out of Chicago, was the day that Nena became part of the Valdez family... and found out how they got down.

"Yeeeaaah, man!" Macho burst out laughing. "You'd think when people discover that the person they fuckin' with is a part of our family, they'd fall back. Naw. They gotta try us. Then they mommas get to cryin'."

"Mommas die too," Javi said, not giving a rat's ass who had to go if any of his people, blood or not, got touched.

"Hey, hey." Yessy let go of Demon. "No gangster shit today. Today is a day of leisure. Family, friends, and..."

"Food!" G-Baby cut in. "I'm frickin' starving! When are we leaving?!"

Just then, Michelle and Nena came out of the hotel. Everyone looked at the Pilsen girl.

"Daaaaayuuuuum!" exclaimed Javi and Macho in unison.

"That's Nena?!" G-Baby asked in disbelief.

"Yep. The new new of Chicago," Yessy joked, remembering how some people said Nena resembled the *ATL* actress, Lauren London.

Nena's hair was flat-ironed, parted up the middle. Michelle did her makeup, giving her a Cleopatra-look. Gold earrings dangled from her ears; three gold chains were around her neck. The shiny, latex, leather bodysuit she had on was like gold giftwrap paper wrapped around her. Her shiny, gold heels had gold spikes jutting out all around them. Her long, talon-like nails were as gold as her lips and eyelids.

Goddamn! She did all that in thirty minutes? Javi asked himself.

Michelle took a flick of Nena, who had all but turned pink. They all took flicks of her then. G-Baby walked up to Nena, circling her a few times.

"Hmmm... mhm... mhmm."

Smack!

"*Ooww*! Goddammit, Gab!" Nena screamed after G-Baby smacked her ass hard.

Javi and Macho both stared in shock, as did Yessy and Michelle.

"I knew Gabi liked girls!" Michelle whispered to Yessy.

"This a phat, juicy muthafucka, joe," G-Baby said, patting Nena's booty cheeks.

Nena grinded her teeth. "Gabriela... Leave my butt alone, you freaky ass bitch!"

CHAPTER 16

STACKS

Neveah cried her eyes out as she sat, balled up in the corner of Stacks' son's mother's house. She was terrified even though she knew the man in front of her was her father.

"Girl, stop all that damn cryin'!" Stacks demanded of her. "You actin' like you don't know who I am!"

"I want my daddy!" Neveah pleaded. "I want my daaaddyyy!"

Stacks' blood started boiling. Hearing his daughter call another man daddy almost sent him spiraling into a frenzy. He felt as though he was a pressure-cooker, ready to explode.

"Dontae… baby, calm down," Jazmine said, holding her own crying toddler on her lap.

"Calm down… she tells me to calm down, even though my daughter is callin' another dude daddy?" Stacks turned and looked at her so evilly that Jazmine immediately got up with their son and ran into her bedroom, closing the door behind her.

Stacks looked at his daughter. Neveah hid her face from him, hoping he couldn't see her.

"Neveah, I'm yo daddy! Me! Not yo' nasty-ass momma's boyfriend! I made you! And until you learn that… you ain't leavin' this room!"

Stacks stomped out of the bare bedroom, leaving his daughter wailing, crying for her daddy to come get her.

EVELYN

"What up?" Evelyn answered when Lil' Five called her.

"Aye, joe. Bruh man wildin', joe," he told her.

"Who?"

"Stacks. You ain't heard?"

"No. Heard what, man? Spit it out!" Evelyn demanded, as she got ready to climb up into her big Volvo 880, preparing to head out to Jersey with Gloria, Payton, Olivia, Kiara, and Jada, all who were just finishing pre-tripping their rigs.

"His ass got into it at a truck stop up Pleasant Prairie, right next to where the Nike Factory Outlet is. So many muhfuckas got laid out, includin' my homies. The cops got Stacks' Benz and found out his identity. His ass ran and stole a whip after he got up outta thea, joe."

Evelyn shook her head, pushing in the clutch pedal then turning the ignition key. 600 horses of ISX Cummins power instantly came to life.

"Dude is really dumb," she said then, sitting in her seat, looking over at Gloria holding Oinky on her lap, as she sat behind the wheel of her shiny 2013 International 9900i Eagle.

"That ain't even the half of it, Eve. The whip he stole... joe... it had his muthafuckin' daughter in it!"

Evelyn gasped. "Hold up! What?! Neveah?!"

"I guess. Sheit, the Porsche truck he took, it was his baby momma, Kenzie's."

"Oh, my God... how?... Like, yo... in what part of life does shit like that happen?"

"I don't know, joe. But his ass is all over WGN News; he a wanted man, Eve."

"Stay away from him. I'll handle it, Lil' Five. When I do, you take over."

"Eeeeee, okay then! Aye, hit my line if you need me to strap up. Fuck that baby snatchin' ass nigga, joe."

Evelyn ended the call and cursed. She called Gloria on her iPhone.

"Yeah, bae?"

"Change of plans. We got a little girl that needs to be returned to her mother," Evelyn told her, then she cut the rig's engine off, hopped out, and headed toward her car with Gloria on the way with no questions asked.

DIABLO

Diablo followed the motorcade of black vehicles from a distance. In his PT Cruiser, he was as incognito as could be. Riding shotgun was his right hand, Botas. In the backseat, Magali sat with an AK-47 on her lap.

After seeing the news, a quick plan came together. Diablo wanted Valdez blood spilled, and he wanted Stacks dead. Magali didn't care about any of the Valdezes. She just wanted Stacks all to herself. In her head, she knew the Xavier guy, who was with Stacks' daughter's mother, would run home to check on Kenzie. Little did he know, one of Diablo's men had been following him while he'd been in his big truck the previous day. He'd stayed on Xavier, even when he climbed up into a drop-top Porsche with a beautiful woman and went to her home, where Xavier stayed for the night.

The sicario also saw a tall woman knock Xavier to the ground earlier that morning. She'd arrived with a bunch of black SUVs. Once she'd gotten Xavier into the black Trailblazer SS, the sicario followed them to Xavier's residence then to a shack in the woods where the woman, Xavier, and a whole bunch of dread heads stayed inside for a few hours. When they emerged, they came out as if they had a target to pursue. The sicario had updated his boss then. Diablo told his man to continue to follow. He was on the way.

"Diablo?" Magali called up to the front.

She saw his eyes look at her in the rearview mirror.

"You gave me your word that Stacks isn't your target."

"What's your point?" he asked.

"My baby needs his father."

He chuckled. "You see on the news about that detective that's been missing? His car found on the side of Green Bay Road, burning?"

Magali nodded. "The news says he was affiliated with the Rojas-Gomez Cartel. He was being investigated."

Botas laughed but said nothing after it.

"Maybe," Diablo said. "Wonder where he went?"

Magali felt a chill go up her spine then.

"I'm not gonna hurt your prieto baby daddy, chula," he told her. "I'm after this Xavier fucker and that ChaCha bitch. The rest will fall soon after."

"But… it's three of us and all of them!"

Diablo chuckled at her. "No tengas miedo, chica. You can't kill the devil nor his associates. You, chula, are my associate. So, sit back with your little cuerno de chivo and look pretty. We're about to have some fun."

STACKS

Sitting alone in the kitchen, Stacks puffed on a blunt of Purple Haze. He was trying to calm his nerves. He had just seen his face on the news. Cops were looking for him, and not only because of the kidnapping and auto-theft. They wanted him for questioning about Rambo's death and the robbery of the Rojas-Gomez Cartel's stash house, which included the murders. He knew that, without a doubt, the Feds were likely to get involved.

His iPhone rang suddenly, startling him. He saw it was Evelyn. He answered.

"Yeah?"

"Open the door!" she demanded.

His eyebrows furrowed. "What?"

157

Evelyn snapped. "¡Abre la fucking Puerta ahora mismo, mamahuevo!"

"Is screamin' at me in Spanish really supposed to make me understand what yo' ass is sayin'?" Stacks said, chuckling as he took another puff.

"Oh, you think it's a fucking game, bitch? Aight!"

Click!

Suddenly, Stacks heard *Bam!* The backdoor flew open with such force that it sounded like the police were barging in.

His Desert Eagle laid on the table, next to the ashtray he used to ash his Dutch Master. Stacks dropped the loud blunt and grabbed his gun, jumping up from the table. He spun around, pointing his cannon at the doorway thar led to the hallway where the back door was.

Ready to blast, Stacks wrapped his finger around the trigger. But then...

Bam!

The front door crashed in at that exact moment.

Boom! Boom! Boom! Boom!

Stacks fired four shots at the kitchen's rear entryway as a warning, then he ran to the living room to see the front door was in pieces.

Outside of the house, Stacks saw Evelyn and some dark-skinned chick with a deep reddish afro through the window. Evelyn had an AK-47 at her side; the darker girl had an AR-15 with a grenade launcher attached to the barrel of it, still smoking.

"Bitch!" Stacks yelled then took aim at her through the window.

He got ready to pull the trigger, then suddenly, from behind, a huge pair of hands snatched him up with such force that he dropped his gun. The hands lifted him up into the air as if he weighed nothing.

What the fuck?!

Stacks' eyes went wide when he looked into the eyes of the biggest man he had ever seen in his life. And he looked like he could fry Stacks with the fire in his eyes.

Evelyn and Gloria made their way into Jazmine's house and saw Stacks being held up into the air by the massive Samoan truck driver.

"Thank you, Tank Roll," Evelyn said to the gigantic, six-foot-nine, four hundred pound, long haired, and tattooed monster.

"No doubt, Evie," Tank replied in his deep, powerful voice, as he continued holding Stacks up by his shirt. "I live for snatchin' pussy ass baby takers like this up."

Evelyn walked up to Tank's side and looked at Stacks.

"Lie once, my friend snaps your neck with his bare hands. Where is Neveah?"

Stacks' teeth grinded as he looked down at her.

Tank shook him violently. "Speak, bitch! Where's the fucking kid?!"

Suddenly, screeching tires outside of the house took their attention off the matter at hand. Immediately, Evelyn and Gloria readied their weapons, pointing out the windows. But the second they saw the motorcade of black SUVs led by ChaCha's SS Trailblazer, they relaxed.

Tank had turned his attention to the window as well. Stacks saw the small window of opportunity and went for broke.

Wham!

With everything in him, he threw his head back then shot it forward, head-butting Tank hard enough to make him roar in pain. The Samoan giant then dropped Stacks to his feet.

"Fuck!" Evelyn saw Stacks snatch his gun and make a run for the kitchen. "Hell no!" she screamed and started firing her chopper at him.

Gloria followed suit, letting her AR-15 spit; she missed Stacks' ass by mere inches, as he bent the corner to the kitchen.

"Let's go!" yelled Jamaica, as he and his goons heard the shooting going on inside of the house.

Twenty dread heads with AKs and ARs ran in. ChaCha and Xavier, with automatic H&K G36s, ran in with them. They were ready to blow some shit down. When they saw Evelyn and Gloria take off running into the kitchen, firing their assault weapons, ChaCha and Xavier and Jamaica ran to assist. The other dread heads went to help Tank, whose nose was badly broken, bleeding profusely.

Xavier bum-rushed past them all, seeing Stacks hightail it through the backyard.

Brrrrrrrr! Brrrrrrrrr! Brrrrrrrrr!

So many shots were fired. Stacks juked to his right, diving behind the single-car garage.

"¡Que se joda!" Xavier growled and ran after him.

"Bro!" Evelyn yelled after him, seeing him take off.

"Go find Neveah!" ChaCha demanded of her, as she and Jamaica flew past her and Gloria with a few goons right with them.

Evelyn and Gloria did as told, running back in to find Kenzie's daughter.

XAVIER

Xavier slid to a stop at the side of the garage and paused. He carefully peeked around the corner; Stacks wasn't there.

A short fence lined the backyard. He looked around carefully, using his good sense of hearing to zone in on Stacks.

ChaCha, Jamaica, and five goons joined him.

"You see him?" she asked Xavier.

Xavier squinted, zeroing in on movement in the next yard inside some bushes. He started raising up his spitter, ready to fire.

"Wait!" ChaCha halted him. "It could be a kid!"

Boom! Boom! Boom! Boom! Boom! Boom! Boom!

Gunshots rang out no sooner than ChaCha finished speaking. Slugs flew at them from the bushes.

Xavier covered ChaCha with his own body when bullets hit right above her head.

"Aagghh! Fuck!" he shouted, as pain exploded in his left shoulder then in his back.

ChaCha screamed as she realized he'd been hit.

Jamaica and his goons hopped up and blew at the bush in a firing squad line. They sent so many rounds at it that it was reduced to twigs.

"Xavier! Papi!" ChaCha rolled him over onto his back, as he groaned in agony.

"Tell me they got him, yo! Tell me!" he growled.

ChaCha looked on as the dreads hopped the fence and ran toward the bush. Jamaica turned his head back and shook it.

"¡Coño!" she cursed.

"I got her!" Evelyn yelled out and appeared just then. "I go…" She paused when she saw her brother on the ground, bleeding out. "Brooo!"

Neveah saw him and immediately started crying. "Daaaddy!"

"I'm okay, baby… I'm okay," Xavier panted, in so much pain.

"Come on! Come get him up!" ChaCha yelled, as she attempted to lift Xavier up on her own but failed.

"Yo! Aye!"

Tank came running just then, startling everyone.

"We got company!" he told them.

No sooner than he told them, machine gun fire erupted.

"Shit! Who the fuck is shooting?!" Evelyn asked, holding the crying little one in her arms, while Gloria held her AR, and Tank held Evelyn's AK.

"It's those fucking sicarios!" Tank told her. "The dude with the scar on his face! He got a gang a muhfuckas outside, and this time, they ready!"

ChaCha cursed again. She had not expected this.

"Daddy! I want my daddy!" Neveah cried, reaching her hands out for him.

Thunderous gunfire filled the air. It sounded like a warzone. Jamaica and his goons returned to where ChaCha and Xavier were.

"Come! Up!" Jamaica helped lift Xavier up. "We don't die hea' taday, tiguere! Not on my watch!"

Jamaica ordered one of his goons to lead in front of the ladies and the others to watch the rear. Tank opted to join the real goons, ready to put in some work.

"Let's move! Now!" Jamaica ordered, then they hurried toward the rear where the alley that ran between Johanna and Joppa provided all of their escapes before the sicarios got to them – or the cops, who were most definitely on the way.

DIABLO

"Nobody lives! ¡Matalos a todo el mundo!" yelled Diablo.

The fifty new shooters he had bought off of a big crime boss in Matamoros, Mexico, all heavily armed like S.W.A.T., and strapped like the military's special forces, advanced on the house after dropping the Jamaicans that had tried to stand against them.

"Hey! Chula!" shouted Diablo when Magali ran past where he was to catch up with his team. "What are you doing?! Let them do their job!"

"¡A la chingada!" Magali snapped. "I ain't no sideline bitch, cabrón!"

All she really wanted was to make sure that nobody hurt her child's father, but unbeknownst to Diablo, she had a move of her own that she planned to put into play. It would solve at least half of her problem and would guarantee that Stacks would be hers, submitting to her all the way.

Diablo followed with Botas right on his tail. When they entered the house, there were so many bodies laid out. Blood was everywhere. The few that clung to life received bullets in their heads, putting them out of their miseries.

Sticking with Magali, who had her AK barrel up, ready to dump on anyone else that was still alive, they all heard one of the shooters shout "¡Agui, Jefe! ¡En el cuarto!"

Magali ran to the bedroom of which the sicario hollered to them about. Thinking Stacks was inside, she ran like a track star to get to him before he started trying to shoot his way out and ended up getting bucked on. When she got to the bedroom though, it was not Stacks that was being held at gunpoint.

Magali started grinning devilishly when she saw Jazmine there. Immediately, when she locked eyes with the dread-headed chick, holding her and Stacks' one-year-old son, Jazmine pissed her pants in fear. She knew exactly who Magali was and was shook like a can of soda.

"P-Please! He's not here! He left us!" Jazmine cried, clutching her son tightly to her, as he screamed in fear.

Magali stepped forward, handing her chopper to one of the sicarios, then stepped right in front of Jazmine.

Jazmine went to take a step back. Magali cocked back and punched her square in the nose. Jazmine howled in pain, falling to the floor with her son.

Magali snatched Dontae Jr. from her then. With a nose that gushed blood, Jazmine tried to get up and get her baby back.

"¡Matala!" Magali ordered, stepping away from her.

Two of the sicarios pointed their weapons at Jazmine. She screamed, reaching for her child.

The sicarios were about to put Jazmine down when Magali heard Diablo stop them.

"Cops are on the way, chula," he told her, then he told his men to grab Jazmine and bring her. "She'll bring that pinche mierda out of hiding," he added, answering the questioning look on Magali's face.

Magali sneered, then she marched out of the bedroom with the crying toddler and his bleeding mother behind.

"Pinche loca," Diablo said to himself, shaking his head at Magali.

"You sure you want her on the team, carnal?" asked Botas, calling Diablo bro and following him out of the house. "She's unpredictable."

"She's a means to an end, brother," Diablo told him, as they got out of the crib. "Don't worry. Stick to the plan and everything will work out."

He and Botas hurried to the PT Cruiser. Magali had just hopped in with Dontae Jr. while his mother was taken to one of the vans with the shooters.

Diablo put his car in drive and floored it. The house exploded from the grenades tossed in as he dipped off. Zion police cars came flying, racing up Johanna from 21st Street.

Assault rifle fire sounded off. Diablo smirked as he heard his killers welcoming the cops to the bloody scene. He glanced in the rearview mirror and saw Magali scowling.

"Hey, chula. Smile. You have another child now, que no?"

He saw her shoot a glare at him, then she turned away, not saying a single word in reply.

~   ~   ~

Tia stirred up the big pot of sweet and spicy chili once more, smiling her ass off at the thoughts of her eventful evening. Alone at home, she was prepping the last bit for the date she had coming over. Besides the chili, the hot-water cornbread in the oven, smooth R&B music crooning, and red velvet cake in a glass cake holder, the sexy LBD – little black dress – and the red high heels she had on her feet, her makeup and hair done up, and her sweet-scented perfume were the icing on the cake.

Knock! Knock! Knock!

The smile on the cafe-au-lait complexioned woman's face spread, and she squealed excitedly when she heard knocking on her front door. She had waited sooo very long for her co-worker to ask her out, and after he finally did, they had a wonderful evening lined up with good food, good music, champagne, and sex.

"Here I come, hot chocolate!" Tia said to herself, as her heels clacked on the polished hardwood floor.

She went toward the back door. She had told Kyle to park in her two-car wide parking space behind the house, accessible by the alley that ran behind it.

Unlocking her door with an ear-to-ear smile, Tia found herself looking at four AK-47s pointed at her instead of her tall, dark, and handsome date.

"Eeeeeee, joe! Lil' mama bad as hell!" she heard and saw it had come from a thick, very beautiful girl with gold hair, standing next to a dark-skinned woman with a spirally afro who was holding a little girl in her arms that looked like she had been crying. Both women stood in front of a very tall woman and a massive guy that looked Hawaiian. "Yo' ass must got chu' a date, huh? Lookin' all sexy 'n shit."

"Aye! ¡Callate la boca, pendeja! Get what we came for!" Tia heard the tall woman snap at the gold-head along with sounds of sirens all over the place.

The gold-hair girl sighed then turned back to Tia.

"Please don't be mad, but we need the keys to that SUV you got, like now. You'll be compensated with waay more than it costs," she said.

Tia then heard the sounds of groaning. Just behind the tall woman and the giant, she saw two men with dreadlocks holding up a man that was bleeding heavily. She'd sworn she heard gunshots earlier but had been too preoccupied with the thought of multiple orgasms to care.

"O-Okay… I'll help you," she stammered.

Tia had no clue why she was running to get the keys to her Ford Expedition, but she ran as fast as her pumps would carry her. She grabbed them from the bedroom, ran back to the back door, and tossed them to the gold-hair chick.

"Thank you and good luck with your date!" she said to Tia in such a pleasant manner. "A brand-new whip and a bag of money are already en route to you for your help."

With that, the group hurried off and hopped up into her SUV. They dipped off through the alley, disappearing from sight.

Seconds after they were gone, Tia saw his Cadillac CTS turn in. As soon as she laid eyes on the man, dressed casually, she pushed the last six minutes from her head and got herself back into date-mode.

God, this man is so fine! I can't wait 'til later! she thought to herself, as her nipples grew hard at the sight of his infectious smile.

"Hey, gorgeous," Kyle said, approaching her with a bouquet of red roses and a box of chocolates.

Tia giggled like a schoolgirl in love. "Hey, handsome. Come on in. Everything is all nice and hot, ready for you."

"I love how that sounds," Kyle said, already knowing what the beautiful woman was on.

He stepped inside. Tia closed her door and got ready to make the man hers before the night was over.

CHAPTER 17

STACKS

Goddamn! These muhfuckas is 'erywhere! he thought to himself as he kept on running, trying to get as far away as possible. About a block away, he started hearing so many gunshots that, for a second, he thought he was back in Chicago and not Zion. The gunfire had him wondering who the hell Evelyn and her people were shooting at. Then, he heard explosions going off. Not long after that, he heard so many sirens and engines gunning, racing to get to his baby mama's house.

Thinking of Jazmine and his son, Stacks cursed to himself. He hadn't wanted to leave them, but he wasn't ready to die yet. He was trying to get rich and was hell bent on doing it. Sacrifices would be made. It was life, taught to him by those that came before him in K-Town.

He kept running, ducking low every time he saw red and blue lights coming in his direction. Up ahead of him, he saw 21st Street. He caught his second wind, thinking of the BP gas station at the corner of 21st and Lewis. He knew he could snatch a ride from there and get gone.

He was halfway to 21st when he heard honking behind him. Stacks jumped to his right, hand going for his pistol, and upped it. He pointed it at the black Dodge Challenger Scat Pack that had pulled up next to him.

The passenger window rolled down, and from inside, he heard, "Hold up, bro. I'm Rambo's homie, dog. Don't shoot."

Stacks' eyebrows furrowed when he heard his deceased homie's name.

"Later for all that tryna figure shit out, my nigga. Hop in and we out. Twelve ain't leavin' 'til they find who did all that shit."

"How I know you ain't twelve, joe?" Stacks asked, ready to just pop dude and take his whip.

"Nigga, I'ma muhfuckin' Almighty Latin King! 5-0 killa' 'til the day I die! Now get in the car so I can keep my word to my Lord homie!"

Stacks found himself moving toward the Challenger. He hopped into the passenger's seat, and immediately, the hefty, long-haired, Hispanic cat sped off, shooting across 21st, heading toward 22nd and Joppa.

"If you was cool wit' my bro, how come I don't know you, fam?" Stacks asked, still gripping his pistol, looking at the guy as he shot across 22nd.

"He told me he tried to tell you about me before that shit went down at Bevier Park wit' them bitch ass Valdez niggas, and you and yo' lil' thottiana and her homo-ass brother was plannin' to get at Victor Gomez's bitch ass," he explained, coming to 23rd seconds later then banging a right to get to Lewis Avenue.

Stacks was bewildered that the guy knew all about that. There was no doubt in his mind now that he was an ally.

The man hit a left on Lewis to head south toward Woukegan. Stacks put his pistol's safety on and relaxed a little more.

"You said Victor Gomez? Who is that?" he asked.

"The nigga that did run the Rojas-Gomez Cartel; it was his dope spot you and yo' people ran up in wit' them Norteños inside."

"Did?" Stacks questioned.

"He's dead. The Dominican that you think you can get at," the guy said, reaching 27th Street, "him and his people killed dude, and his bitch ass pops, and his grandma. They don't play no games, my nigga."

"How the fuck do you know all this, fam?" Stacks demanded to know. "Who are you?!"

The guy chuckled, as he slowed down to the speed limit.

"They call me Narco, bro, and I'm the nigga that's gon' make you rich like you been tryin' to get. But it's gon' require you to handle a few things for me."

Stacks stayed quiet for a minute. He studied the brown skinned man. He detected nothing even close to bullshit coming from him, and if dude was talking about killing, then that was right up his alley.

"Aight. What chu' talkin' 'bout, Narco?" he asked then, ready to hear the deal.

Narco broke it down, keeping it to the pound. The more he spoke about it, Stacks' smile got bigger and bigger.

"Yo' ass over there smilin' 'n shit, but them niggas ain't no joke. On my crown, you see what they do to people that try them."

"I know. Don't worry. I don't got shit to lose, and I know where that green-eyed nigga operate his business from," Stacks said. "This gon' be easy as pie, joe. On the Fin."

Narco chuckled. "I hear you, my nigga. I like that in you. Keep that same energy and you'll be aight," he said then cut the conversation short when he turned the music up and blasted Twista and the Speedknot Mobstaz's *Warm Embrace.*

JAVI

Down in Homewood at Frankstown and Blackadore, Javi parked the Phantom behind Macho's Mulsanne, across the street from a pale-yellow two-story house one house away from the traffic light. Immediately, being right there brought back so many memories of the childhood days that he, his brother, and sister had spent living in the house that had belonged to Macho and Tool's deceased grandmother.

Hide-n-Seek, Cops and Robbers, water gun and water balloon fights all summer, along with hunting for garden snakes in the backyard. The basement of the house still had the old go-karts, minibikes, and the four-wheelers they used to race around the block with until cops came and tried to catch them but failed when they went off road where Crown Victorias couldn't go.

Macho and Tool owned their g-ma's house, and after they had it completely restored back to the original way it was back in the 90s, it became where they went in order to take a real vacation, to be back close to their Taino and African roots. There was so much culture inside that even Martin Luther King Jr., Rosa Parks, and Marcus Garvey would feel at home. When their grandmother succumbed to lung cancer, their two aunts and uncle allowed the house to get run down and vandalized. The brothers put an end to that, banned the three from ever stepping foot back on the property, then they had the house restored. Right after City, Lee, and Dee, who were the contractors that fixed up the house, finished, Macho and Tool both got 8106 tatted on them so that they would forever take with them where they grew up in what they called their castle in the hood.

Javi looked at the old Hernandez home and smiled. Michelle knew how much her fiancé loved his cousins' g-ma's house. All the stories that she had heard, hell, she loved it.

In the back with Demon and Diamond, Nena felt a sense of home, as she looked at the house. She was amazed at how she was in the company of ridiculously wealthy goons with bank accounts that looked like phone numbers, yet unless you knew this about them, many would swear they were just some clean-cut, humble guys with swag and some really nice houses, cars, and trucks.

Javi got out and went around to the passenger's side, opening Michelle's door then the suicide rear door. Like a gentleman, he held out his hands and helped both of the pregnant women out of the luxurious ride. Their dogs hopped out and stood at Michelle's side, wagging their tails excitedly.

Just pulling up was Perry in his G-Wagen with Felicia up front. Behind them, in a big Ford F-350 dually truck, was Perry's oldest cousin, City, and City's wife, Chardonnay.

City's twin younger brothers, Cee and Dee, with their ladies, rode up behind their big bro on custom painted crotch-rockets, done up with a lot of chrome engine parts, wheels, and high-performance exhaust pipes.

Everyone parked and greeted each other. Nena was introduced to the Steel City Mafia members just as a glossy blue Bentley GT pulled up with pitch black tints all around.

The driver's window rolled down. The seventh member of the SCM smiled broadly, revealing her pearly whites.

"Yeeeoooooo!" shouted Lacey, a stallion of an Italian beauty, parking in the middle of the street and hopping out her Bentley, rocking a bright white, shoulder-less bodysuit with jeweled LV signs all over it, white LV stilettos, and her jet black hair hanging loose down her bare shoulders.

A long, thick, white gold Cuban link chain with an LV charm made of blue diamonds hung around her neck. White gold Tiffany & Co earrings were in her ears and on her wrist, a white gold, Cartier watch fitted with blue diamonds in the bezel and in the dial. Lacey was dripping hard and looking damn good doing it.

The only female member of the Steel City Mafia stood five foot ten without heels. She had body – hips, tits, and ass, all real. Her only augmentation was her lips. A little filler in them enhanced her sexy Mediterranean looks. She was often joked with; people saw her as JWoww from the show, *Jersey Shore*.

Lacey sucked her teeth and playfully punched Macho in his arm.

"Ow!" Javi suddenly hollered out, as pain hit his shoulder and his back. "What the fuck?!"

Everybody looked at him. Demon and Diamond tilted their heads, looking at him peculiarly.

"The hell wrong with you?" asked Macho.

"I don't know. I just felt intense stingin' in my shoulder and back."

Michelle walked up to him and rubbed his tender spots. "All good?"

"Yeah. Thanks, bae."

DIABLO

Diablo and Botas laughed as they sipped cold Coronas in the garage of a house far out in the woods, up in Antioch.

"You should've shot both of his bitches in the head. I bet money he still doesn't know how close he was to dying right with that puta," Diablo said, speaking of the hit he sent Botas on, resulting in the death of one of Xavier Valdez's honey-dips and the other chick taking a few bullets in her leg. "I can't wait to catch them and end it all."

"Neta, güey," Botas replied. "Nobody knows where that dude, Javi, is nor his girl. His house is guarded heavily, so is his yard. I got people looking for his brother and sister, *carnal*, pero they have no clue where any of them are."

Diablo nodded. "We've got nothing but time, brother. We'll catch them eventually. Death comes for everyone sooner or later."

"Simon, güey. So, what about the fucking prieto? We got his kid and his bitch. You think he'll man up for their lives?"

"He ran away and left them for the wolves. What do you think, cabrón?"

Botas shook his head. "Pincehe mierda."

"We'll leave it up to la chula to decide what to do with them," Diablo said then took a swig of his beer.

Two gorgeous Mexican women in tight dresses and heels entered the garage just then. One had a bag of cocaine; the other had a bottle of José Cuervo.

"¡Orale, güey! The bitches come with party favors!" Diablo cheered.

"¡Simon, carnal! Let's party, homes!" Botas shouted excitedly, ready to get high, drunk, and dive into some wet Mexican panocha.

MAGALI

Smack!

"Call him, bitch!" Magali screamed, smacking the tied-up Jazmine in her face again. "I swear to God I'll fucking hack you into pieces!"

With her face swollen and red from getting smacked and punched on for the last twenty minutes, Jazmine still wouldn't give her baby daddy up. And it had Magali astounded.

"You gonna die for him?" she asked Jazmine, trying a different angle. "He left you! And yo' son! To die! Use yo' muthafuckin' head, pendeja, or it's coming off!"

Jazmine heard Magali's words. They stung her to the core. She knew Stacks had run, leaving her and their son at the hands of killers. She just didn't have it in her to betray anyone, even someone that deserved it.

"Okay," Magali nodded. "You want to play Captain-Save-A Lame, huh? Aight. I'll be right back, shorty."

Jazmine watched Magali leave the room. Before she closed the door, she set Jazmine's Galaxy on the table next to the door.

The second the door shut, Jazmine sprang into action. She tipped herself over until she fell out of the chair which, luckily, Magali hadn't tied her to. She wormed her way to the door, using her body strength to get herself up. With her teeth, she was able to twist the lock in the center of the doorknob, locking it. She then hopped to where her phone was. Thankfully, the screen was still lit and unlocked. Quickly, Jazmine used her nose to go into her contacts and scrolled to the name she was looking for. As soon as she found it, she pressed 'Call' on it.

EVELYN

"Goddammit, yo!" Evelyn felt pain in her shoulder and in her lower back, as she sat with Gloria in the basement area of a house belonging to ChaCha's paid, under the table doctor.

Downstairs with the two was Tank and a few of the dread heads. Upstairs, Xavier was in surgery. ChaCha refused to leave his side, even with the doctor telling ChaCha that his injuries were not life threatening.

Kenzie had been called and was on the way via dread head escort. ChaCha had called Danny, Ricardo, Roselyna, and the old heads, notifying them of the situation, but she made it known that she did not want Javi to be told. He would lose it, then so would Macho, and Nena might miscarry from grief.

"You okay, baby?" asked Gloria, turning to face her girlfriend.

"Yeah. Every time one of us gets hurt, we feel it. Like a twin or triplet type thing."

Evelyn's iPhone rang just then. She saw the number on the screen and recognized it. Frowning, she answered the call.

"If you're with yo' piece of shit baby..."

"Eve! I need your help!" Jazmine cut her off with urgency in her voice. "Please! They have me and my son! Dontae left us when these Mexicans ran up in my house! My son is somewhere else!"

Evelyn shot upright. "You were there?!"

"I was in my bedroom with my son! This Mexican bitch is tryin' to make me give him up! I'm not built like that though!"

Just then, Evelyn herald pounding.

"Shit! She's back!" Jazmine panicked.

Evelyn then heard a loud blast.

"Bitch! Who the fuck you talking to?!" Evelyn heard a woman yell.

"Dontae!" Jazmine cried. "My baby!"

Evelyn could hear a toddler crying. Then, she heard Jazmine begging for her son.

Smack!

The sound of hand to flesh was unmistakable. Jazmine yelped, then Evelyn heard a thud, as if Jazmine had fallen to the floor. She put her phone on speaker, which got everyone's attention. Gloria, Tank, and the dreads stood up and listened as so many cries and pleas for mercy came.

"Who the fuck is this, joe?"

Evelyn heard the other woman's voice addressing her.

"This is yo' worst nightmare if Jaz or Dontae Jr. gets hurt," Evelyn told the chick.

She heard a laugh. "Oh, yeah?"

Smack!

"I'm not havin' no nightmares," the woman said.

"What do you want from her?" Evelyn asked. Then, to Gloria, she whispered, "Hurry up and go get Mena! We need to trace Jaz's number to get her location!"

"I want the bitch's baby daddy," Evelyn heard, as Gloria ran to do as told. "Bring him to me, and I'll let them go."

"Who are you?" Evelyn asked then.

The woman laughed. "I'm yo' worst nightmare if you don't hurry the fuck up and find the father of my growing child!"

The call ended then, leaving Evelyn baffled. She looked at Tank, who shook his head.

"Doesn't anyone use condoms anymore?" he asked.

CHAPTER 18

THE FAMILY

Tool had arrived on a chromed Hayabusa 1300 with his gorgeous, dark skinned Belizean chick on the back of the customized crotch-rocket. His younger brother greeted him out front, as Macho waited for his dogs to be dropped off by the hotel's sitter.

He greeted Tool's chick, whose name was Tamalita; the two entered the house to join the party.

Macho waited out front for the sitter, who had texted that she was just down the way. Javi came outside as he waited, dapping his cuz up.

"When we leavin' for Jersey?" Javi asked.

"Early in the a.m. I figured we'll leave about four or five, get there by nine or so; we off the books with this one, so it's you 'n me on the way back."

Javi nodded. "Fine with me."

The sitter pulled up and let Macho's pit bull and Yessy's rottweiler out. She waved to Macho and Javi, as the dogs ran up to them, then she pulled off.

"Nena ridin' that way too to pick up some Maybachs for my sister. We gotta make sure her hot-head ass gets enough sleep."

"Fa' sho. Let's get back to everybody," Macho said, patting Dream's and Maliante's heads. "Yessy made her special BBQ sauce, yo."

"Eeeee, joe! I finna smash so many chicken wings 'n shit, cuzzo! Let's go!"

XAVIER

Xavier felt numb from the pain medication entering his body through the IV in his arm. The surgery was over; the bullets had been removed, and what could be repaired was fixed. He was then taken to a big bedroom to recover from the procedure. ChaCha went and got Neveah from Jamaica. She screamed with excitement to see her daddy.

"Hey, lil' mama," Xavier said to the little one, as he took her into his arms.

ChaCha and Jamaica stood by the door, watching the two with smiles.

"Hi, Daddy! I love you!" Neveah hugged his neck and held him.

"I love you too, pretty angel." Xavier kissed her cheek and hugged her back.

ChaCha heard footsteps behind her. She and Jamaica turned and saw Gloria. Seeing the worried expression on the Dominicana's face, ChaCha sighed.

"What happened now, Gloria?" she asked.

"We need you downstairs, ChaCha," Gloria told her. "Another kid is in danger."

ChaCha shook her head. "Maldita sea!"

Xavier heard ChaCha curse. He and Neveah looked over at her and Jamaica, listening to whatever Gloria was telling them. ChaCha then turned to Xavier.

"Tenemos que ir, papito," she told him, sounding very frustrated. "More problems."

"What happened now?" Xavier asked.

ChaCha filled him in. Xavier grinded his teeth in anger.

"What the hell is with this dude? Beats his daughter's mother, leaves his son's mother and his son to die at the hands of hitmen. Yo', on Tommy... Please! If... no... when y'all catch him... I want to be the one to handle him."

"Neveah! Xavier!"

Kenzie ran into the room just then, overjoyed to see the loves of her life there together, safe and sound.

"Mommy!" Neveah shouted and hopped up as Xavier released her.

Kenzie scooped her little girl up and kissed her face so many times. She carried Neveah and sat next to her man. Xavier pulled Kenzie into his arms and sobbed, thanking God that they were all back together again.

Kenzie looked over at ChaCha and Jamaica.

"Thank you. Thank you so much, y'all," she wept.

"Somos familia, Rojita," ChaCha replied, then she nodded to Xavier before she went with Gloria, leading Jamaica with her.

THE FAMILY

Yessy and G-Baby did their thing on the grill – ribs, chicken, brats, and burgers; rice, corn, and potato salad was made by Felicia. Lacey baked powder-sugar topped brownies, making a special THC infused batch for herself and Perry.

Nena and Michelle sat outside on the back porch, watching the dogs roam around the small backyard. They were freed from having to do anything due to their pregnancies.

City's woman, as well as Cee's and Dee's, got in where they could, helping bring food to get cooked or taken to the old school warming oven in the kitchen.

The guys sipped beers and kicked it out front on the porch. They reminisced on the days of childhood. Macho and Perry got into a debate about who had been the best dirt birt, four-wheeler, and go-kart racer when they were shorties.

"Maaan, hell naw, yo! You buggin', cutty!" Perry said incredulously. "When I had my Banshee, I smoked ya' ass every time we raced! On the homies, cuz!"

"So, you admit that without the Banshee, you are trash?" asked Macho with a taunting grin.

"Oooooweeee! Them sound like racin' words, yo!" City shouted, hyping them up. "I got five bands on Macho!"

"Daamn, cuz! You bet against me?" Perry asked, looking at his big, hefty, bushy bearded, and dread headed cousin.

"Hell yeah. Macho is a wheel man, cutty. You already know that."

"Fuck all that." Cee dug in his pocket and pulled out a knot of cash. "I got ten gees on cuzzo. What up?"

"I got ten on P Dub too. Sorry, Macho," said Dee, looking at his homeboy.

Macho smirked. "You will be."

"What about you, Javi?" Perry asked. "Who you think got more skills?"

"Me!" Javi replied, taking a swig of his brew.

The four SCMs looked at the man for a minute, then they all burst out laughing.

"Cuz, yo' ass will never beat me," Macho proclaimed. "¡Jamas!"

~ ~ ~

Down in the basement of the old house, Macho led the guys to where ghost hunts used to happen. In the very back, five dusty dirt bikes, all Kawasakis, set on kickstands. Macho, Perry, and Javi each grabbed a 450cc. City opened the rear cellar door for them to roll out into the backyard. The dogs bumbled in, curious as to what was going on. When Michelle and Nena saw the three pulling out dirt bikes, they both glanced at each other. Then, Michelle called Yessy on her iPhone, telling her that her man was about to do some crazy shit.

Out front in the street, the three lined up next to each other and kickstarted their engines. City, his brothers, Tool, Lacey, along with the neighbors, all stood outside, watching. Macho told them that the first one around the block and back won, plain and simple. No helmets and no pads were on any of them.

Cee's and Dee's women, Tiffany and China, stepped out into the street to start the race.

"Three… two… one… go!" they shouted in unison.

Macho rode off like he thought he was Motorcross champion, James Stewart, popping a wheelie in the process. Perry hit it, as did Javi.

"You got this, baby! Get 'em!" Michelle yelled to Javi, as the three blew up Frankstown Avenue.

Macho shifted gears without the clutch, focused completely, as he rocketed on.

Perry got closer to Macho's tail. "I'm right here, niggaaa! Woooo!"

Javi was a few feet behind the two Steel City Mafia goons. For some reason, their bikes seemed faster than his.

Aight. Okay. I know what to do, Javi thought to himself, seeing the brown house coming up that he remembered utilizing, running from the cops when he and Macho got into fights around the way.

Macho and Perry battled it out like, at the end of the race, the prize was everlasting life. They bent around Frankstown, to Bennett Street, cutting a hard right where a school set on the corner. Ahead of them was a quarter mile, more or less, of a straight stretch. Traffic was light on the two-way street; a few businesses lined the street, all the way up to the Bennett and Oakwood Street intersection, which included Perry's dump truck yard.

The two came upon a rival dump truck company after the school. In between a tiny one-way strip called Conemough and Bennett was an old Texaco gas station that barely ever got any business yet had been open since Macho and Tool were youngsters.

As the two raced on, from off the dump truck company's lot, a bunch of tires suddenly rolled out into the street. Macho and Perry gasped, cursing as they squeezed the hand brakes. But Macho couldn't stop fast enough and hit one of the wide front steer tires.

"Macho!" Perry shouted, seeing his best friend get launched off the bike just as he himself narrowly avoided hitting a tire.

Macho landed hard on the ground, skidding along the asphalt, leaving skin behind.

Perry jumped off of his dirt bike and rushed to his boy. Macho was okay, but he was bloody and bruised. Perry looked over at the truck company's garage, where its two service bay doors were open, and two chromed-out Peterbilts set inside.

A tall, bald, light skinned man with a beard and muscles like a WWF wrestler walked out of the garage, holding two thick chains, linked to thick, leather, spike collars, around the necks of two big, blue-furred pit bulls. Both vicious blue devils barked aggressively, trying to pull away from the huge man.

Another tall, bald ,bearded man, this one skinnier by far, came out behind the dog-wielding man, holding a Mossberg pump shotgun.

"P muthafuckin' *Dub!*" Big Muscles shouted, grinning tauntingly. "What up, lil' cutty? You and ya' mans aight?"

Macho got up off the ground as a few cars slowly crept past.

The drivers saw the man on the pad in the front of the garage holding a shotgun. Tires screeched as they desperately hurried to get away.

"I'm all good, swold," Macho said, shaking it off. "I'ma assume this was an accident."

Swold shrugged. "Go ahead. Makes me no never mind, homeboy. I'ma assume ya' homie gon' stop steppin' on my toes, tryna take money outta me and my brother's pocket."

Perry got furious then. The two men, Swold and his older brother, Floyd, who had a funny resemblance to the NBA star, Lamar Odom, were close to their forties but had been beefing with Perry since he'd started his dump truck company. It was over money for the most part. The big man that contracted all the hood cats/drug dealers turned company owners for high-dollar work had chosen Perry over Swold as his top go-to company.

The root of the problem was an age old family rivalry. The Royce family and the Revilo family had been beefing since the old days. It'd still revolved around money. The Revilos moved heroin; the Royces moved cocaine. Being considered family to the Valdezes, Perry and his people were set. The Revilos didn't like that.

"When you assume, you make an ass out of you, not me," Masho replied. "Mamahuevo."

Perry laughed. "Y'all old muhfuckas mad, huh? A youngin like me gettin' all the money? Not leavin' ya' old ass no crumbs?"

"Oh, it's funny? Get 'em!" Swold let go of his dogs.

They both rushed at Macho and Perry. Neither of them ran. Suddenly, a dirt bike came sailing from out of nowhere. It hit both dogs seconds before they could reach either of their targets. They yelped in pain from the impact. Laid out on the asphalt, broke up, neither of the so-called vicious pit bulls could get up.

Javi appeared just then, as Floyd pumped the shotgun, ready to blow at his and his brother's opps. He wasn't alone though.

Screeching to a stop, the Bentley Mulsanne appeared, stopping right in front of the three. From the other direction, City's F-350 pickup skidded to a stop.

Yessy, G-Baby, Michelle, Felicia, and Nena hopped out of the Mulsanne with Dracos fitted with drums.

City, Cee, and Dee, along with Tiffany, China, and Lacey hopped out of City's big dually truck. In the pickup, Demon and Diamond, Maliante and Dreams were in mode, waiting to be commanded to attack. Their eyes were on Swold and Floyd; the pit bulls were not a threat to them or their humans.

"I think you need better dogs, cutty," said Perry, shaking his head, looking at Swold's dogs whimpering on the ground. "Shoulda came to me."

Swold and Floyd were heated. They were outnumbered by at least eleven.

Hearing the whirring of a crotch-rocket approaching, the two looked and saw a big dread head pull up on an all-chrome bike with a chick on the back. She held an AK574U fitted with a fifty-round clip full of .45 rounds.

"Oh, shit!" Swold panicked, as she raised it up and pointed it at him and his brother.

Brrrrrrrrrrrrrrrrrrrr!

Tamalita shot into the garage, sending slugs flying into the grille of Swold's Peterbilt, then she shot the grille up on Floyd's Peterbilt. The bullets destroyed the engines instantly. Engines were very expensive.

The Revilos looked at the mob in front of them in the middle of the street. Traffic had stopped; nebby travelers were dying to see something crack off.

The ladies advanced then. Swold and Floyd were terrified as the mini-AK wielding woman stepped onto their property.

Yessy and G-Baby pointed their Dracos at the two dump trucks; Michelle, Nena, and Felicia pointed at three others. They started blasting, Swiss cheesing the expensive trucks until all twelve of each one's tires were flat, lubricants spilling out, fuel leaking, windows blown out.

"Okay! Okay! Yoo, chill!" Swold pleaded, as he and his brother's fleet was destroyed.

The ladies ceased fire – but not before they'd caused at least a quarter-million dollars' worth of damage.

Without any more words, Javi, Macho, and their posse dipped off, leaving the Revilo brothers with bewildered expressions. Traffic started rolling again. People rode past, clowning the two, taking pictures, laughing their asses off. Floyd looked over at Swold and shook his head.

"One day, bro. We gon' get P's bitch ass, yo," he said. "And his people."

Swold nodded. "One day. One day soon."

CHAPTER 19

MAGALI

Magali threw her head back and cried out in bliss, as she rode the stiff cock of one of Diablo's sicarios. She had no attraction at all to the paisano, but she had urges that needed to be satisfied. He at least wasn't ugly, which was why she was even wet.

"Fuck! Yeah, chula! Get this chile!" the dark brown skinned man groaned, as Magali rode him fast like he was a racehorse.

Magali didn't want to talk. She clapped a hand over his mouth to shut him up, then closing her eyes, she pictured it being Stacks that she was riding. And it seemed to supercharge her arousal.

She got wetter. Hornier. Hotter. The sicario's dick got harder from her sudden increase in moaning and crying out. Magali again threw her head back, as she cupped her breasts, massaging her nipples. Seconds later, she exploded, cumming all over the sicario.

Magali caught her breath and got up. The hitman, though, hadn't finished. He protested his frustration to her.

"¡Donde estas, chula? ¡Yo quiero venir tambien!"

"That to me sounds like you need some lotion," Magali replied with a smirk, as she started getting dressed.

The sicario muttered, "Puta," under his breath.

"Chinga tu madre, pendejo," Magali shot back.

Pissed, the sicario hopped up out the bed, angry and naked.

"¡Que dijestes, perra?!" he snapped.

Magali burst out laughing when she saw his tiny pecker.

"Que chiquito chile que tu tienes," she clowned. "Fucking worm."

Suddenly, the window next to the bed shattered, then the man's head exploded like a pin poking a balloon. His brains splattered all over; the walls behind him were painted in crimson.

Magali screamed in fright and took off, snatching the door open. But on the other side, a very large dog with clipped ears and tiger striped fur sat there. As soon as it saw Magali, it started growling viciously, gnarling its sharp teeth.

"Oh, shit!" she shrieked, heart dropping damn near out of her ass.

A tall, beautiful woman with the bluest eyes appeared just then, holding Dontae Jr. She looked up from the toddler to Magali. In her eyes, Magali saw pure fury. She then saw Jazmine behind her, being helped to walk by an older, light-skinned man with a scruffy beard and thick, long, graying dreadlocks. She caught a glimpse of Jazmine mean-mugging her, as she and the old Jamaican passed by.

"Life's very precious," the tall woman said, as Dontae Jr. giggled after she kissed his cheek. "You should've left when you had the chance, dumbass."

Magali then saw a young, golden-brown chick with long, golden-blonde hair step through the big dog and the tall chick. Magali's eyes went wide with fear when she saw the girl had a machete in her hands…

CHACHA

The look of sheer fright in the chicana's eyes came right before the sound of a loud, wet fart. A foul stench wafted into ChaCha's nostrils in seconds.

Pablo barked then sneezed the rancid odor out of his nostrils.

Evelyn started walking toward the terrified Mexican, gripping the handle of the machete tightly.

"Wait! Wait! Hold up, joe!" Magali pleaded, taking steps back.

"I swear! I wasn't gonna hurt the baby nor ol' girl. I promise. I just wanted my baby daddy!"

"Kidnappin' babies ain't how you do that, mamahuevo!" spat Evelyn, getting ready to cut the bitch's head off.

Magali made a break for it, running toward the window, ready to dive through it and deal with whatever awaited after hitting the ground from two stories up. The whole time, she couldn't believe that they were in Diablo's house for the life of her.

Where the fuck is everybody?! she thought in a panic.

ChaCha stood where she was and watched Evelyn hurl the machete at Magali with such force that the blade stuck right into her back, hitting her spine.

Magali screamed, falling forward and banging her face off of the window ledge as she instantly became a paraplegic. She fell to the floor, her busted nose gushing blood, teeth knocked out. She had no feeling in anything but her upper body.

"Coje el bebe y vete afueda," ChaCha told Evelyn, handing her Dontae Jr.

Evelyn wanted to see Pablo rip the girl up, but she obeyed ChaCha, taking the little one out to be with his mother.

Once Evelyn and Dontae Jr. were gone, ChaCha shut the door. She looked at Magali. She was trying to crawl her way up to the window to pull herself out.

"¡Mata!" ChaCha commanded her presa canario.

Pablo ran at Magali and chomped down on her head. Magali screamed in agony as she felt his jaws crushing her skull. ChaCha could hear it cracking. Magali's screams stopped after five more seconds. Her body went limp.

"¡Buen trabajo, Pablo! Good job!" ChaCha went and yanked Evelyn's machete out of the dead girl's back.

"Payback's a bitch, traga. Rot in piss," she said then led her dog out, passing all the dead sicarios that silenced assault rifles took out before anyone ever realized they were fucked.

DIABLO

Diablo, Botas, and four surviving sicarios ran for their lives through the woods. A hit squad of dread heads pursued them; dogs barked as they chased after them. One of the sicarios screamed in pain, as they were caught and mauled by a couple of the rottweilers, tearing him apart like lionesses on a helpless antelope.

Gunshots rang out. Two more of Diablo's men went down, as slugs peeled their caps back. Diablo, Botas, and one more sicario were left. Botas pulled out his .45 Colt 1911, turned, and fired a shot.

"Aagghh!" the last sicario cried, as the bullet hit him in his leg.

He fell to the ground, cursing Botas for the snake move. Seconds later, two dread heads caught him and blew him to pieces.

Brrrrrrr! Brrrrrrr! Brrrrrrr!

Slugs flew at Botas and Diablo like the wind. Bullets whizzed by their heads, slamming into trees, knocking chunks out of them.

Less than a minute later, they reached a lake. Without even thinking, they both dove in, diving as deep as they could.

Diablo swam like Michael Phelps, desperate to get away. Botas followed, but not even five seconds later, he felt the sting of bullets hitting him in his back. His screams, muffled by being underwater, were unheard by Diablo, as he continued swimming for his life. He made it to the other side, surfacing just as he nearly ran out of breath. From the years he'd spent in the Mexican Special Forces, his survival instincts had kicked in, allowing him to push himself to the brink.

Climbing out of the dark water, Diablo looked back and did not see a single one of his men behind him. But at the other side of the lake, he saw the mob of dread heads there, looking at him. He was too far for their bullets to reach, luckily for Diablo.

He saw one of them make a motion with two fingers from their eyes then to him.

"Tu madre, pinch prieto," Diablo mumbled then got up out of there before any more surprises showed up.

KENZIE

Tears fell down Kenzie's face, as she looked down at her sleeping boyfriend. A decision she'd just made had her devastated. She had to leave. Since she'd come into his life, nothing but bad things had followed. With him almost losing his life to protect ChaCha, during a daring rescue to get Neveah back, Kenzie couldn't bear the thought of what would happen the next time some shit happened. To him or any of his family.

"Mommy? Where're we going?" Neveah asked, standing next to her with her Barbie bookbag on her back.

Two big duffle bags were next to Kenzie's left foot. She was ready to go, to get far away, far enough to not let her drama hurt Xavier anymore.

She took her daughter's hand into hers. Looking down at her little girl, Kenzie put on a smile, though her heart cried tears of forlornness. The melancholy in her heart had Kenzie feeling like she was actually about to die.

"We have to go, baby," she told her daughter, just above a whisper.

"But what about Daddy?" Neveah's voice started breaking, as her eyes filled with tears.

Kenzie then reached down and picked her baby girl up. "Daddy needs to rest. We're gonna let him get some sleep. Okay?"

Neveah was a smart little girl. She didn't believe her mother for a second.

"I want Daddy to come, Mommy." Tears rolled down her precious face.

"I know, baby. One day," Kenzie said then set Neveah back down, grabbed the bags, and turned toward the door.

Before Kenzie left out of the room, she looked at Xavier. He looked so peaceful.

I love you, baby. Please don't forget about us, she thought to herself then led her daughter out of the room, exiting out of the house and out of Xavier's life, to the Uber that awaited at the curb.

CHACHA

Jazmine couldn't believe what she was seeing. No way was it real. She swore she had to have died in that house and was in hell, tricks being played on her.

But she wasn't.

After getting a doctor check-up, Jazmine was escorted to the private airport in Waukegan. A lavish Gulfstream G550 waited on the tarmac, as ChaCha drove her G-Wagen up to it.

Standing next to the stairway of the jet, two big Dominican men held four duffle bags. After hopping out the Mercedes truck with Dontae Jr. in her arms, ChaCha and Jamaica walked the mother and toddler to the jet.

The two men opened the bags. Jazmine saw more cash inside than she'd ever seen before in real life. Her eyes nearly popped out from how wide they went.

"Our pilot will take you anywhere you want to go," ChaCha told her. "In the country or out. In the bags, you have four million in clean cash. Your baby daddy will never burden your life again, unless you reach out to him, which would be foolish."

Jazmine nodded in agreement. "He left us to die. I will never contact him again."

ChaCha nodded. "I hear you talkin', Ma. Be smart. Go start over, go to school, set up a college fund for your little boy. Be someone for yourself, not for a square-ass bum like dude."

Nodding her head, Jazmine sighed. "Thank you. So much."

ChaCha kissed her finger and touched it to Dontae Jr.'s cheek. She smiled at him, as he smiled at her.

"Go ahead. Go and live better," she told Jazmine.

Jazmine carried her son up into the jet. ChaCha's bodyguards carried the money in behind her. The stairs lifted up until the plane was sealed up. The jet started moving, taxiing toward the runway.

ChaCha and Jamaica watched the jet take off into the dark sky. In seconds, all that was visible was its blinking lights.

ChaCha sighed then looked at the old head. "Now to deal with Eve."

Jamaica nodded. "We wait though. A lot has 'appened taday."

Agreeing with him, ChaCha decided to wait. She and Jamaica hopped back into her G-Wagen. Before she pulled off, she answered a call from Shabba.

"Yes?"

"Boss lady. De woman was very tankfull for de new cah and de money. She tanked ya' very much."

ChaCha smiled, happy the woman whose Expedition they'd had to commandeer to get away from the cops was appreciative to accept the repayments.

"Thanks, Shabba. I'll need you, Bullet, Face, and Kingston to head to Pittsburgh as soon as you can. Javi and Macho have a run to make, and I don't want any more highway mayhem."

"Straight away, Cha," Shabba replied then ended the call.

"Me go to me woman's house, boss," Jamaica then said, yawning. "Me need a massage and a hot meal."

ChaCha chuckled. "Me too, rude bwoi," she replied as thoughts of Danny entered her mind. She put her truck in drive and headed toward the gate. "I'll be heading to see the boss, so tomorrow, I'll be unavailable."

Jamaica chuckled. "Okay."

"What's so funny?" ChaCha asked, coming to a stop, as the gate began to slide open.

"No'ting, Ximena. No'ting at all," Jamaica said, capping his ass off.

ChaCha narrowed her eyes at him but said nothing more, as she exited out of the airport, ready to take the old head to his chick's crib and head south to go see the only man she had ever given her heart to.

JAVI

Javi's eyes opened when the alarm went off at three-thirty in the morning. Michelle woke up with him. She sighed as he got up to get some things to go shower.

"I really can't come with you?" Michelle asked.

"Naw, bae. This is our first run for Guera. We don't know her client. I'm not puttin' you nor my baby in harm's way if shit pops off."

"Why do y'all have to be the ones to make these runs, Javier? Like, you all have other drivers that are goons that y'all trust. Do the boss thing and delegate the responsibility to someone else. I need your body next to me, baby."

Javi stopped what he was doing. He looked at her and smiled. Walking up to her, he sat on her side of the bed, kissing her forehead.

"Our family's name was built off of how the ol' heads handled biz by their own hands. Nobody does it like how we do. It's what sets us apart from other families, cartels, mobs, and other organizations, Michelle. My family, we've been

192

tippin' the scales in our favor for as long as cocaine has been around. This shit that we do, it's our legacy. You don't put your legacy in another person's hands. Fuck who can't, or doesn't, agree."

She could do nothing but smile at that. His words had such simplicity yet had summed up how his family had amassed the multi-billion-dollar fortune it was worth. They made their own moves, because that was how they wanted to do it. Period!

"Promise me you gonna be careful, Javi. Please."

He nodded. "Te lo juro por dios, I'll be careful, amor."

MACHO

"Porque carajo no puede ir contigo?!" Yessy yelled, swinging an extra-large down pillow at Macho.

Macho stepped back before it could hit him. "See. You buggin' already."

"No me importa un carajo, Antonio! Me quiero ir contigo!"

Macho looked at his lady in her silk nightie – hair loose, face screwed up, fists balled. In their suite, she'd hopped right on his ass when his alarm woke them and their dogs up. To find out that he wasn't allowing her to go like she always did had Yessy livid.

"Yessy. Amor. Calmate, Ma. It's not that serious," Macho said to her in a soft tone, walking toward her.

Yessy let him put his arms around her. He was her heart. Completely. And she was his.

"Yessinia Moralez, chill! It's only to Jersey and back. The shit's goin' to these bikers out in New Kensington."

Yessy's eyebrows furrowed. "The 8 Ball Boys?"

Macho nodded.

"Wow. Fucking fake-ass, Hell's Angels wannabe, racist pricks! Guera has you dealing with them?! What the fuck is wrong with you?"

"I'm psycho. Duh!" Macho grinned at her.

Yessy burst out laughing. "¡Tu 'ta loco!"

"I know I'm crazy." Macho kissed her lips. "But so are you." He kissed her again.

"When do you have to be on the road by?" she asked.

"Five."

"Good." Yessy rushed him back to the bed and jumped on top of him. "We got time for you to make it up to me for not taking me. And if you say anything other than, 'Your wish is my command, oh beautiful queen, Yessina,' I will bite you in your sleep."

Macho burst out laughing, as he laid on his back under his woman.

"Your wish is my command, oh beautiful queen, Yessinia," he told her then in a flash, flipped her over onto her back. "My sweet, sweet, sexy, always wet and ready for me Yessinia," he added then moseyed his way down south, pushing her nightie up, exposing her bareness.

"Good boy," Yessy giggled. "Now hush up and eat breakfast. It's hot and ready for you."

CHAPTER 20

JAVI

After sexing his fiancée down, without getting puked on, Javi went and hopped into the shower. Michelle took her prenatal supplements, fed and watered the dogs, then as Javi showered, she cheffed up some cheese eggs and some sausage links.

She set him and herself up some plates. Javi threw on a plain, black, V-collar shirt, black jeans, and black Tims then went out to join his woman at the table.

Seeing just two plates made, Javi kicked himself, muttering a curse.

"What?" asked Michelle with a raised brow.

"Nena's goin' too. She needs to eat."

"Why is she going, but I can't?"

"Bae, she's goin' to Jersey for Eve; she in a whole 'nother truck. Remember?"

Michelle groaned, frustrated. "Okay, Javier. You want me to make her some too?"

"Naw. I'll cook. Just call her over. I need to make sure she keepin' my niece or nephew healthy."

NENA

Nena made her way over to their room. She was dressed in tight fitting, acid-washed jeans, a navy-blue, long-sleeved shirt with an orange Chicago Bears logo on the front, white, low top Air Forces, her hair in a ponytail, and hoop earrings in her ears; even as plain Jane, Nena was just bad!

Javi made her take a few bottles of prenatals that Michelle had to spare. After they all ate, Javi kissed his woman passionately then patted the dogs' heads. Michelle hugged Nena and demanded that she drive safe. Nena got a dog kiss in her face by Demon, then they left out of the room.

Michelle plopped down on the bed and sighed. Diamond hopped up onto the bed with her and laid her head on Michelle's lap. Michelle patted her face, cheering up a little bit.

Knock! Knock! Knock!

Michelle got up to go answer the door. As soon as she opened it, she saw Yessy and G-Baby, both dressed in jeans, t-shirts, and Nikes, with their hair in ponytails. Maliante and Dreams sat at their sides, looking for Demon and Diamond.

"Um…. y'all goin' somewhere at four-thirty in the morning?" Michelle asked.

"Yup. And so are you," Yessy replied. "Get dressed, yo."

JAVI

Javi and Macho walked Nena to Evelyn's Volvo and assisted her in pre-tripping the tractor and trailer. Once she was good to go, they sent her on her way.

Macho then led Javi toward a whole other stand-alone garage, opposite where their custom Peterbilts were.

"What is we doin'?" Javi asked, wondering why they were going there instead of to their rigs.

"Goin' to work, tiguere. We ridin' together; it's only one load," Macho replied, reaching the garage entrance door and entering a number into the padlock on the side of it.

The door unlocked. Macho stepped inside first, turning on the lights. Javi entered, looked and saw what they were rolling in, and cursed.

"Maaan, come on, cuz! Really?" he asked incredulously.

Macho burst out laughing. "No tenga miedo, nigga. Somos tigueres. You afraid of a truck?"

"That's not a fuckin' truck, cuz! It's a damn devil!"

Parked all by its lonesome was El Viejo. The old man was a creepy looking, 1985 Peterbilt 359 Extended Hood. Its black paint and its stainless and chrome exterior parts and wheels had long ago lost their glossy finish and shine. The 'V'-shaped windshield drop-visor and the shiny, pointed, stainless steel, seven-inch diameter exhaust stacks, mounted at both driver's and the passenger's doors, gave the thirty-year old Pete a devilish look.

Behind its cab was a sixty-inch, flat top sleeper berth. The old rig's frame was longer than usual, via custom stretching. It sat three hundred inches long and had a lowered stance, giving it a hot rod semi look.

Javi looked up at El Viejo and caught chills. The dinosaur of a semi reminded him of those old movies where trucks came alive by themselves and started running people over.

Macho looked over at his cuz and shook his head. "That's crazy, yo, Homies, you ain't scared of the bullets, bombs, knife fights... But yo' ass scurd of a truck."

Javi waved his cousin off. "No quiero escuchar esa 'mielda."

"Uh huh. I know," Macho chuckled then went to start the pre-trip inspection while Javi hung back, staying away from the old man until he had no choice but to get in the death trap truck.

Macho checked all the lubricants and fluids in the engine bay. Then, he climbed inside the big twin turbo Caterpillar 3406 E motor with a surplus of high-performance Pittsburgh Power diesel upgrades. Macho and his brother had completely rebuilt the 359 from its already hooked up touches. It'd been owned by Juanito, bought right out of the dealership, in 1984. El Viejo had trafficked billions of dollars of cocaine in the time he'd been on the road. He'd been shot up, set on fire, crashed, and towed multiple times. Nothing could kill him.

From Juanito, it'd gone to Danny after Macho's father, Tana, passed on it. Danny fortified it and used it as his trap-truck. When he went to prison, Macho and Tool added it to their stable then added their own modifications to it.

El Viejo was as safe for drivers and riders as soldiers inside of a M1A1 Abrams battle tank. He looked like a creepy old truck, but in all actuality, he was far from just that.

Javi watched his cousin close the long, square engine hood, then after a quick look under the truck, he climbed up into the cab and started the big electronic Cat engine.

El Viejo started up. He shook as 1,400 horsepower woke up. The rig roared, sounding angry. Javi swore it was like waking an old, cranky man up from his slumber, one with a shotgun on his lap and a hatred for all humans on his property.

Chills again shot up Javi's spine. The 359 scared the bejeesus out of him.

Macho was still laughing as he got out to finish checking over El Viejo.

The garage bay door began opening up just then. As it got higher, Javi saw Tool was there, hopping off of his chromed Hayabusa. He entered the garage, saw the look on Javi's face, then turned to see the comical smirk on his younger brother's face. Tool started laughing.

Ten minutes later, the pre-trip was done. El Viejo was good to go. This was already known because the Murrysville yard had twenty-four-hour ASE certified diesel techs that kept every truck and trailer in the fleet in top condition.

"Man, get cho' scary ass in, yo!" Macho shouted as he climbed up into the driver's seat while Tool gestured an invite by the open passenger's door.

Javi shook his head, took a deep breath, and walked toward El Viejo, hesitantly climbing up into the cab.

"Oh, shit? What the hell?"

He was dumbfounded to see the complete contrast of the old Pete's exterior and the interior. It was like a brand-new truck inside – chrome, leather, woodgrain, custom stylings. The glossy floor was wood; the driver and passenger seats were high-quality Bentley leather with custom diamond-stitched inserts. The steering wheel was a chromed, three spoke, wood grain gripped GT classic style design that tied in the wood dashboard, accented in chrome gauge bezels and chrome switches. The tall shifter to the eighteen-speed transmission was all chrome, topped by a woodgrain knob. Custom door panels housed JL Audio 6x9 speakers, while tweeters were wired up in the ceiling.

"Eeeee, joe! This muhfucka is hard!" Javi exclaimed, getting all the way up inside. When he stepped back into the sleeper berth, he thought his eyes were deceiving him. "Aww, yo, y'all went crazy on this, cuz."

There were leather, diamond-stitched walls; both rear corners had three twelve-inch JL Audio W7 subs in custom-made fiberglass enclosures. In the middle center of the sleepers' rear wall, a window that could slide open looked out the back of El Viejo, over his fifth-wheel and his rear wheels.

The bed had been widened and a big comfortable mattress laid on its base, topped with Italian 1,000 thread count sheets and a Gucci monogrammed blanket with leather Gucci pillows.

The sides of El Viejo's sleeper also had whore-doors. They opened up to the outside, allowing whores to jump in and out after satisfying the driver. But the whore doors El Viejo had served a completely different purpose.

"Naw, stay scared, nigga," Macho teased, as Tool climbed up into the passenger's seat. "It's the big, scary Peterbilt! It's gonna run yo' Illinois born ass over!"

Javi just stared at Macho, as Tool chuckled.

"Will ya' shut up and drive?" he asked, sitting on the bed, kicking off his Tims.

"Sure." Macho hit the gas, revving El Viejo up.

The engine was so loud that Javi had to cover his ears and so powerful that the whole truck shook.

Macho released the tractor's parking brake as he clutched the shifter into low gear. Tool reached out and hit a button on the Clarion head unit.

Macho crept El Viejo out of the garage, into the darkness of early morning.

The Clarion's touchscreen popped out and flipped up. Tool went to the playlist; while in the old school Pete, only older music was allowed. Tool selected one titled *Ridin' To The Money* and sat back in his seat. Macho steered El Viejo toward the exit, passing by his and Javi's trucks.

"My mans is comin' to get ya' truck, lil' cuz," Tool told Javi just as Macho's favorite O.G. cut, KRS-One's *Step Into A World (Rapture's Delight),* came on.

Javi nodded his head and laid back The beat hit seconds later, and the powerful speakers came to life, pounding so hard that it vibrated the ground.

MICHELLE

Michelle stood next to Yessy and G-Baby with their dogs behind them. From the lobby window, they all watched Macho's old rig ride by, bass hitting so hard from inside that they could feel it.

"I know one thing, Yessy. Your man better not bring my fiancé back with no eardrums," Michelle told her homegirl.

Yessy chuckled. "It's bound to happen."

They kept looking out the window until El Viejo had reached the line of PH&D rigs checking out at the security booth.

"Come on. Let's go," Yessy then said.

The girls and the dogs headed out, hurrying to where Yessy had a plain Range Rover Supercharged sitting in a spot next to her man's Bentley. They piled in. Yessy started the supercharged V8 engine, put it in drive, and slowly rolled out of the spot, careful to stay far back from the Pete.

"What exactly are we gonna do?" Michelle asked from the backseat with her Sicilian mastiffs, the rottweiler, and pit bull laid out around her.

"Same thing we always do, Ma," Yessy told her. "Watch our dudes backs and kick their asses when they do some dumb shit," she said, making her way up behind another PJ&D rig that was now behind El Viejo.

G-Baby laughed. "Not sure we can handle Tool though. He a big-ass nigga, man," she threw in, pulling a battery powered 2-way radio out of a small bag.

"Paah'leease. Tool's a big softie," Michelle threw in, as Yessy inched up with the refrigerated food transport. "At least for the ladies he is."

"Who's the chick he brought to the barbecue?" Yessy asked.

"Another model. You know how he is," G-Baby chimed in. "Bottles and models is Tool's motto. It used to be Antonio's too."

"Keyword… used to be," Yessy corrected, coming to a stop, as the rig stopped at the booth. "Put that radio on Channel 19, Gabi."

The sounds of El Viejo roaring caught their attention. They caught sight of him rushing off down the small access road, heading to the main road. Fire shot up out of the loud exhaust pipes every time Macho shifted a gear.

"Who really loves such an old, creepy-ass truck like that, yo?" Michelle asked as the rig in front rolled off, exiting the yard.

"Macho," Yessy and G-Baby said in unison.

"And Tool," Yessy added.

"Los tigueres de la ciudad de steel," Michelle chuckled. "I'm glad my baby is related to those two crazy muthafuckas, yo."

The ladies laughed at her. Yessy threw the deuces up at the ex-Navy Seal in the guard booth and exited, turning onto the access road, preparing for the ride east to keep her bae from blowing things up.

CHACHA

ChaCha was speechless. She was stunned. Her heart cried for Xavier. The tears in his eyes were a rare thing to see. He was truly torn apart. The note in his hand was like holding his own heart in his palm after it'd been ripped out of his chest.

"I don't get it, cuz. Why does she not understand that she isn't responsible for me gettin' shot?"

He read the note left by Kenzie again.

My heart. Since I came into your life, I have caused you nothing but pain. Now, you're laid up with two bullet holes in you because of me. I cannot continue to allow you to hurt anymore, so I have to go. I love you, Xavier, and so does Neveah. I hope you'll always remember us, but it may be best you don't, so you can move on. You deserve better.

Kenzie

ChaCha wiped away his tears with her hand. She was nearly on the brink of tears herself. Pablo, sitting at her side, even whimpered, feeling her distress.

"I'm so sorry, Papa," she told Xavier, as she pulled him into her arms to comfort him. "I'm sorry. I don't understand it either, but I guess one day, we will be able to. All we can do is pray that Kenzie finds the peace she needs to be happy and content."

Xavier nodded in agreement but thinking about the news of Stacks getting away… again… he started steaming.

"Hey. No. Do not do that," ChaCha said, knowing what was on his mind already. "Un dia, ese mamabicho se va a morir. Lo juro por dios, Papa. He has an angel watching over him right now, but one day, Xavier, I swear he will fucking die."

He grinded his teeth in sheer rage. He really had nothing to say. He made a silent promise to himself that he would not rest until Stacks was in pieces, scattered all across the country.

Just then, a couple of knocks on the door got their attention.

"¡Entra!" ChaCha shouted.

The door opened, and Xavier saw Vanessa. She gasped, clapping a hand over her mouth, shocked and saddened to see that her boo was laid up like she'd heard.

"Xavier! Oh, my God, baby!" she cried, rushing over to him on the opposite side of where ChaCha sat. "What happened to you?!"

ChaCha sighed. She stood up and looked at her cousin. "I'll leave you two alone. Papa, asegurate de llamar a Nena. Okay?"

"I will, cuz," Xavier replied, as Vanessa kicked off her flats and climbed onto the bed with him.

"Pablo, ven," ChaCha told her dog.

Pablo obeyed and followed his human out of the room. ChaCha closed the door. She leaned up against it then broke into tears.

For a minute, she sobbed. She had already been en route down to Salem, down southern Illinois, when Xavier called her about Kenzie taking Neveah and leaving. She'd turned right around to go comfort him. She had never seen Xavier so gone over a woman except for Vanessa. And now that she was back in the picture, ChaCha actually hoped that her baby cousin would be good for him. Just like a woman's heart, a man's heart was easy to break, no matter how tough they were outside. Love could be a beautiful thing. But it could also cause someone to commit suicide.

EVELYN

Evelyn leaned against the trunk of her Alpina, waiting for Lil' Five to pull up. With her was Gloria and the twins, Kiara and Jada. Posted in the parking lot of an old diesel repair business that had shut down long ago, down in Waukegan off of U.S. Route 41, the four ladies were on point.

Idling off to the side was Kiara's brand-new 389 Peterbilt car-hauler. Parked in back of it were three Chevy Silverado 1500 pickup trucks. They were fully loaded, waiting for their new owners to come get them.

Minutes later, Lil' Five's Range Rover turned into the lot. It rode up and parked a few feet away. Lil' Five hopped out, fresh in Louis Vuitton, rocking icy jewelry. With him were three dark-skinned dread heads that looked like mirror images of each other. Evelyn recognized them from the day she had to pop at the black pickup truck in front of Stacks' dope spot. They were triplets and seemed to be down for Lil' Five more than Stacks.

"What up, Eve?" Lil' Five approached and gave her a hug. "Ladies! How y'all doin' today?" the handsome, yellow dread head asked with a cheerful smile that made all four of the women see him as an adorable young heartbreaker.

The Alabama twins were already visualizing Lil' Five sandwiched in between them. Evelyn couldn't help but to imagine Lil' Five's lips on her. Even Gloria found herself swooning over the young Ghost.

"Fine, like yaself," Kiara said in her southern twang. "I mean! And yaself?"

"I'm gucci. Ready to find out what I was called here for." He looked at Evelyn for the answer.

She nodded her head toward the three pickups. "The keys are in them," she said, a double meaning in her words. "If you accept them, I want every single person who knows Stacks hunting him the fuck down like the diseased creep that he is. If you accept and don't do this, I will come for you. You know who I am, Lil' Five. Do not fuck with me."

Lil' Five nodded. "I understand. Stacks is a piece of shit. So is his cousin."

Evelyn's eyebrow rose up at that. "His cousin, Prince?"

Lil' Five's eyebrows furrowed. "You know him?"

She nodded. "What's to him?"

Gloria wondered the same thing.

Lil' Five pulled his iPhone out and went on the internet. He typed in Prince's government name then showed the two ladies what Google provided.

"Wow..." Evelyn was amazed.

"Fucking mielda," Gloria cursed, curling her lip up in disgust.

Kiara and Jada stayed where they stood but could hear their boss' words.

"And Stacks was in it too, joe," Lil' Five told them, scrolling down to a bunch of mugshots of people involved.

Evelyn and Gloria saw Stacks' picture and shook their heads.

"People like them don't deserve to have, nor be around, kids," Evelyn said. "Find him. Keep him alive, Lil' Five, and my family will bless you."

"Fa'sho. We on it, joe. On Ghost," Lil' Five said, exiting the net and sending a group text to every Unknown he had in his phone. "Aye! Red! Gold! Black! Hop in them Chevies and let's go!" he yelled to the triplets.

The three each hopped up into a pickup. Evelyn told Lil' Five how many bricks each one had hidden in their beds and in their frames. The young Lord's eyes went wide in shock.

"Eeeeee, jeeooooe! On Ghost, even if I get 'em off fa ten gees each, that's..." He did the math in his head, but Evelyn beat him to it.

"Thirty million. A hell of a price for one man's head," she said, then her eyes narrowed. "Do not fail."

Without any more words, Lil' Five nodded then hopped back into his Range. He led the triplets out of the lot, and they all disappeared from sight.

"You really trust him with three thousand kilos of your family's perico, baby?" asked Gloria.

Evelyn nodded. "He's hungry but not enough to bite the hand that feeds him."

"What about lick?" Jada asked with a devious smile.

"I gots somethin' that lil', sexy muthafucka can lick," her twin said.

"Take y'all asses to work," Evelyn said. "Nena, Payton, and Olivia's already on the way. Kiki, go get in your truck, take Jada to get hers, and go."

"Yes, ma'am, boss lady. We's a goin' ta work now," Kiara sassed jokingly.

The twins climbed up into the rig. Kiara pulled off and made a wide turn out and roared up the little road.

"You and me," Evelyn said, as she and Gloria got into her car. "We have one more thing to do, then we head east to join them."

Gloria smirked. "I'm the one that shot him outside the hotel."

Evelyn gasped, turning to look at her. "What the fuck? You?"

Gloria looked at her. "You are mine. ¡Para siempre, cabróna! Motherfuckers that try to take my lady are gonna die!"

Evelyn wasn't even angry. A second later, she started smiling.

"My bitch a muhfuckin' gangsta, joe," she chuckled, as she put the Beemer in drive.

"Yo te amo, Eve," Gloria told her, taking her right hand into hers, kissing it.

"I love you too, baby. Now let's go handle this biz and get back to the money," Evelyn said and turned out of the lot, plotting bloody murder after exposing him for the foul human being she'd discovered him to be.

CHAPTER 21

XAVIER

"Hey, baby!" Nena answered excitedly.

"What's good, Ma? How you feelin' today?" Xavier asked, as he dried himself off after stepping out of the specialized handicapped shower.

"Even better since you remembered I exist."

Xavier chuckled. "Wouldja knock it off? Can't nobody forget yo' crazy ass, Azalea. Where you at though?"

Nena told him she was an hour or so out from Harrisburg, PA. She told him about being invited to the barbecue, the race, and how she got to shoot up a dump truck with Yessy, G-Baby, and Michelle after some dudes tried to get down on Macho and Perry.

"The fuck? Why ain't nobody call me about this?" Xavier asked. "And why the fuck is you gunnin' them niggas shit up with my baby in yo' stomach?"

"I'm a ride or die bitch, joe. Fuck, you forgot? I am La Nena, a.k.a. The Realest Bitch Alive! Michelle is my people. Javi is my people. You are his brother, and you are my heart. Do I need to say more?"

Xavier started laughing. "Naw, Ma. I dig. You just leave the G-shit to my bro 'n 'nem, aight? At least 'til my baby's born."

"I'll see what I can do," Nena giggled.

"You a asshole."

They talked for a few more minutes, then they ended the call with plans to spend some time together once Nena was back from all the runs she was going to be on for the next few weeks.

Xavier was about to call his brother and ask why his pregnant fiancée allowed his own pregnant chick to shoot assault rifles in the middle of a street in broad daylight, and with an audience watching, when a tap at the door held him up.

"Yeah?" he called out.

The door opened. Vanessa stepped inside wearing a fuzzy robe and a mischievous smile on her face. She saw he was still naked and licked her lips.

"Uh oh," Xavier chuckled. "Someone is insatiable, I see."

Vanessa untied her robe and let it drop to the floor. "I can never get enough of that good-good, baby," she told him, as she walked up to him. "And I never will be able to," she added just before sinking down to her knees before him to take his hardening dick into her mouth and show him even further that she was who he needed in his life.

~   ~   ~

Da Brat's *Funkdafied* pounded as Macho blew east along the Pennsylvania Turnpike. Tool was videochatting with his model-chick while Javi did the same, still laid out in El Viejo's sleeper.

"I love that idea, baby! For real! And it's been so long since I've been there! Ooooo. I can't wait!"

Javi noticed that, in the background, he could tell Michelle was in a vehicle.

"Where you goin' so early in the morning?" he asked her.

"Stop bein' nebby, nigga," she replied then gave him a wink and a kiss.

"Get fucked up for goin' to see another dude if you want, yo," Javi playfully threatened.

He saw her eyebrows rise up. "Says the guy that has two women pregnant at the same damn time."

Oh, shit... I forgot about Angela. I need to check on her. Muhfuckas got her held hostage 'n shit.

"I'ma tell ChaCha's people to let her go," Javi told his woman.

"I already did."

Javi looked at her with puzzlement. "Did? What did you do, Michelle?" he asked in an accusing manner.

"Let her go and gave her some money. Told the bitch if I ever see her again, it's curtains."

"So... you want for there to be a child of mines just out there?"

"Next topic, Javi! We'll figure it out when she has the baby, man! Damn!"

Reaching Harrisburg, Macho switched from the Turnpike to I-78, taking it the remainder of the way. In Easton, PA, he stopped for fuel then finished the last leg of the trip, taking 78 into Jersey, right to Elizabeth.

As he'd predicted, like a seasoned trucker could, they arrived at the massive city-sized Port of Elizabeth just after nine-thirty.

Macho went to the entrance lanes that were filled with trucks and without trailers, waiting to gain access, to pick up loads, or drop off loads that were entering the country or waiting to be loaded on a cargo vessel and shipped out.

"Nena ain't got no foot-power, cuzzo," Macho said to Javi, who was still back in the sleeper, as he spotted Evelyn's green and gold luxury auto-transporter in one of the entrance lines.

Javi got up and went into the cab, seeing the shiny truck as well. He reached for the mic to the CB and called out to her.

"How 'boutcha, green Valdez mobile parkin' lot?"

Seconds later, Macho, Javi, and Tool heard Nena's voice.

"No way this is Javi. Ain't no way, joe."

Tool chuckled at the obvious surprise in her voice.

"Oh, it be me, Pilsen girl."

Nena replied, "How in the hell did y'all catch up to me?"

"One word... Macho."

"Figures. Goddamn speed demon."

Macho burst out laughing. "Don't blame me," he said after Javi held the mic up for him to speak. "I got 1,400 reasons to... fly like an eeaagle! Ooohhh!"

Laughter erupted over the CB as other truckers heard him clown.

"Hey, my man, Macho's in the house!" a trucker shouted out.

"Machitooo! Que paso, bro?" another hollered.

"Heeeey, Machooo," a female cooed. "I missed you, handsome. Where you been?"

"At home with his wife, bitch!" Nena snapped. "Stop talkin' like that before I come slap the shit out cho' ass, joe!"

Macho, his brother, and Javi burst out laughing at Nena. Javi spoke into the mic again.

"Whoever you are, you just got treeaated! Boom! Boom! Boom! Boom!" he shouted and started laughing.

~ ~ ~

Rashonda smacked her lips as she pulled off from the booth she'd just checked out of the port at. The girl that had snapped on her over the CB radio when she was trying to get at Macho had her pissed. The chocolate, blonde haired belle had been trying to get at the thuggishly handsome goon for quite a while. She always ran into him on the road, mostly in Jersey docks. She was well aware of who he was, as were most of the truckers that frequently ran around the east coast.

Every time Rashonda saw Macho, triple X-rated thoughts entered her mind. He made her so wet and didn't even know who she was. She had intentions to change that real soon.

Rolling forward in her older Freightliner Century Class, pulling a fifty-three-foot-long intermodal container trailer full of imported goods, Rashonda headed out of the port, following a mass of semis leaving out as well. She glimpsed to her left and saw the super old Peterbilt that Macho was behind the wheel of. She saw a dread head in the passenger's seat and just the face of a guy standing between their seats from the sleeper.

Her heart fluttered when Macho looked her way. He reached up and tugged down on the cord above his head to the left, tooting the air horns.

Rashonda blew him a kiss before she rolled past him, reaching the road.

Making a wide turn out, Rashonda headed along with a congested flow of commercial traffic. She shifted gears on her two-speed transmission smoothly, never once touching the clutch. Years of over the road driving was under her belt.

Glancing over at the center of the dash, Rashonda knew she needed fuel before getting back onto the Jersey Turnpike to head back home to Maryland where her load was also going.

A sign for a Pilot fuel station came up. Minutes later, she reached the fueling spot, turning into the diesel pump only location. A few other rigs were getting diesel fuel. She maneuvered her rig around the outer perimeter, swinging seventy-five feet of eighteen-wheeler out and parking perfectly at the pump in between two flashy PJ&D Transport rigs.

Rashonda put her electronic log device onto 'Fueling' then got her five-foot-eleven inch tall frame out of her truck with her Pilot fuel card in hand.

Just as she slid her card into the pump's slot, screeching tires made her look toward the front of her rig. A black Range Rover had appeared, its sound system bumping loud and hard enough that Rashonda could feel the bass under her Timberlands.

The driver's door flew open. A very beautiful woman in a t-shirt, jeans, Air Max 90s on her feet, and her long hair in a ponytail hopped out with leather workout gloves on her hands. She had the look of a woman on a mission in her eyes. Her mission was Rashonda.

YESSY

Yessy grinded her teeth, as she walked toward the tall, thick, dark-skinned woman.

"Uh, you need somethin'?" the blonde head chick asked, as Yessy got within two feet of her.

Bink! Bink! Bink! Wham!

Four lightning-fast swings put Rashonda on her ass in a diesel fuel puddle. Yessy hit her so hard and fast that seconds after, Rashonda still hadn't realized what had just happened. All she knew was that her jaw hurt, she saw two of everything, and her butt was wet.

She looked up at Yessy. "Wh-What the hell, yo?! Fuck I do to you?!"

Yessy grabbed Rashonda by her silky mane. Rashonda yelped in pain.

"Leave him alone, puta!" Yessy growled through clenched teeth. "He is mine!"

She then slammed Rashonda's face into the base of the diesel-pump machine, breaking her nose. Rashonda was knocked unconscious from the hard blow.

Yessy looked at the PJ&D trucker that was watching from the passenger's side fuel tank of her rig. She smiled, nodding her head at Yessy. Nodding back, Yessy went and jumped back into her Range, joining a laughing G-Baby and Michelle.

"Hell naaw!" G-Baby shouted, laughing so hard that tears filled her eyes. "¡Esta tipa ta loca!"

Michelle laughed so hard that she could barely breathe.

Yessy mashed the gas and peeled off, dipping out of the Pilot, heading back to the port to wait for El Viejo to come back out.

"Turn the radio back on, Gabi," Yessy told G-Baby, which was how they'd heard Rashonda flirting with Macho in the first place. "Another bitch flirts with my man, I'm stompin' her ass! On God, son!"

XAVIER

Vanessa squealed and giggled at the feeling of Xavier's face in her ass crack. He licked and slobbered all over her puckered-up asshole, fucking her mind up. She gripped the bedsheets in her hands, face down, ass up high. Music played through the makeshift aftercare room's speakers; Justin Timberlake's *TKO* bumped, turning Xavier up.

Vanessa came a minute later. Her juices squirted on Xavier's chest, soaking him. She rolled over onto her back and demanded he get up in it. He obeyed her, climbing on top.

He slid into her wet-wet, filling her up, stretching her out. His gunshot wounds weren't even close to being on his mind. Percocets had him flying high, dick hard as steel as he started stroking the pussy.

Vanessa wrapped her legs around him. Xavier leaned down and kissed her while keeping his rhythm. She fell even more in love with him. The physical attraction, mental, emotional, and spiritual were all so strong. The sex was hot. He had her body and her mind.

"Xavier! Oh, God, I fucking love you, baby!" she cried out, as he brought her to another orgasm.

It came out before he even realized it.

"I love you too, Ma," Xavier told her, as he felt his nut coming. "I've always loved you."

The words were music to her ears. They gave her the strength to overpower Xavier, muscling him onto his back.

213

She got on top of him, sliding her soaking wet womanhood over his length. She took his hands into hers, intertwining their fingers. Xavier looked up at her.

"Damn 'Nessa," he said in amazement, in true awe of how unbelievably gorgeous she was. "You are so beautiful, bae. For real. I can't even believe we back in tune with each other after all these years."

She smiled at him. Leaning down, Vanessa pressed her lips to his, as Public Announcement's old hit, *Yippie-Yi-Yo*, came on. She put so much passion behind her kiss. Her heart was in it, as well as her mind. Vanessa felt one with him. Mind, body, and soul, Vanessa was his, and Xavier was hers.

Pulling back a few seconds later and looking down into his eyes, Vanessa smiled at him.

"You and me, we're meant to be, Zay. You've always been mine, and I've always been yours."

"Yeah? Always?" he asked.

"Yes." She put her forehead on his, her eyes inches away from his. "We are one, two, and three."

Xavier burst out laughing. "Yo, you're wild as hell!"

Vanessa laughed. "This is true, baby, but I'm wild for you," she told him, raising back up with his dick still hard inside of her. "Now let me show you how wild I can get, Papi."

And she did, for the next two hours, until they ran out of gas. Vanessa fell fast asleep in his arms. Xavier laid there for a while, music still playing. As Blaque's *808* played, he thought about Kenzie – her smile, her passion, the love she had for him. He thought about Neveah. He smiled at the image of the little girl smiling at him. He missed them already, but Kenzie made her choice. Xavier had never been the type to chase chicks, even if she had affected him in ways no other woman had. But he'd be lying if he said her taking off like that didn't hurt him to the core.

Coming back out of his thoughts, the warm, beautiful, naked woman in his arms, that he had so much history with, was who he knew he should be making his wife.

Whoa... my wife? he then thought, shocked that he even had it in his mind to do something like that.

It scared him to make Vanessa Mrs. Valdez, but it also excited him. But what about Nena? And Keisha? He hadn't even reached out to her since the shooting. There was no way he could try to make the woman in his arms his lifelong partner with so much mess revolving around him. Could he?

CHAPTER 22

MACHO

Macho maneuvered El Viejo through the gargantuan port. Yarder trucks, forklifts, and other rigs moved about, working as one to keep the trillion-dollar logistics chain moving.

With directions from Guera to go right to the ship her load was to be unloaded off of, Macho headed toward the rear of the docks where his load would bypass Customs inspections.

Moored alongside the edge sat an enormous cargo ship. Painted up toward the upper bow was *Queen Valdez*. The huge vessel had been owned by the Valdez family for decades. It'd been all over the world and had transported trillions of dollars in goods in the time it'd been built to the current day.

Macho saw a port supervisor's SUV coming his way. Parking in a spot alongside a wall of stacked trailer containers, across the way from the ship where a crane unloaded containers, setting them onto bare trailer's chassis frames pulled by little yarder trucks, he waited for the man to roll up.

A hefty African American guy in a flannel shirt, jeans, and steel-toe boots got out of the Expedition and made his way to Macho's door.

Tool watched as the sky crane continued working. Javi sat on the bed, nodding his head to *Notorious Thugs* by Notorious B.I.G. and Bone-Thugs-N-Harmony.

Macho opened his door as the man walked up. A brown paper bag loaded with stacks of cash found its way into the supervisor's hands; he nodded his head, and without a word, he went back to his SUV and pulled off.

~   ~   ~

Half an hour later, the container with Guera's Venezuelan-grown and produced cocaine was off-loaded from the ship and laid on top of a chassis. The yarder driver pulled off from under the crane and looped around to where El Viejo sat. Stopping next to the old Pete, the driver hit a button on the yarder's dashboard. The hydraulic-powered fifth wheel that yarders were built with rose up to lift a trailer on landing gear – to make moving it fast and easy for the driver – lowered back down to set it back on the ground, and then brought where it needed to be. The trailer's legs touched back down on the ground. The driver slid through the rear door of the little truck, unhooked the air and electrical lines, unlocked the fifth wheel's jaw, then with a nod to Macho, he got back in the yarder's driver's seat. He pulled from under the loaded trailer and rolled away to go grab another trailer.

After positioning El Viejo in front of the trailer and backing the Pete's rear-end under it until the trailer's kingpin slid into the tractor's fifth wheel, Macho put on some work gloves and got out to couple up. Tool climbed over into the driver's seat and waited to assist his brother with the lights and brake checks.

At El Viejo's driver side, just behind the sleeper, Macho unhooked the three lines that came up through the stretched frame, in between the sleeper and the fifth wheel, of which the front of the trailer rested on.

As he reconnected the 'red' emergency air-line glad hand and the 'blue' service line to the trailer's air line connections, the window in the rear of El Viejo's sleeper slid open.

"You's a hardworkin' dude, cabrón," Macho shot back.

"My mama is your cousin, cabrón," Javi laughed as his cuz gave him the finger.

Macho plugged in the green electrical line in between the airlines then made sure the handle jutting out from under the fifth wheel was all the way in and in the locked position.

He went to the back of El Viejo where the trailer's landing gear legs and turn-crank were. He dipped under the trailer first. With light from his iPhone, Macho looked up into the fifth wheel's slot where the trailer kingpin slid in and out. He saw the hook like jaw was locked around the kingpin shank, securing it inside so the trailer would not break away during the ride. That would be very bad with the ten million dollars' worth of cocaine inside.

Crawling back out, Macho unhooked the turn-crank. He put it into low gear and started turning. His iPhone rang as he felt the heavy weight of the trailer get lighter. Pulling it out of his pocket, he answered it with one hand while continuing to raise the legs up with his other hand.

"Yes, my love?" he answered, hanging the crank back on its hook and going to the little exterior door at the bottom corner of El Viejo's sleeper.

"Hiii, sexy tiguereeee!" Yessy sang out. "Whatcha doin?"

"Makin' us some money," Macho told her, opening the door and grabbing a little mallet hammer. "What are yooouuu doin'?"

"Oh…. just sitting here… thinking about you."

"Oh, really?" Macho asked as he walked along the driver's side of the trailer toward the rear to check the wheels and tires. He heard the sound of his brother release the trailer's parking brakes, which charged up its air brake system. "What you thinkin' about, freca?"

"Wouldn't you like to know?" Yessy teased, giggling.

Macho chuckled as he checked all four tires and inspected the wheels and lug nuts. "I sure would."

"Hmmm…. But if I told you, you're so far away that you wouldn't be able to do anything about it."

Macho laughed. "Am I really that far away?"

Silence. He heard nothing as he stood at the back of the trailer, signaling up to Tool for him to hit the lights.

"What does that mean?" Yessy asked a whole minute later.

Macho gave his brother a thumbs up for the left turn signal and the right.

"Nothin' at all, baby," he laughed. "What're you and Gabi and Michelle doin'?"

"Um... chilling. Why?"

Tool hit the four-way flashers and got a thumbs up. After he pushed the brake pedal, making the brake lights come on, Macho nodded and went to check the passenger's side trailer wheels and tires.

"Just asking. You three be up to no good whenever y'all link up."

"Maaaan, I know you ain't talkin', yo! You, your brother, and Javi?! Y'all asses be doin' the most whenever y'all get together, Antonio!"

Macho burst out laughing, as he went up to the exterior tool door in El Viejo's sleepers' passenger side lower corner, putting the mallet back.

"So?" he said. "Somos gangstaz, lil' mama. You forgot?" he questioned, opening the passenger's door and climbing up into El Viejo.

"How could I forget?" Yessy laughed. "Anyways, how long 'til you all get back? I needs me some lovin', Papi."

"I think you already know when I'll be back, punk. Nos vemos muy pronto, beautiful. Love ya!"

Macho ended the call, chuckling to himself.

"She know we know?" Tool asked, as he shifted into low gear while he released only the trailer's parking brakes.

"My lady is very smart. She'll figure it out," Macho told him.

In the sleeper, Javi answered a call from Xavier, as Tool tested the trailer's brakes by tugging on it with El Viejo while the brakes were still on.

"Qué lo qué hay, 'mano?"

"Bro, why you got Nena dumpin' on niggas out in the middle of Bennett?" Xavier asked.

"I didn't make her do that shit. You better ask Yessy or Michelle."

Xavier sighed. "Yo, maan... Kenzie left, bro."

"Left? What chu' mean?"

Tool pulled off, done with the brake check, ready to exit the port.

"She left me, man. Took Neveah and got ghost. She felt that me gettin'.... she felt like since she came into my life that she's the reason shit been poppin off."

Javi shook his head. "That's crazy. You don't know where she went?"

"The doctor showed me footage from the cameras outside; she got into an Uber with li' mama. That's all I know."

"I'm sorry, bro. I know you really cared for her. You gon' try to find her?" Javi asked as Tool joined a line of trucks in the exit lanes.

"Naw. I think it's best she find her peace without me. If it was meant to be, it would be, yah mean?"

"I do. What about Nena?"

"Nena always gon' be my baby. But I'ma take the dive with 'Nessa."

"Word?"

"Yessiir! We about to go eat. She in the shower right now."

Tool pulled up to the booth to check out.

"Y'all still rollin'?" Xavier asked, hearing chatter.

"Leavin' the port. Where's Eve?"

"I have no clue. Her phone's off."

Javi groaned. "We gon' have to sit her down and have a talk, bro. Her ass wildin'."

"I think everybody's wildin' right now. Go on ahead though. Get at me when y'all get back to the 'Burgh."

"Yup."

Javi ended the call just as Tool pulled forward, rolling El Viejo off toward the road. Macho got up and had Javi switch with him, so he could lay down and catch some rest. Before he closed his eyes, he brought up Guera's contact info in his iPhone to send her a text.

Got your groceries. Thank you for choosing Numero Uno. Your business is appreciated.

Less than a minute after sending it, Macho received a thumbs up emoji and a pair of red lips blowing kisses emoji, followed by a *grassy-ass, guapo*.

Macho closed his eyes to catch some sleep before they got back to Steel City.

PRINCE

Prince groaned as he struggled to get dressed. He was ready to go after sitting in the hospital for so long. He was ready to get back to the money with his younger cousin.

A knock at the door came. He looked toward it as it opened. Evelyn stepped in wearing a denim bodysuit, Timberlands, her hair in a ponytail, and clutched in one hand, a Louis Vuitton tote bag.

"Hey, handsome! Look at you! Finally ready to get up outta here, huh?" she asked, closing the door behind her.

"Hell yeah. I been missin' out on money like crazy, lil' mama," Prince told her as he slowly stood up from the bed. "You lookin' all good 'n shit. Lemme find out you's 'bout to see yo boyfriend after me."

Evelyn chuckled. "Hmmm… we'll see. That depends."

"Depends?" His eyebrows furrowed up. "Somethin' is dependin' on if you got another man or not?"

Evelyn walked toward him. "Yep," she replied simply, setting her tote on the bed. "It all depends on if you're really a fucking creep ass pimp like I've heard."

"A pimp?" Prince burst out laughing. "Yo' ass tweakin', joe. What I look like bein' a pimp, Eve?"

She took her iPhone out of the bag and brought him up on Google again. "You look like this guy that got arrested, charged, and convicted of predatory sexual assault, domestic violence, prostituting of underage girls, rape, and false imprisonment."

Evelyn showed Prince his own mugshot. She studied his face, watching his facial expression go from puzzled to shocked, then he looked up at her with trepidation in his eyes. She could see by how his Adam's apple moved that Prince had just swallowed hard.

"Hold on... just wait a sec, Eve," Prince pleaded as she put the phone back into her bag.

"Wait? Why? So you can come up with a lie?" she asked, and faster than his eyes could follow, Evelyn snatched out the new Sig Sauer MPX submachine gun from her bag, fitted with a sound-suppressor, a beam, and a forty-round magazine.

Prince nearly pissed himself when she pointed it at him.

"Eve! Come on, baby. It's not me! I wouldn't do no foul-ass shit like that! I took the weight for my cousin! He was pimpin' little ass girls!"

Evelyn shook her head at how he had just snitched like a bitch.

"Your cousin, Stacks, right?" she asked though she already knew.

Prince's eyes bugged wide then. "H-How do you know my cousin's name?"

"He took advantage of you while you were in a coma; he tried to extort me for my family's yayo, threatening to take my people out if I didn't supply him," Evelyn told him. "And I took over his crew. Lil' Five works for me now; he is the man with the plug on the purest Dominican yayo a young nigga will ever get they hands on. And as for you and yo' bitch ass, creep ass cousin... y'all are dead men walkin' if you step foot anywhere inside Cook County."

"You can't kill a ghost, shorty.'"''

Evelyn heard the words spoken, but Prince's lip hadn't moved. His eyes rolled to his right. Evelyn followed them and saw him standing there, the man that continuously escaped death, in the doorway, pointing two Glocks with extended clips right at her.

STACKS

"Ooooo, man. I wish y'all could see the looks on y'all faces right now! On Vicelord, y'all look shook, joe!"

He smirked at Evelyn. The stupefied look on her face gave him great satisfaction as it looked like she might soil herself.

"Cool, cuz! Yo, let's get up outta here, joe!" Prince said, scrambling to get out of the jam.

Boc! Boc! Boc!
Boc! Boc! Boc!

With both guns, Stacks lit his cousin up, putting six holes in his face and chest.

Evelyn went to point the MPX at Stacks, seizing the opportunity, when shots rang out from outside of the room.

Stacks howled in pain as four shots slammed into his chest when he spun around. Despite the pain, his body armor saved his life. He managed to hold onto his guns and ran toward the window.

"Hell no!" Evelyn shouted, pointing her submachine gun at him.

But right as she was about to take his head off, more shots came flying into the room. She saw a Hispanic man with long hair run in, blasting at Stacks with an automatic AR-15.

223

The window shattered then. Evelyn turned and saw Stacks jump right out of the window.

"Holy shit!" she gasped, knowing they were up on the second floor.

The man glanced at Evelyn, knowing exactly who she was. She saw him, his eyes, and they instilled fear inside of her. She froze, unable to move, barely able to breathe.

Then, she heard an engine rev up then tires screeching.

DIABLO

Ignoring the Valdez princess, Diablo ran to the window and saw Stacks limping toward a black Scat Pack Dodge Challenger.

Without a word or care, he took aim at Stacks and started firing, hitting him in his left arm before the passenger's door opened up, and he got in.

"*Chingao!*" Diablo cursed then continued firing, shooting at the car's roof.

The bullets pinged off of it, not a single one penetrating the invisible armoring. Diablo cursed again. The car's rear tires smoked as the driver mashed the gas pedal. Diablo angrily watched it speed off out of the hospital's lot.

"Freeze! Drop your weapon!" he heard shouted from behind him.

Diablo started grinning. Slowly, he turned around with his AR gripped tightly, held in front of him.

"I said drop it now!"

Diablo saw three armed security guards in the room, all of them pointing their semi-automatic 9mms at him. He glanced to his left and saw the Valdez family princess was nowhere in sight.

"Last time! I said…"

Brrrrrrrrrrrrrrrr!

Diablo squeezed the trigger and hit the security guards in their faces. He didn't stop shooting until they were on the floor, bleeding from all the holes he put in them.

"Fuck the cops," he said to himself. "Real ones and wannabes," he added.

Diablo started toward the doorway when he heard a noise. With a quickness, he spun to his left, and he saw her. She was standing next to the hospital bed where a dead man laid next to.

"Ah, yes, la princesa Valdez," Diablo said, pointing his AR at her. "I've been looking for your brothers, but I'll settle for you, chula."

He saw her smirking then, not even attempting to raise her gun up at him.

"Something funny?" he asked, taking aim at her face.

"Yeah... You, mamahuevo, bulletproofing a fucking dually pickup truck," she said to him.

Diablo chucked. "Did the job, chula. Now enough with the small talk. How 'bout you drop that gun and join me? You can give your hermanos a call and have 'em come pick you up at my place, eh?"

"How 'bout mamate un bicho y muere, bitch," she replied.

"Or I can just kill you here, puta," Diablo shot back, finger around the trigger. "Either way, I'm outta here in a second."

"Oh, how true that statement is, pendejo."

Diablo heard another noise the second she finished her sentence. He looked to his right and saw a dark-skinned chick with a spirally afro charging at him with a machete.

EVELYN

Evelyn watched as he tried to put his gun on Gloria, but she was too fast and already up on him. She swung the machete hard at his face. The blade ripped right through it, severing the top half of his head.

His body dropped to the floor. The bottom half of his brain slipped out of his sliced skull. Blood poured out, pooling onto the floor.

"Where is the other one?!" Gloria asked, frantically looking for Stacks after seeing Prince's body by Evelyn's feet.

"He jumped out of the window; he's gone," she told her.

"Coño, man!" Gloria cursed. "Fuck it! ¡Vamos! We have to go. Now!"

Evelyn took one last look at Prince, then she and Gloria hauled ass out of the room, making a beeline for the emergency stairway exit just as a horde of armed guards filled out of the elevator, right next to the stairs that the two Dominicanas had just slipped past them for.

CHAPTER 23

LOS TIGUERES

"Glad you could join us, ol' head," said Tool, dapping Shabba up, who had just pulled up in an Escalade with three other Rastas to the little off-brand Ma 'n Pop truck stop in Easton, PA.

Tool had made a stop to top off El Viejo's tanks. His cousin and brother were both K.O.'d in the ol' school Pete, resting peacefully before El Viejo's loud jake brake woke them up. While Tool was filling up the driver's side fuel tank, the Escalade pulled up and out came the Kingsford, charcoal-black Rasta goon with his squad.

"Ya, mon. Me meant ta catch up witcha' in Pittsburg, but 'de boss lady 'tol me 'ta get straight 'ta ya' before 'ya got inta trouble."

Tool laughed. "Now what would give her that idea?" he asked sarcastically.

Shabba burst out laughing at the Dominerican goon.

~   ~   ~

The trip west to the 'Burgh went smoothly. Tool drove the rest of the way back to the Steel City. As he got off of the PA Turnpike in Monroeville, the dreads broke away, heading off for their next mission. Nobody felt the need for armed escorts at home. It was home after all.

Glancing in his mirror though, Tool saw they still had a tail. But compared to the dread heads, the one he saw hanging back far enough, trying to be inconspicuous, was the best protection one could get.

Following his brother's directions, Tool made his way out to New Kensington. By the time he entered the area, it was half past ten at night.

Hopping off a small intercity highway, Tool transferred onto a two-way road that ran for miles through a deep valley. Only El Viejo's headlights lit up the road ahead of him. Every so often, a small house or field came up, but mostly, the valley road was just hills and mountain terrain on both sides. Tool and Macho were very familiar with the long, desolate stretch though. To those that were in the game, it was simply known as the drug route.

Macho laid on the bed, playing a Zombie-killing game on his iPhone. Javi nodded his head to Trick Daddy's *'I'm A Thug*. Tool kept El Viejo at a steady speed along the drug route. Cops were not known to post along it, mostly because of the dangerous individuals that controlled the entire territory. The cops tended to come after bodies were reported or after the gunshots ended.

Almost twenty miles later, the valley opened up into a big, round zone. Off to the sides, directly across from each other, were two businesses; the one at the left was a concrete mill, and across from the big plant was a commercial vehicle parking lot filled with cement trucks and other vehicles belonging to the plant.

A few tall, steel light poles placed around the yards provided just enough light to illuminate them. Javi unclicked his seatbelt, as Tool hit the jake-brake and down-shifted gears, working the foot brake to slow El Viejo down. Macho got up and stretched, getting ready.

Coming to a slow enough speed, Tool made a wide left turn in. Right away, he and Javi saw a line of motorcycles off to the right, backed up to a tall stone wall. Toward the left, there were four box trucks and a couple of cargo vans.

An office building was connected to what had to be a warehouse, just off the size of it. A tall garage bay door was at the right, directly in front of El Viejo.

Standing outside were three big, burly, white men wearing biker leather vests, jeans, and boots. One gestured for Tool to turn around and back into the warehouse. No sooner than so, the bay door began to rise up. Just before he swung El Viejo to the left to hit a U-turn, Tool, Javi, and Macho all caught glimpses of a large group of men inside the brightly lit storage area.

About-facing, Tool lined El Viejo's trailer up with the bay. He stopped, shifted into reverse, then watching in both of his mirrors, he started slowly backing the trailer into the warehouse.

Javi's eyes were glued to the passenger side mirror. On his side, he saw a live version of *Sons of Anarchy*.

"Why exactly is Guera supplyin' these crackers?" Javi asked as the warehouse light filled El Viejo's cab.

"They need coke; she murdered their other supplier, put the squeeze on them, and taxed them," said Macho, as he came and kneeled between his brother and cousin.

"Sooo… We're deliverin' her yayo to what are probably some very angry white boys?"

"Yep," Tool replied, as the nose of the old Peterbilt entered the building. "Racist too," he added, coming to a stop seconds later.

As he put the shifter into neutral and pulled out the tractor's and the trailer's brake knobs, applying the brakes, the bay door began to close. Tool cut El Viejo's engine off and opened his door.

"Stay here, lil' cuz," Macho told Javi, as he went to get out through the driver's door behind his bro.

"What chu' mean stay here?" Javi questioned.

Macho looked at him. "We're in Pittsburgh to keep you safe, yo. If shit pops off with these clowns and somethin' happens to you, ya wife gon' be pissed at me, then Yessy, G-Baby, and ChaCha gon' get on my bumper. I don't need, nor want, that. So, just keep ya eyes open. Me entiende, cabrón?"

Javi nodded. "Yeah, man."

After his cuz got out and closed the door, Javi climbed over and got into the driver's seat. He kept his eyes shifting from mirror to mirror. At the first sign of trouble, he was hopping out and lighting shit up.

~   ~   ~

Jack Hoss, leader of the 8 Ball Boys biker gang, sat in the miniature monster Chevy Silverado pickup truck inside of his warehouse with his driver, watching. After the semi had backed into his spot, his gang of twenty-five all gathered at the rear of the trailer, waiting for the drivers to get out.

When Jack saw the massively tall dread head round the driver's side of the trailer with a slightly shorter but more muscular man with braids coming from behind him, he instantly grew furious.

"What the hell?!" he said out loud. "The wet-back bitch kills off Cordero, forces us to buy from her at ridiculous prices, then sends monkeys to bring our shit?!"

Shaking his head behind the wheel, Sullivan tisked. "Ain't that about a bitch."

"Tell ya' what," Jack said, opening his door, "we're gon' make the bitch regret fuckin' with the 8 Ball Boys. Come on, Sully. Let's go greet these fuckers in ol' white man fashion."

Many of the bikers were angered by the presence of the two colored guys in their spot. Some were ready to pull out their guns and kill them. Others wanted to clip their bike chains, hang the two, then send them back to where they came from in a box.

"Gentlemen, gentlemen, gentlemen," they heard the muscular guy with braids say. "Good evenin' to you all. We come bearing gifts."

They saw the tall dread head work the combination lock on the container's doors, unlocking it and taking it out of the door latch holes.

Jack walked up. His crew parted for him and Sullivan, like Moses did for the Red Sea. The fire in his eyes displayed his rage for the two negros in his building.

"Y'all ain't here to bump 'yur gums," he said to the two, noticing how similar they looked, deducing that they had to be related. "Hop on up in that trailer and show me my shit, boy!"

The man with the braids looked at him, locking eyes. He then laughed. "Yes, suh, massa! I's gon' climb up in dat dea trala' 'n shows 'ya what we's a got fa' ya', suh!"

The dread head started laughing.

Jack sneered at him, then he climbed up into the container with Sullivan behind him.

Macho used bright light from his iPhone as Sullivan used a bowie knife, which had been concealed in a leather sheath under his shirt, to pry open one of the wooden crates. Inside were bathroom fixture parts and piping. Jack's eyebrows furrowed up.

"Where the hell is my coke, ya son of a bitch?!"

"Maybe look under the pipes, pendejo," Macho replied with a raised eyebrow of his own.

Sullivan moved the top row of the flow pipe. Indeed, under it, there were plastic wrapped blocks stacked ten high in rows of ten. Jack nodded his head then called to his men.

"Let's go get our shit 'n get these monkeys outta here, men! Let's go!"

After all fifteen crates were unloaded, Macho followed the two racists out of the trailer. The second his Tims touched the ground, Sullivan turned and swung his bowie knife at Macho. Macho knew it was coming.

He bent back, missing getting his face sliced.

Tool cocked back and rocked the closest man to him then jammed his elbow into the face of another, who he had known was going to sneak him. Macho shot back forward, fist balled. He hit Sullivan so hard in his jaw that it nearly ripped off.

"Get them!" Jack yelled, as he whipped out his cannon.

His crew upped their guns, ready to fire, until…

Brrrrrrr! Brrrrrrrr! Brrrrrrrr!

From under the trailer, bullets flew at them from an assault rifle. Macho saw his young cousin under it, dumping at the bikers with an SK.

"Shit, shit, shit!" Jack ran like a coward as the assault rifle fire blew so many of his crew down.

A bunch took cover, narrowly missing getting their heads blown off. They took out their guns and started firing.

Macho and Tool ducked under the trailer, as Javi kept the bikers that had escaped his line of sight ducked off. He'd seen their leader run toward a pickup truck.

He ceased fire then. "I think we should go now."

"I concur," Macho replied.

Javi hopped up and sent a few more rounds at the bikers, while Macho and Tool hurried to climb up into El Viejo. Javi backpedaled to the passenger door and jumped up inside just as some of the bikers began shooting back.

"Cuz! Drive!" Macho demanded, as he and Tool went into the sleeper and raised up the bed.

Under it, there was a secret gun rack built in under the tool compartment. They grabbed the two other old school SKs inside. Javi fired up El Viejo's engine, slammed the shifter into second, then punching in the parking brakes, he mashed the gas and made the powerful Pete launch forward. Ten tons of old school 359 plowed through the bay door like it was made of paper.

Javi right away got into survival mode; as he blew up out of the building, he saw a massive group of men that he hadn't seen in the garage running toward the bikes. Two of them had the unfortunate luck of coming face to face with El Viejo's grille.

"Squish, squish, bitch!" Javi said as he felt the two bodies splatter under El Viejo's front wheels.

The motorcycle riding goons started shooting as Javi hurried out of the lot. He swerved a hard right onto the valley road, heading back in the direction they'd come from.

"It's on y'all, yo!" Javi shouted over El Viejo's roaring engine as he speed shifted gears. Amazed at how fast the damn semi was, Javi started laughing, geeked up to be driving a vehicle that had helped build his family's empire. "I fuckin' love this truck!" he then said to himself.

On the driver's side, Macho opened up the sleeper's whore door. Tool opened the whore door on the passenger's side. Javi yelled back to them, seeing a sea of headlights behind them.

"Here they come!" Javi yelled.

"Aye, yo! Play some music, cutty!" Macho yelled back, seeing some bikers speeding up on his side.

Javi's eyebrow rose. "What?!"

"Turn the music on, cabrón!"

Javi turned the volume all the way up.

Whodini's *One Love* came on.

"No! Change it!" Macho shouted, as the bikers got close enough to take aim with their pistols to fire.

"Man, come on, cuz!" Javi shouted back, glancing in the mirror.

"Change it, Javi!"

Tool was laughing his ass off at his little T'd up brother.

Javi switched the song.

Ice Cube's *Hello* featuring Dr. Dre and MC Ren came on.

"Yeaah, muthafuckas!" Macho shouted and tugged on the trigger, making the old school chopper spit round after round at the bikers. "I started this gangsta shit! And this the muthafuckin' thanks I get?! Hello!"

Brrrrrrrrrrrrrrrrrrrrrrrrrr!

Six bikers flew off of their Harley's as slugs ripped through their bodies. Their bikes went flying, causing a chain reaction of bikers crashing. The ones lucky enough to avoid collision opened fire.

"You missed me, bitch!" Macho shouted after he hurried to slam the whore door back shut.

Javi thought he was tripping. Muzzle flashes from pistols and machine guns on his side lit up the night… but no bullets entered the truck's sleeper.

"This muhfucka bulletproof too?!" he asked himself incredulously.

Macho opened the whore door again just as *Ain't No Fun* by Snoop Dogg, Warren G, Kurupt, and Nate Dogg began.

"Wooooo! Guess who's back in the muthafuckin' house! Wit dis SK fa you muthafuckin' clowns!"

Bocka! Bocka! Bocka! Bocka!

Macho laughed as one of the bikers started shooting at El Viejo's rear wheels.

"Eh eh! Stop it!" he said then squeezed on the guy, hitting the chopper's fuel tank.

The bike exploded. The rider flew off, engulfed in flames.

"Anotha one! DJ El Tiigueree!" Macho clowned.

He was about to light more bikers up when, suddenly, they fell back.

"The hell? Where y'all goin'?" He looked out of the whore door and saw them shoot at the trailer's tires.

On his side, Tool saw them doing the same.

The tires blew, and immediately, the bare steel webb wheel rims began to drastically decrease El Viejo's speed. Showers of bright sparks flew from the grinding steel wheels.

"Yo! I'm losin' speed!" Javi shouted, seeing that he was now at just over seventy-three miles an hour when he was doing nearly one hundred a minute ago.

"Javi!" Tool yelled up. "Hit the blue button on the dash!"

Javi looked and saw the little button. He pushed it. For a few seconds, he thought nothing happened. He had no clue that the button generated an electrical current, traveling through a wire, out of the dash, and down the front of El Viejo. It ran under the rig, toward the back of the sleeper going to the fifth wheel. Hidden from unsuspecting eyes were two strong blow-off valves. As soon as the current reached the valves... The fifth wheel skid plate blew off. The trailer slipped off the rear of El Viejo. It hit the ground hard, front end digging into the asphalt. It flipped forward, standing straight up in the air, then just as Javi picked up speed again, the trailer came down on its roof, hitting the ground so hard that the container's sides blew out. Tool and Macho repositioned themselves at the rear window. Javi's jaw was nearly in his lap.

"What the fuck?!" he shouted, astounded to have just witnessed some movie special effects type shit.

Macho and his brother laughed.

"Maybe now he see why El Viejo is the shit, huh?" he asked Tool.

"Quite possibly, 'mano," Tool replied.

They both focused their attention back to the bikers. A few on choppers were still coming. But now, the box trucks and the cargo van were giving chase.

Countless guns fired out the back of El Viejo. Macho and his brother just watched.

"Naa naa naa booo booo! Y'all mamas eat doo doo!" Macho shouted.

Tool shook his head. "You's a nut, bro."

Javi laughed his ass off at his cousin. "Fuckin' crazy ass half-breed."

"Okay! Okay! You wanna play?!" Macho continued clowning as the 8 Ball Boys continued chasing and shooting. "Okay then! Let's play, mamahuevos!"

He was about to open the window when, suddenly, a big explosion sent a massive fireball up into the pitch-black sky.

Macho and Tool both looked at the cargo van, as it flew off of the road, landing in a heavily treed area.

"The hell?" Macho wondered, puzzled as to what exploded.

Tool squinted, trying to see what had just happened.

One of the box trucks exploded just then. It went flying off in a big ball of fire. Then another. A third exploded then the fourth.

Macho and Tool were tripping. Javi started laughing, seeing the explosions in the mirror.

"Maaaan, what the hell is y'all shootin'?" he asked.

"That wasn't us," Tool told him.

"Oh, shit… wow… look, bro," Macho said, pointing at a set of hyper-white headlights. "Tell me that is not them."

Tool burst out laughing. "I do not believe I can do that, lil' bro. Because it is most definitely them."

THE LADIES

"Wooo! Yeeaah, bitch! Get all they asses, yo!" Yessy yelled, as she kept her Range Rover steady while Michelle, standing up through the sunroof, fired an M4 fitted with a M-203 grenade launcher.

G-Baby hung out of the passenger's window, firing a fully automatic AR-15 fitted with monkey-nut drums.

Brrrrrrrrrrrrrrrrrrrrrrr!

The Chicagorilla Rican let the spitter work. Eight more bikers went down.

Michelle started sniping the remaining bikers, popping heads like she was playing *Call Of Duty: Black Ops* zombie missions. Some got so scared that they purposely swerved off the road, skidding their bikes on the shoulder. They'd rather lose some skin than their heads.

"Bye bye, mamahuevos!" Michelle yelled, as they sped past the ones that managed to escape her and G-Baby's wrath.

"Okay, get back inside, future blimp," Yessy told her, patting Michelle's booty.

Michelle sank down into the backseat where the dogs were all hyped up.

The Range Rover's Bluetooth system intercepted an incoming call as City High's *Caramel* featuring Eve played. Yessy glanced over at the LCD screen. Macho was calling. G-Baby snickered, seeing his name, as she set her AR down.

"Uh oh," Michelle said, seeing the call display as well. "Think they're mad?"

Yessy saw El Viejo's right turn signal come on as signs for an exit came up.

"Yes... I most definitely do," Yessy told her then answered the call. "House of the juicy booty burger, can I take ya' order?"

G-Baby and Michelle laughed as Yessy followed El Viejo off of the valley road onto another dark two-way route.

"Really, bae?" the ladies heard Macho say.

"Really what, Papi?" Yessy asked, trying hard to keep from laughing.

"I'ma kick yo' ass."

"Want a booty-burger first?"

The girls laughed their asses off.

"Javi said you in trouble, Michelle," Macho told her.

"I bet," Michelle responded then laughed.

MICHELLE

"Aww! Come on, bae. Why you mad at me?" Michelle asked, poking out her bottom lip.

"Because," Javi replied, leaning against El Viejo's grille.

"Because what? I helped you and your cousins out."

"By standin' up through a sunroof and shooting box trucks with grenade launchers... with our baby in yo' belly."

Back in Murrysville, Javi had gotten El Viejo parked back in his garage. Inside, next to the old man, was Yessy's Range

Rover. Macho, Yessy, G-Baby, Tool, and the dogs were by the Range, posted up. Macho had called Guera, told her what happened. She apologized for his and his peoples' trouble, offering to compensate them for their trouble. Macho declined. He told her it was fun, and he couldn't wait to do it again.

"Hey! I'm just makin' her strong before she even comes out!" Michelle said defensively.

"He," Javi replied, correcting her.

"What?" she asked, raising an eyebrow in confusion.

"We're havin' a boy," he clarified.

Michelle sucked her teeth, crossing her arms over her chest.

"You do not know that," she told him.

"Yes, I do."

"Whatever. Can I have a kiss?" Michelle asked, wrapping her arms around his waist.

"No."

"What the fuck you mean no, goddammit?! You better kiss me right now, nigga!"

"No."

"Javi! Gimme a kiss!"

"No."

"Javier!"

"Ssshhhhh."

Macho, Tool, and the ladies were laughing so hard that they couldn't catch their breath.

Michelle went to steal a kiss. Javi dropped low, slipped out of her arms, and started dipping on her. Michelle gave chase, screaming at him.

"Give me a kiss, motherfucker!"

"Nope! You're beat!" Javi laughed his ass off, as he dove to the ground and rolled under El Viejo, hopping up on the other side.

"Javi! ¡Te lo juro por dios!" Michelle yelled. Demon and Diamond ran over to her, tails wagging in excitement. "Get your ass over here and kiss me!"

Suddenly, El Viejo's engine started up. Michelle looked up at the open driver's window and saw Javi behind the wheel.

"Javier Omar Valdez! I swear if you…"

Javi clutched into gear and rolled off, spinning the rear tires as he gunned it out of the garage. He left behind thick, black, diesel smoke, tooting the air horn.

Michelle shook her head, putting her hands on her hips. The dogs stood next to her, watching Javi do a whole U-turn in El Viejo, facing where she stood.

Macho, Tool, Yessy, G-Baby, and the dogs walked up next to her.

"Why is your future husband stealing my truck?" Macho asked, as they watched Javi rev the engine, making flames shoot out of the pipes.

"I don't know, but he's gonna make me kick his ass if he doesn't give me a kiss, yo! On God, nigga!"

Javi then rolled El Viejo back over to them. He parked a few feet from Michelle then got out. He rounded the front of the Pete, stepped up to her, and roped her into his arms. Javi gave her what she wanted. He kissed her with more passion than she could ever remember before. It made her body yearn for him.

"Well, damn!" G-Baby said. "He finna get her preggo before she has the first one!"

They laughed.

Javi pulled back after a minute long kiss. Michelle trembled in anticipation. Her heart sang for him.

"I love your crazy ass, Javier," she told him, as she gazed up into his eyes.

"I love you more, lil' mama." He pecked her lips again. "How about we take a real vacation?"

"To where?" Michelle asked, her eyes lighting up at the thought of a real getaway with the love of her life.

Javi grinned. "We goin' to La Republica Dominicana," he told her. "I already got us a jet ready to fly us out."

"But we didn't pack. And what about the dogs?" Michelle asked, as she patted her dog's head.

"We can buy brand new everything in Italy first then go to the D.R. for our wedding."

Michelle gasped. "A wedding in the D.R.?! Oh, Javi!"

She threw her arms around him and hugged him tightly.

"I guess that you like that idea?" he chuckled.

"I do! Hell yeah!"

"Aye, cutty," Macho called to Javi.

Javi turned toward his cuz. "Yo?"

"We'll all be there to see y'all tie the knot. You two deserve this," Macho said, walking up to Javi. "Blessings to both of y'all, yo. Homies. I love y'alls crazy asses."

"Aww! Y te amamos tambien, tigueraso," Michelle replied, hugging Macho in a sisterly way.

"Go ahead. We'll keep things in order while y'all gone," said Tool, walking up with the ladies and the dogs. "We gotta few things to handle."

He dapped Javi up and hugged Michelle. Yessy and G-Baby did the same just as a black Escalade pulled up to them. A chauffeur hopped out and came around. He opened the passenger's side rear door and gestured for them to enter the luxurious executive style SUV.

"Aye, cuz. Don't go blowin' up a bunch of things while we gone, yo," Javi told Macho. "I need you at our wedding. So, don't die or get on FBI's most wanted list."

Macho laughed. "Naw, yo. Me and bro finna wrap up the first lil' bit of you and Michelle's troubles, then we gon' fly out. Go on now, lil' nigga. Don't worry 'bout nothin'. It's our turn now, nigga, and Hoooomies, cuz. We finna tuuurn the fuck up, yo!"

EPILOGUE

One Year Later...

"Hiii, mamita! Ay, Dios mio, you are so cute!" Angela gushed excitedly over her beautiful two-and-a-half-month-old daughter, Amara. The precious, smooth, brown infant had awakened from her afternoon nap and yawned. "Aww! I love you so much, Amara. Tienes hombre, mamita?"

Angela carefully picked her daughter up out of her little musical swinger and carried her through the big condominium she and her daughter had made home in downtown Atlanta for the past two months after Amara was born.

With money in the bank, Angela had no problem affording the expensive digs. It still surprised her though. For months, she had been held against her will in a very luxurious mansion in Jamaica, then one day, the woman who had the heart of the man that Angela wanted for herself had appeared. Angela thought her time had come and cried her eyes out. She was just weeks away from giving birth.

But then, Michelle had surprised her by releasing her, and with her freedom, Angela got a big bag of money then was forbidden to ever let her face be seen again.

Angela didn't play with it. She initially planned to go to Puerto Rico but changed her mind and ended up going to the A after remembering how good Atlanta was to those that had gwap.

She got herself a condo, started an online retailing business, then she had her baby.

Amara being born was bittersweet. She was a bundle of joy yet a daily reminder of the love she would never get to have. But nevertheless, Angelea loved her daughter and was going to be the best mother ever to her.

She sat Amara in another swing seat in the open-concept kitchen. Going to the custom marble cupboards, Angela opened one close to the fridge and got her breast milk pump out. She hooked herself up and filled a bottle up, then she fed her daughter, burping her afterwards.

Amare yawned, ready to go back to sleep.

Angela took her back to her crib and laid her in it. She smiled lovingly at her little one then decided to take a shower, so she could get ready for bed. It had been a long day but a good one. She sold a lot of merchandise and made a huge profit.

Angela drew herself a hot bubble bath in her big jacuzzi tub. She put on some music, undressed, then sank down into the steamy lavender-scented water.

She leaned back and let herself enjoy the massaging water jets. She moaned from how good they felt.

Then, he popped into her mind.

"Javi," she purred, as her kitty started yearning.

Angela spread her legs and started playing with her pussy. Remembering all the times Javi dicked her down had her wishing for one last romp.

"¡Ay!!" she cried out minutes later, as she exploded.

Angela's body went limp as her release drained her. She closed her eyes to revel in the fact that the father of her child was a ridiculously rich and handsome man. A smile grew on her lips, then as she inhaled a lung full of sweet, scented soap, a strong pair of arms grabbed her head and held it in place.

She screamed, eyes popping open. Then, her heart dropped when she saw the person standing by her jacuzzi, assisted by the pair of arms holding her.

"¡¿Que carajo?! ¡¿Que 'stas haciendo aqui?!" Angela demanded to know, struggling against who had her in a headlock.

The woman started smirking at her, looking right into Angela's eyes.

"I'm startin' what I couldn't finish, bitch," she said.

Then, the person behind Angela twisted as hard as they could manage and snapped her neck...

"Don't worry about Amara, puta. She'll be with family," were the last words Angela heard before everything went dark.

~ ~ ~

"Never! This me right here, bruh?!" Stacks asked, super geeked when he was handed the keys to the Lamborghini Huracan.

"You been makin' me tens of millions, Lord. You deserve gifts like this, my nigga."

Stacks looked at Narco and was lost for words. Ever since he had agreed to put in some work and take out some competition, Stacks had become a made man. Though unable to go to Chicago, he was plugged up and had made a name for himself in Milwaukee. At first, when Narco had brought him up to the Mil, Stacks couldn't fathom trying to move coke and dope out there, but Narco had some say-so out in his city, and many others, whether they were Kings, GDs, Maniac Latin Disciples, or Cobras, respected Narco since he was their connect. When he announced to all for Stacks to be allowed to get money in the Mil, he had been welcomed in and quickly built up his clientele.

After a year of moving weight, Stacks was as up as he had always wanted to be. He had a big-ass house out in River Hills, a bad-ass bitch that was a ride or die to the fullest, and had started three businesses. Life was so good that he could retire years before he was even thirty years old.

"Man, good look, joe. Wifey gon' be tryna' drive this muhfucka all over the Mil," Stacks chuckled.

"Not a good idea," Narco said, giving Stacks a weary look. "Shorty will get her ass robbed faster than cops can show up to a shots fired call in yo' neighborhood."

Stacks laughed. "Aight, King. Lemme go on 'n head back home. The wife's cookin' me dinner, and my stomach touchin' my back. On Vicelord, joe."

Narco dapped him up, then Stacks hopped into the exotic hyper car. He started the big V10 engine up and revved it loudly, getting goosebumps from the sound.

Stacks threw up his gang sign at Narco, and Narco threw his crown up. Pulling off, Stacks left Narco's big house and got on the road to get back to his crib.

Nodding his head to the beat of Rich Homie Quan's *Type Of Way,* Stacks' mind was on his next moves. He still had a small storage unit full of bricks of cocaine, ice, and heroin to pop off. The trap spots he had throughout the Mil were pumping hard, doing numbers. Tens of thousands were coming in every day, and he didn't even have to lift a finger.

Up ahead, the traffic light was turning red at Capital Drive and Green Bay Road. Stacks brought the Lambo to a stop and silently mouthed the words to the song.

Five seconds into his wait, an eighteen-wheeler suddenly screeched to a halt in front of him, stretching across both lanes, blocking him.

"What the fuck?" he said to himself, furrowing eyebrows, creeped out by the old black Peterbilt rig.

The passenger's side of the long trailer started sliding to the rear just then. Stacks' eyes went wide with surprise when he saw seven masked figures standing inside the trailer, all pointing Dracos at him.

Tap! Tap! Tap!

Stacks froze when tapping on his window made his ear ring. Terrified, he looked to his left and saw another person wearing a mask, and in his hands, he was gripping a big

M134 Mini-Gun with a belt of 7.62mm NATO rounds fed into it.

"Shit," Stacks cursed, as he saw the man smile sinisterly through the mouth hole.

Xavier squeezed the trigger and let the gas-powered street sweeper spit. So many rounds flew out the long barrel. The pieces of body and destroyed car it left behind when he put nearly five hundred rounds into the Lambo were so scattered that it looked like an explosion went off inside.

"Bitch ass nigga," Xavier muttered when he let go of the trigger. "Rest in piss," he added, then he ran to where El Viejo idled and jumped up into the curtain-side trailer with the Steel City Mafia goons.

Macho chirped his 2-way radio, giving his women the go-ahead. Behind the wheel, with G-Baby and Felicia in the 'ol school Pete with her, Yessy roared off, leaving a bloody mess in the street for Milwaukee police to clean up and act like they were investigating...

~   ~   ~

Mikey opened his eyes but couldn't see anything. He took a deep breath and smelled staleness in the air along with what smelled like rubbing alcohol.

What the fuck?! Where am I?! he wondered.

He tried to move but discovered that his wrists and his ankles were tied. He could feel then that he was tied in a spread eagle-type of way, legs out, arms out.

Mikey tried pulling again, but the chain restraints only clanged against metal, causing a ruckus.

He started getting scared then. He had no memory of anything at all. He couldn't even remember where he had been before he got to... wherever he was.

Then, suddenly, it came rushing back to him. He had been about to make a break for it with his sister after gathering all the money he made, moving stolen cocaine and dope that came from a Rojas-Gomez stash house with his sister, Stacks, and Rambo. It had been a bloody day. They all upped their body counts that day and were up – until mistakes were made.

The last thing the young, skinny, long-haired, Mexican boy remembered was dressing in drag, his true identity, then being set up by his own sister and taken by Mexican hitmen to God knows where.

"Fucking bitch! She set me up! I'ma kill that bitch, joe!" Mikey said to himself, voice hoarse, throat sore as hell.

The sound of a door opening just then made Mikey freeze. It closed then. He heard footsteps coming toward him.

"I see you're awake now, eh?" he heard a man say. "How are you feeling?"

"Where the fuck am I, joe?! Why am I tied up?!"

"Well, technically, you're handcuffed, and you are in a place where I perform miracles."

"Miracles? Man, uncuff me and let me go! Fuck is wrong wit' chu'?!"

Slap!

"Watch your mouth, you little punk! I run this show! I'm the pimp, and you are the whore! Shut up, bitch!"

Mikey grinded his teeth in anger. He wished so badly he was free to strangle the guy.

"That's better. Now, your operation was a first for me, so I've…"

"Operation?!" Mikey cut in.

Slap!

"Don't interrupt me while I'm talking! Now! As I was saying, your surgery was my first. I fucked up and you were put into a medically induced coma for the past four months in order for you to heal."

"What are you talking about?!" Mikey demanded.

He then felt the blindfold covering his eyes being untied. Blindingly bright light hit his pupils and immediately made him close them up. He cursed as his head started throbbing.

"Yeah, a little bright. Sorry about that," the guy said.

Mikey, little by little, opened his eyes. Once he was able to process the light, he opened them all the way.

His vision was blurry. He tried to focus in, but all was fuzzy. The cool liquid dropped into his eyes cleared everything up for him a minute later.

He blinked his eyes then looked around. Seeing what looked like an operating room from the fifties, he grew nervous.

"Hey? Mikey?"

He turned his head to the right and saw a caramel-brown skinned man with hazel eyes and curly hair. He was heavyset, wearing scrubs with blood on them.

"The fuck?! Who are you?!"

The guy smiled. "They call me the miracle man. Welcome to Rio de Janeiro, young man... or should I say... young lady?"

"What?! Bitch ass nigga, I'm a man!" Mikey snapped.

"You were a man," the guy said with a twisted smirk.

Mikey's eyebrows furrowed up with confusion. He saw the guy leave and grab a little remote then press a button.

A mechanical whirling sound got Mikey's attention. He looked up then and saw a long mirror being lowered down. He saw himself, covered with bandages around his chest and his lower region.

"Hope you like it," the guy said, then he took the upper bandages off.

Mikey gasped when he saw that he had breasts.

"And that's not all, my friend," the man said, undoing the lower bandages.

Mikey screamed. Gone was his penis, replaced by a vagina.

"What the fuck did you do to me?!" Mikey shouted.

"I gave you what you wanted. You wanted to be a bitch, so the people you owed sent you to me to make it happen," the guy said.

Mikey started crying then. He couldn't believe what he was seeing. He had been given a sex-change operation against his will.

"Aww, come on, little lady. Don't cry. I'll make it all better for you."

Mikey turned his head and saw the guy was getting undressed. In less than a minute, he was ass naked with an erection that had Mikey screaming in fear.

"Don't fight this shit. Just let it happen. I gotta break you in, you know? Lots of people have been anticipating you being ready," they guy said and started climbing up on top of Mikey. "Now close your eyes. This shouldn't hurt... for too long."

Mikey screamed at the tops of his lungs, "Noooooo!"

The guy smacked him. "Shut up, ya' little bitch!" he snapped then slammed himself into Mikey and started breaking him in without a care in the world about how badly he was hurting the cross-dressing snitch.

THE END

Lock Down Publications and Ca$h Presents
Assisted Publishing Packages

Due to an increase in the price of services we have increased our prices. The prices below reflect the price increase as of 11/1/24.

BASIC PACKAGE	UPGRADED PACKAGE
$699	**$1000**
Editing	Typing
Cover Design	Editing
Formatting	Cover Design
	Formatting
	Upload eBooks to Amazon
	Upload Paperback to Amazon
ADVANCE PACKAGE	**LDP SUPREME PACKAGE**
$1,400	**$1,700**
Typing	Typing
Editing (line editing/content)	Editing (line editing/content)
Cover Design	Cover Design
Formatting	Formatting
Copyright Registration	Copyright Registration
Proofreading	Proofreading
Upload eBooks to Amazon	Set up Amazon Account
Upload Paperback to Amazon	Upload eBooks to Amazon
	Upload Paperback to Amazon
	Advertise on LDP's Amazon and Facebook Page

***

Other services available upon request.
Additional charges may apply

Lock Down Publications
P.O. Box 944
Stockbridge, GA 30281-9998
Phone: 470 303-9761
Email: lockdownpublications@gmail.com

Submission Guideline

Submit the first three chapters of your completed manuscript to ldpsubmissions@gmail.com. In the subject line add **Your Book's Title**. The manuscript must be in a Word Doc file and sent as an attachment. Document should be in Times New Roman, double spaced, and in size 12 font. Also, provide your synopsis and full contact information. If sending multiple submissions, they must each be in a separate email.

Have a story but no way to send it electronically? You can still submit to LDP/Ca$h Presents. Send in the first three chapters, written or typed, of your completed manuscript to:

LDP: Submissions Dept
P.O. Box 944
Stockbridge, GA 30281-9998

DO NOT send original manuscript. Must be a duplicate.
Provide your synopsis and a cover letter containing your full contact information.

Thanks for considering LDP and Ca$h Presents.

NEW RELEASES

BLOODLINE OF A SAVAGE 1-3
THESE VICIOUS STREETS 1-3
RELENTLESS GOON 1-3
BY PRINCE A. TAUHID

THE BUTTERFLY MAFIA 1-3
BY FUMIYA PAYNE

A THUG'S STREET PRINCESS 1&2
BY MEESHA

CITY OF SMOKE 3
BY MOLOTTI

GET IT IN SLUGS 1 &2
BY B. STALL

STANDING ON HER BUSINESS 1&2
BY DG SANTANA

STEPPERS 1,2&3
THE REAL BADDIES OF CHI-RAQ
BY KING RIO

THE LANE 1&2
BY KEN-KEN SPENCE

THUG OF SPADES 1&2
LOVE IN THE TRENCHES 2
CORNER BOYS
BY COREY ROBINSON

TIL DEATH 3
BY ARYANNA

TIPPIN' THE SCALES 4 | DIESEL

THE BIRTH OF A GANGSTER 4
BY DELMONT PLAYER

PRODUCT OF THE STREETS 1-3
BY DEMOND "MONEY" ANDERSON

NO TIME FOR ERROR
BY KEESE

MONEY HUNGRY DEMONS 1-2
BY TRANAY ADAMS

HUB CITY MENACE 1-3
BY J. WHITE

A THUGGISH PASSION 1&2
LAND OF DA HOOLIGANZ 1-4
KILLAZ ON STANDBY 1&2
BY IRA B.

FO'EVA ROLLIN 1&2
BY ASSA RAYMOND BAKER

THE LEVEL UP 1&3
BY LUXURY KING

Coming Soon from Lock Down Publications/Ca$h Presents

IF YOU CROSS ME ONCE 6
ANGEL V
By Anthony Fields

A THUGS STREET PRINCESS 3
By Meesha

CORNER BOYS 2
By Corey Robinson

THA TAKEOVER
By Keith Chandler

BETRAYAL OF A G 2
By Ray Vinci

SAVAGE FAMILY EMPIRE 1&2
SOULLESS GOON 1,2&3
THE DIRTY SIDE OF MONEY 1,2&3
By Prince

FOR MY ENEMY'S SAKE
AMBITIONS OF A SLIDER
FRESH OFF DA PORCH
By IRA B.

THE TRUCKLOAD 1-4
TIPPIN' THE SCALES 1-3
BAD BITCHES WIT GUNZ 3
PROBLEM SOLVED 2
By Christopher "Diesel" Hornezes

TIPPIN' THE SCALES 4 | DIESEL

Available Now

RESTRAINING ORDER 1 & 2
By **CA$H & Coffee**

LOVE KNOWS NO BOUNDARIES 1-3
By **Coffee**

RAISED AS A GOON I, II, III & IV
BRED BY THE SLUMS I, II, III
BLAST FOR ME I & II
ROTTEN TO THE CORE I II III
A BRONX TALE I, II, III
DUFFLE BAG CARTEL I II III IV V VI
HEARTLESS GOON I II III IV V
A SAVAGE DOPEBOY I II
DRUG LORDS I II III
CUTTHROAT MAFIA I II
KING OF THE TRENCHES
By **Ghost**

LAY IT DOWN I & II
LAST OF A DYING BREED I II
BLOOD STAINS OF A SHOTTA I & II III
By **Jamaica**

LOYAL TO THE GAME I II III
LIFE OF SIN I, II III
By **TJ & Jelissa**

IF LOVING HIM IS WRONG…I & II
LOVE ME EVEN WHEN IT HURTS I II III
By **Jelissa**

PUSH IT TO THE LIMIT
By **Bre' Hayes**

TIPPIN' THE SCALES 4 | DIESEL

BLOODY COMMAS I & II
SKI MASK CARTEL I, II & III
KING OF NEW YORK I II, III IV V
RISE TO POWER I II III
COKE KINGS I II III IV V
BORN HEARTLESS I II III IV
KING OF THE TRAP I II
By **T.J. Edwards**

WHEN THE STREETS CLAP BACK I & II III
THE HEART OF A SAVAGE I II III IV
MONEY MAFIA I II
LOYAL TO THE SOIL I II III
By **Jibril Williams**

A DISTINGUISHED THUG STOLE MY HEART I II & III
LOVE SHOULDN'T HURT I II III IV
RENEGADE BOYS 1-4
PAID IN KARMA 1-3
SAVAGE STORMS 1-3
AN UNFORESEEN LOVE 1-3
BABY, I'M WINTERTIME COLD 1-3
A THUG'S STREET PRINCESS 1&2
By **Meesha**

A GANGSTER'S CODE 1-3
A GANGSTER'S SYN 1-3
THE SAVAGE LIFE 1-3
CHAINED TO THE STREETS 1-3
BLOOD ON THE MONEY 1-3
A GANGSTA'S PAIN 1-3
BEAUTIFUL LIES AND UGLY TRUTHS
CHURCH IN THESE STREETS
By **J-Blunt**

CUM FOR ME 1-8
An LDP Erotica Collaboration

TIPPIN' THE SCALES 4 | DIESEL

BLOOD OF A BOSS 1-5
SHADOWS OF THE GAME
TRAP BASTARD
By **Askari**

THE STREETS BLEED MURDER 1-3
THE HEART OF A GANGSTA 1-3
By **Jerry Jackson**

WHEN A GOOD GIRL GOES BAD
By **Adrienne**

THE COST OF LOYALTY 1-3
By **Kweli**

BRIDE OF A HUSTLA 1-3
THE FETTI GIRLS 1-3
CORRUPTED BY A GANGSTA 1-4
BLINDED BY HIS LOVE
THE PRICE YOU PAY FOR LOVE 1-3
DOPE GIRL MAGIC 1-3
By **Destiny Skai**

A KINGPIN'S AMBITION
A KINGPIN'S AMBITION II
I MURDER FOR THE DOUGH
By **Ambitious**

TRUE SAVAGE 1-7
DOPE BOY MAGIC 1-3
MIDNIGHT CARTEL 1-3
CITY OF KINGZ 1&2
NIGHTMARE ON SILENT AVE
THE PLUG OF LIL MEXICO 1&2
CLASSIC CITY
By **Chris Green**

TIPPIN' THE SCALES 4 | DIESEL

A GANGSTER'S REVENGE 1-4
THE BOSS MAN'S DAUGHTERS 1-5
A SAVAGE LOVE 1&2
BAE BELONGS TO ME 1&2
A HUSTLER'S DECEIT 1-3
WHAT BAD BITCHES DO 1-3
SOUL OF A MONSTER 1-3
KILL ZONE
A DOPE BOY'S QUEEN 1-3
TIL DEATH 1-3
IMMA DIE BOUT MINE 1-6
DYING FOR LIKES
By **Aryanna**

A DOPEBOY'S PRAYER
By **Eddie "Wolf" Lee**

THE KING CARTEL 1-3
By **Frank Gresham**

THESE NIGGAS AIN'T LOYAL 1-3
By **Nikki Tee**

GANGSTA SHYT 1-3
By **CATO**

THE ULTIMATE BETRAYAL
By **Phoenix**

BOSS'N UP 1-3
By **Royal Nicole**

I LOVE YOU TO DEATH
By **Destiny J**

I RIDE FOR MY HITTA
I STILL RIDE FOR MY HITTA
By **Misty Holt**

TIPPIN' THE SCALES 4 | DIESEL

LOVE & CHASIN' PAPER
By **Qay Crockett**

TO DIE IN VAIN
SINS OF A HUSTLA
By **ASAD**

BROOKLYN HUSTLAZ
By **Boogsy Morina**

BROOKLYN ON LOCK 1 & 2
By **Sonovia**

GANGSTA CITY
By **Teddy Duke**

A DRUG KING AND HIS DIAMOND 1-3
A DOPEMAN'S RICHES
HER MAN, MINE'S TOO 1&2
CASH MONEY HO'S
THE WIFEY I USED TO BE 1&2
PRETTY GIRLS DO NASTY THINGS
By **Nicole Goosby**

LIPSTICK KILLAH 1-3
CRIME OF PASSION 1-3
FRIEND OR FOE 1-3
By **Mimi**

TRAPHOUSE KING 1-3
KINGPIN KILLAZ 1-3
STREET KINGS 1&2
PAID IN BLOOD 1&2
CARTEL KILLAZ 1-3
DOPE GODS 1&2
By **Hood Rich**

THE STREETS ARE CALLING
By **Duquie Wilson**

TIPPIN' THE SCALES 4 | DIESEL

STEADY MOBBN' 1-3
THE STREETS STAINED MY SOUL 1-3
By **Marcellus Allen**

WHO SHOT YA 1-3
SON OF A DOPE FIEND 1-4
HEAVEN GOT A GHETTO 1&2
SKI MASK MONEY 1&2
By **Renta**

GORILLAZ IN THE BAY 1 4
TEARS OF A GANGSTA 1/&2
3X KRAZY 1&2
STRAIGHT BEAST MODE 1&2
By **DE'KARI**

TRIGGADALE 1-3
MURDA WAS THE CASE 1-3
By **Elijah R. Freeman**

SLAUGHTER GANG 1-3
RUTHLESS HEART 1-3
By **Willie Slaughter**

GOD BLESS THE TRAPPERS 1-3
THESE SCANDALOUS STREETS 1-3
FEAR MY GANGSTA 1-5
THESE STREETS DON'T LOVE NOBODY 1-2
BURY ME A G 1-5
A GANGSTA'S EMPIRE 1-4
THE DOPEMAN'S BODYGAURD 1&2
THE REALEST KILLAZ 1-3
THE LAST OF THE OGS 1-3
By **Tranay Adams**

MARRIED TO A BOSS 1-3
By **Destiny Skai & Chris Green**

KINGZ OF THE GAME 1-7
CRIME BOSS 1-4
By **Playa Ray**

FUK SHYT
By **Blakk Diamond**

DON'T F#CK WITH MY HEART 1&2
By **Linnea**

ADDICTED TO THE DRAMA 1-3
IN THE ARM OF HIS BOSS
By **Jamila**

LOYALTY AIN'T PROMISED 1&2
By **Keith Williams**

YAYO 1-4
A SHOOTER'S AMBITION 1&2
BRED IN THE GAME
By **S. Allen**

TRAP GOD 1-3
RICH $AVAGE 1-3
MONEY IN THE GRAVE 1-3
CARTEL MONEY 1&2
By **Martell Troublesome Bolden**

FOREVER GANGSTA 1&2
GLOCKS ON SATIN SHEETS 1&2
By **Adrian Dulan**

TOE TAGZ 1-4
LEVELS TO THIS SHYT 1&2
IT'S JUST ME AND YOU
By **Ah'Million**

TIPPIN' THE SCALES 4 | DIESEL

KINGPIN DREAMS 1-3
RAN OFF ON DA PLUG
By **Paper Boi Rari**

THE STREETS MADE ME 1-3
By **Larry D. Wright**

CONFESSIONS OF A GANGSTA 1-4
CONFESSIONS OF A JACKBOY 1-3
CONFESSIONS OF A HITMAN
CONFESSIONS OF A DOPE BOY
By **Nicholas Lock**

I'M NOTHING WITHOUT HIS LOVE
SINS OF A THUG
TO THE THUG I LOVED BEFORE
A GANGSTA SAVED XMAS
IN A HUSTLER I TRUST
By **Monet Dragun**

QUIET MONEY 1-3
THUG LIFE 1-3
EXTENDED CLIP 1&2
A GANGSTA'S PARADISE
By **Trai'Quan**

CAUGHT UP IN THE LIFE 1-3
THE STREETS NEVER LET GO 1-3
By **Robert Baptiste**

NEW TO THE GAME 1-3
MONEY, MURDER & MEMORIES 1-3
By **Malik D. Rice**

CREAM 2-3
THE STREETS WILL TALK
By **Yolanda Moore**

THE STREETS WILL NEVER CLOSE 1-3
By **K'ajji**

LIFE OF A SAVAGE 1-4
A GANGSTA'S QUR'AN 1-4
MURDA SEASON 1-3
GANGLAND CARTEL 1-3
CHI'RAQ GANGSTAS 1-4
KILLERS ON ELM STREET 1-3
JACK BOYZ N DA BRONX 1-3
A DOPEBOY'S DREAM 1-3
JACK BOYS VS DOPE BOYS 1-3
COKE GIRLZ
COKE BOYS
SOSA GANG 1&2
BRONX SAVAGES
BODYMORE KINGPINS
BLOOD OF A GOON
By **Romell Tukes**

CONCRETE KILLA 1-3
VICIOUS LOYALTY 1-3
BLOODY MONEY BAGS
By **Kingpen**

THE ULTIMATE SACRIFICE 1-6
KHADIFI
IF YOU CROSS ME ONCE 1-3
ANGEL 1-4
IN THE BLINK OF AN EYE
By **Anthony Fields**

THE LIFE OF A HOOD STAR
By **Ca$h & Rashia Wilson**

NIGHTMARES OF A HUSTLA 1-3
BLOOD AND GAMES 1&2
By **King Dream**

GHOST MOB
By **Stilloan Robinson**

HARD AND RUTHLESS 1&2
MOB TOWN 251
THE BILLIONAIRE BENTLEYS 1-3
REAL G'S MOVE IN SILENCE
By **Von Diesel**

MOB TIES 1-7
SOUL OF A HUSTLER, HEART OF A KILLER 1-3
GORILLAZ IN THE TRENCHES
OOPS CRY TOO 1&2
THE DAUGHTER OF A CARTEL BOSS
By **SayNoMore**

BODYMORE MURDERLAND 1-3
THE BIRTH OF A GANGSTER 1-4
By **Delmont Player**

FOR THE LOVE OF A BOSS 1&2
By **C. D. Blue**

KILLA KOUNTY 1-5
TENDER
By **Khufu**

MOBBED UP 1-4
THE BRICK MAN 1-5
THE COCAINE PRINCESS 1-10
STEPPERS 1-3
SUPER GREMLIN 1-4
A GANGSTA'S SON
By **King Rio**

MONEY GAME 1&2
By **Smoove Dolla**

TIPPIN' THE SCALES 4 | DIESEL

A GANGSTA'S KARMA 1-5
By **FLAME**

KING OF THE TRENCHES 1-3
By **GHOST & TRANAY ADAMS**

BAD BITCHES WIT GUNZ 1&2
PROBLEM SOLVED
By **"Christopher Diesel" Hornezes**

QUEEN OF THE ZOO 1&2
By **Black Migo**

GRIMEY WAYS 1-3
BETRAYAL OF A G
By **Ray Vinci**

XMAS WITH AN ATL SHOOTER
By **Ca$h & Destiny Skai**

KING KILLA 1&2
By **Vincent "Vitto" Holloway**

BETRAYAL OF A THUG 1&2
By **Fre$h**

COUNTDOWN OF A KILLA 1&2
SEX, MURDER AND GOD 1&2
GUNS DOWN, BOTTOMS UP 1&2
By Lo-Life

THE MURDER QUEENS 1-7
By **Michael Gallon**

FOR THE LOVE OF BLOOD 1-4
By **Jamel Mitchell**

TIPPIN' THE SCALES 4 | DIESEL

HOOD CONSIGLIERE 1&2
NO TIME FOR ERROR
By **Keese**

PROTÉGÉ OF A LEGEND 1,2&3
LOVE IN THE TRENCHES 1&2
By **Corey Robinson**

THE PLUG'S RUTHLESS DAUGHTER 1&2
By **Tony Daniels**

BORN IN THE GRAVE 1-3
CRIME PAYS
By **Self Made Tay**

MOAN IN MY MOUTH
By **XTASY**

TORN BETWEEN A GANGSTER AND A GENTLEMAN
By **J-BLUNT & Miss Kim**

LOYALTY IS EVERYTHING 1-3
CITY OF SMOKE 1-3
By **Molotti**

HERE TODAY GONE TOMORROW 1&2
By **Fly Rock**

WOMEN LIE MEN LIE 1-4
FIFTY SHADES OF SNOW 1-3
STACK BEFORE YOU SPLURGE
GIRLS FALL LIKE DOMINOES
NAÏVE TO THE STREETS
By **ROY MILLIGAN**

PILLOW PRINCESS
By **S. Hawkins**

TIPPIN' THE SCALES 4 | DIESEL

THE BUTTERFLY MAFIA 1-3
SALUTE MY SAVAGERY 1&2
By **Fumiya Payne**

THE LANE 1&2
By Ken-Ken Spence

THE PUSSY TRAP 1-5
By **Nene Capri**

DIRTY DNA
By **Blaque**

SANCTIFIED AND HORNY
by **XTASY**

BOOKS BY LDP'S CEO, CA$H

TRUST IN NO MAN
TRUST IN NO MAN 2
TRUST IN NO MAN 3
BONDED BY BLOOD
SHORTY GOT A THUG
THUGS CRY
THUGS CRY 2
THUGS CRY 3
TRUST NO BITCH
TRUST NO BITCH 2
TRUST NO BITCH 3
TIL MY CASKET DROPS
RESTRAINING ORDER
RESTRAINING ORDER 2
IN LOVE WITH A CONVICT
LIFE OF A HOOD STAR
XMAS WITH AN ATL SHOOTER